A MAGICAL IMPERATIVE

The #1
Unseen

A Magical Imperative

EDITH PAWLICKI

*For Aunt Edie who told me (in 2006!) that
she likes parenthetical asides as well and
whose home is in Japan.*

REGARDING FACTS & PRONUNCIATION

Nara is a beautiful (and real) city in Japan. The park, temples, shrines, and streets are as described. The restaurants, businesses, and homes are fiction woven from memories, while Hayashi University is wholly imagined.

This book presented the challenge of making sure English readers understand the story while also conveying the language barrier that our main characters face and incorporating some elements of Japanese culture that are shown through language. To ensure the reader has the same understanding as the point of view character, speech and thought are written in English, with exclamations and loan words in Romanized and *italicized* Japanese. Meanings are clarified in the glossary.

Japanese has five consistent vowel sounds (a dash over the vowel means hold the sound longer):

a, ā – short a, as in baa, far, and papa

i, ī – long e as in sleep, sheep, and keep

u, ū – long u as in due, sue, and crew

o, ō – long o as in so, though, and toe

e – short e, as in eh, men, and pet; *ē* – long a as in pay, say, and day

The diphthong "*ai*" is long i, as in "try" and "sigh." The consonants are similar to their English equivalents, though "r" is softened until it is almost an "l," and "ts" is closer to "s" than "t." Consonant + y + vowel ("kyo") is pronounced similarly to "Leo" or "Rio."

GLOSSARY OF JAPANESE WORDS

anime – Japanese animations

anō – an interjection to show thinking, similar to "well"

bentō – Japanese boxed lunch (whether homemade or prepackaged from the store)

biwa – a traditional stringed instrument similar to a lute

bonsai – miniature potted tree

-chan – a casual suffix usually used for younger women or children

che – a mild expletive, more commonly used by women

conbini – a Japanese convenience store, which has a variety of groceries and prepared foods as well everyday necessities

ēto – an interjection to show thinking, similar to "um"

genkan – the recessed entryway to a home or other building where shoes are removed

hiragana – Japanese syllabary (similar to an alphabet, but each symbol represents a syllable rather than a partial sound)

hyaku-yen – 100 yen (roughly $1); 100-yen stores are popular in Japan

kanji – Chinese characters used for Japanese writing

karaoke – an entertainment where people sing along to the instrumental music of popular songs

katakana – Japanese syllabary reserved for foreign loan words and names

-kun – a casual suffix usually used for younger men or boys

futon – cushion; often refers to a traditional mattress with a duvet cover *mochi* – rice cake, a soft, usually sweet snack made from glutinous rice flour

miso – seasoning made of ground, salted, and fermented soybeans

moshi-moshi – main greeting used to answer phone calls

nattō – fermented soybeans

noren – short curtains that hang from the top of a doorway

obā – grandmother

oba – aunt

oden – a soup featuring large chunks of boiled food such as eggs, fishcake, and daikon radish that is especially popular in winter

okyaku-sama – honored guest, often used to address customers

omiai – an arranged meeting, similar to a blind date

onigiri – rice ball, a common snack of usually a filling inside steamed sticky rice wrapped in seaweed (*nori*)

oni – Japanese demon

samurai – the military caste

-san – a polite suffix that can be used to address anyone (usually the default suffix)

-sama – an extremely polite suffix (used for people in positions of power or towards customers)

sake – rice wine

sakoku – an isolationist foreign policy enacted by the shogunate from the 17th into the 19th centuries

senbei – round rice crackers, often about the size of a palm and sometimes featuring decorative images

-sensei – a suffix to indicate someone's proficiency; usually used for any kind of instructor and doctors

seppuku – a kind of ritual suicide favored by the *samurai* class where a blade is used to disembowel oneself rather than face imprisonment/dishonor

shibori – indigo tie-dye

shimekazari – a New Year decoration traditionally made of braided rice straw and various colorful accents

shitsurei – the beginning of *"shitsurei shimasu,"* meaning "excuse me"

shōgun – title of the military leaders of Japan during the twelfth through nineteenth centuries

shoji – a square lattice with translucent paper used for doors and windows

soba – buckwheat or buckwheat noodles

sobacha – an herbal tea made from roasted buckwheat grains (*soba*)

wakame – a type of seaweed

yen – Japanese currency (roughly equivalent to the cent)

zabuton – cushion for sitting on the floor ("za" meaning sitting, and "buton" meaning the same as "futon")

CHARACTER NAMES

The scene break "images" are character names in Japanese. For those who are curious…

Non-Japanese names in *katakana:*

Aurelie: オーレリー (Ōrerī)

Deborah: デボラ (Debora)

Lisette: リッセット (Rissetto)

Japanese names in *kanji:*

Kazuki: 和希 meaning "hope•peace"

Emiko: 恵美子 meaning "favor•beauty•child"

Kento: 健人 meaning "vigorous•person"

Shigeru: 茂 meaning "lush"

1. CALLED

オーレリー

DESPITE being a creature out of myth, Aurelie Dubois utterly disregarded nonsense like magic, the supernatural, and gods. No, that was misleading. Her faith in science and science alone was *because* she was a creature of myth.

The rickety wooden house where she had grown up had been ruled by stories, all of them false.

Humans may look like us, but they have snakes in their hair! That's why it grows long.

Humans steal Unseen children. They leash us like dogs and force us to hunt for mushrooms!

Human breath is poisonous to Unseen. If they breathe on you, you will die in three days!

Aurelie had been terrified, and on the rare occasion

that a human hiker wandered too close to the family homestead, she had immediately climbed a tree and called the branches close. (As a child, she had believed in magic, but she now realized none of them had been looking for a small child twenty feet up a beech).

When her mother had first declared that they were going to live among humans, Aurelie had vomited from sheer stress. Her mother had explained over and over that while there was a grain of truth to the stories, their essence had been warped and twisted. Yes, human hair grew strangely long, but no, there were no snakes in it. Unseen might very well have a better sense of smell than humans, but you couldn't see how sensitive a nose was by looking at it. And the epidemic caused by the last human to wander into Unseen territory had indeed caused most of the clan to die, but the man had died of the same illness. Their breath wasn't poison.

And yet, Aurelie's mother had never dared expose her species and history to any human, not even to Aurelie's stepfather. They had claimed to have been part of a wilderness cult (which was perhaps the truth), and even after they had gotten social security numbers, Aurelie's mother refused physical exams for herself and her daughters.

As a teenager, Aurelie had the dubious pleasure of attending a public school, and she soon learned that she didn't need to put effort into misdirection and lying—people made up stories to explain away anything that was odd.

Her short hair? A life choice to indicate her sexual

orientation. (This hadn't bothered Aurelie at all, for she felt the same attraction for humans, regardless of gender, that she'd feel for a chimpanzee... None at all). The contradiction of her nearly black eyes and her white-blonde hair? Contacts, bleach, or both. Her impossibly waspish waist, due to the fact she had two less ribs than homo sapiens? A corset or plastic surgery. (Yes, in recent decades, some human women actually got rid of ribs in order to resemble a doll they idolized. Now there was a phenomenon that Aurelie had no desire to study further).

By the time Aurelie entered college, she understood how easy it was to be tricked, and she decided that she could no longer tolerate being fooled herself. At first, she had hoped to pursue her answers in biology, but when she realized the labs—with their blood tests, cell scrapings, and DNA sequencing—were impossible for her, she had turned to history. In fact, ironically, fairy tales. Countless hours in windowless library rooms (to keep sunlight off the delicate documents), her hands in white cotton gloves as she turned brittle pages, seeking truths buried in the folly.

And the truth was, human societies were often selfish. Just as Hansel and Gretel's stepmother was unwilling to spare food for unwanted children, humans were unwilling to set aside land for unwanted animals. Oh, sure, in recent decades, most governments respected endangered species, but they still put profit above sustainability. If Aurelie petitioned the US government to set aside land for Unseen, that would last until coal was discovered in the mountains (at best) or they would all wind up in a lab so that humans could discover their secret to long life (at worst).

Admittedly, Aurelie would have liked to understand that better herself. She had plenty of questions about the Unseen, for as a species they had never been properly documented, tested, or studied. But she could live with the questions if the uncertainty allowed her to travel the world unmolested.

Even now, Aurelie stood brazenly in the early-autumn sunshine before an ancient Buddhist monument, a five-story pagoda. She was in Nara, Japan, the opposite side of the world from where she'd been born. The whole city exuded culture, refinement, and innocence (that too was the opposite of her birthplace).

Some Japanese did look at her a little long, but she was willing to cut them slack on account of her height (almost six feet), her hair (which verged on incandescent), and the fact it was the middle of a pandemic. She hadn't seen another foreigner since escaping quarantine (at least, not an obvious one). Despite the stares, not even the immigration inspectors had suspected her true nature. This was aided, of course, by the US passport in her pocket and the Japanese visa glued inside it—how could two governments have missed the obvious fact that she wasn't human?

Even better than the lack of suspicion though, whatever speculation the Japanese did, they did it *quietly*. Aurelie was loving the polite reserve, the intentionality, and the order that permeated everything from customs lines to restrooms to the strangely cute warning signs about the Nara deer.

Oh, the deer! Delicate beasts that only reached Aurelie's waist, with sandy brown fur and chocolate eyes, even Aurelie could almost believe they were descended from a mythical creature that had carried a god to this place.

Well, at least until the deer *senbei* came out! The ripping of a packet full of their favorite rice crackers drew Aurelie's gaze—and a mob of deer—to a short Japanese woman wearing a pink mask and a floppy white hat. The *senbei* sharer (victim?) was already being nipped at by two extra pushy deer.

"Oh, oh," she exclaimed and tried to back away—but the deer followed, for she was still holding the *senbei*. Aurelie wasn't much for strangers, but she knew animals, and the woman looked pitiful. She pushed her way to the woman's side and stood her ground. The deer hesitated, vaguely confused by her intrusion. Aurelie bowed to them, as she had seen other visitors do, and was embarrassingly delighted by the begrudging head dips the deer offered in return. The Japanese woman bowed as well and gave half her crackers to Aurelie. Together they managed to distribute the *senbei* without further mauling, and laughter burbled up from a place Aurelie had forgotten.

She bowed to the woman when they finished, intending to take her leave, but the woman asked, "What country?"

"Ah, sorry?" said Aurelie.

"You. Are. What country?"

"Oh—oh, the US. Um, *Amerika-jin*."

The woman switched to Japanese. "Ah, American, are you? How nice, how nice. You like Japan?"

"Oh, yes," said Aurelie, "it's beautiful."

"Beautiful, yes, Nara is so beautiful. You know about the pagoda?"

"Um—no, not really…"

The friendly woman started an enthusiastic lecture, some of which Aurelie missed, but she managed to gather that the five-story pagoda was *only* in its sixth century. It really ought to have been in its thirteenth if the original hadn't been destroyed in a war.

Aurelie started to comment that war or no war, it seemed unlikely a wood structure would last that long, but she realized in the nick of time that this was a humble brag, so she clasped her hands in awe, and said, "Amazing."

And she meant it. From the elegant sweep of the eaves, so crisp against the blue sky, to the dark wood that had weathered centuries and the pristine white plaster, the pagoda felt special. And it was only one of dozens of centuries-old buildings, all feats of architecture, even if they had been built today. Despite the pandemic, there were several dozen visitors milling around, admiring the beauty. There was something deeply moving about the whole tableau.

Even though she didn't believe in magic or the supernatural or gods, this whole place felt extraordinary.

The air crackled around her. Tension was building inside.

And, strangest of all, a scent of cardamom and

cinnamon was seeping through her mask.

和希

THE washer played its jingle, and Kazuki paused the film just as a man's black-and-white face filled the MacBook screen, the whites visible around his eyes and sweat beaded on his nose and upper lip.

As he walked to his combo washer-dryer, Kazuki wondered if the actor had been sweating or if he had been spritzed for effect. Probably spritzed—how else could he evince the pain of forced suicide?

A few of the damp clothes tumbled into Kazuki's blue basket; he reached into the machine for the rest.

Those clan elders in the film were something else. Judging a man as worthless because he couldn't follow their tradition. Kazuki knew that humiliation personally.

He slammed the washer-dryer and immediately winced.

It wasn't the machine's fault that Kazuki, contrary to early expectations, had become a supporting character. No, worse: an extra. Unnamed, even in the credits.

He walked to his balcony and forced himself to open the door gently.

The warm autumn sunshine bathed his face, and the scent of roses and autumn leaves overwhelmed him, driving all thoughts from his mind. Setting down his basket, he grasped the cool aluminum railing and leaned forward, trying to breathe the scent more deeply.

Come to the park, something whispered to him. Kazuki tightened his hands on the railing, fighting the alarming impulse to jump off his balcony and run there. Not that he'd be doing any running if he did jump; Kazuki's apartment was on the third and highest floor of his building.

The scent faded—and surely Kazuki had imagined it in the first place. Roses and autumn leaves? Well, maybe autumn leaves, but there were no roses in October.

Still, he wanted to go to Nara Park. Kind of random, but his only plan had been rewatching the old *samurai* film. He might as well go to the park instead; he loved the primeval forest behind the Kasuga-Taisha. And it was a nice warm day; the park might be crowded, but it was perfect hiking weather.

Resolution made, he went to leave, but his eyes caught on his laundry. He forced himself to hang it, but his fingers jerked and snapped impatiently, as if they had minds of their own.

When he finished the laundry, Kazuki grabbed a *bentō* at his neighborhood Lawson and took a bus to just north of the national museum. But instead of heading east as he'd intended, where the Kasuga-Taisha was nestled amongst the colossal trees, he turned west toward the five-story pagoda.

He was sure it would be glutted with tourists, but he—actually, he had no idea why he was going there.

And then he saw her.

A foreign Unseen.

オーレリー

THE tall pine to her right seemed to blur before her eyes, and Aurelie blinked rapidly. The sweet spice must be drifting up from the restaurants on Sanjo-Dori. Aurelie remembered seeing a curry place—or maybe someone was selling spiced nuts.

That scent! It was making her feel so strange! A little dizzy. Almost intoxicated.

Her blood sugar must be low—it was probably near lunch time. She had bought a couple *onigiri* so that she could picnic in the park. She'd find a bench to sit on—she saw some past the pagoda, but two families were near them.

Aurelie's heart tightened, as it always did, when she saw children—without a male Unseen, it was a physical impossibility for her. Her sister had tried with human males, "just in case," but in the end, they were too genetically distinct to have offspring together (more so even than donkeys and horses, who could at least bear infertile mules).

Aurelie yearned for a family, for a partner and child, even as she cringed from the idea. The life her mother had escaped still gave her nightmares sometimes; she'd *never* tolerate a binding.

Aurelie avoided children and lovers, and all that she would (could?) never have. She strode blindly away from the pagoda and the family, seeking a lonelier bench.

Not lonelier: alone. Safe.

和希

KAZUKI froze forty feet away from the foreigner. It was too far away to see details, but he knew. He was utterly positive that she was Unseen.

Even though there weren't Unseen anywhere in the world but Japan. According to lore, the last of the Unseen had been driven to Japan by their enemies, and the fate of their family was the fate of the species.

Nevertheless, this female was an Unseen, and not one he had met. And *Obā-chama* had gone to great lengths to introduce Kazuki to every potential mate in the country.

Shortly after puberty finished, most Unseen were called and bound to their mate. Call it hormones or fate, somehow sexually mature Unseen knew exactly who they wanted to be with. They were drawn to each other, and then bound by sex. After, they had an almost telepathic connection.

But not Kazuki. He wasn't the only one—there were four or so others in the clan who had never been called—but it was still considered odd.

And it eliminated him from positions of leadership.

If this woman was a member of his clan, *Obā-chama* would have introduced them. Unless... *What if she's already bound?*

Her scent—impossibly, the roses and autumn leaves from earlier—reached him, and Kazuki practically swayed with desire. The idea that she might be off-limits, bound to one of his cousins, made him so furiously jealous that he decided it couldn't be.

And—*there's no way* Obā-chama *would allow that hair.* It was about the same length as Kazuki's own—

the longest length that Unseen hair grew—but instead of black, it was a blonde so pale that it seemed to glow. Unseen features tended to be sharp and narrow; combined with that hair, she would look too Caucasian. Kazuki's hair was naturally dark, but he knew several of the family dyed theirs so that they blended in better with the human Japanese around them.

The woman adjusted her mask, and her bell-like sleeve fell back to reveal long, slim fingers and a delicate wrist.

Even for an Unseen, she was unbearably elegant. She wore loose, long trousers, concealing legs that would unsettle humans with their slimness, but a wide belt accented her tiny waist. Kazuki wouldn't be surprised if he could span her midriff with his hands.

She pressed her hand to her forehead as he watched, then cast an annoyed glance behind her.

He followed her gaze to Sanjo-dori, the touristy street that led from the major train station to Nara Park, but he couldn't tell what was irritating her.

She suddenly started striding away, deeper into the park.

Kazuki hurried after her, but he suddenly thought even if she was foreign, even if she was unbound, why should it be any different with her than it had been with the women of his clan?

Kazuki pretended to be easygoing, but he hated the pity, the disappointment, the rejection. As much as he wanted to talk to her, to find out where she was from, and how this was even happening, he feared her answers. So he stayed three meters back, not ready for the fantasy he was building to crumble down.

オーレリー

AS Aurelie went further into the park, the spicy, sweet, earthy aroma seemed to grow stronger. Guided by instinct rather than the cutesy map that was crumpled in her right hand, she came to a wide pond with a picturesque gazebo in the middle. It was empty.

She walked—or maybe floated, for all she could tell—over the blonde wood bridge and settled on the bench that wrapped around the outside of the gazebo.

After a moment, she shoved her mask and the worse-for-wear map into her purse and pulled out one of the *onigiri*. She was befuddled by its plastic wrapping.

An arm reached past her, and the scent of cardamom overpowered her.

"*Shitsurei...*"

Aurelie met the eyes of the Japanese speaker—they were as dark as her own, and Aurelie had no defense against them.

和希

THE foreigner didn't look back once as Kazuki followed her, nor did she pause, until she sat on a bench in Ukimidō, a small pavilion built over a pond.

He felt his face grow hot—he was probably blushing. There was no one but the two of them in sight: it was time for him to speak to her.

Despite his resolution, he walked as silently as possible on the thin wooden bridge to the pavilion and hung back as she settled on a bench.

She pulled a *conbini onigiri* from her purse and fumbled at its plastic wrapping.

Kazuki smirked; there was no way she was from Japan if she couldn't figure out how to open the *onigiri*.

He suddenly realized how big this was. She was a *foreigner*. Discovering the first foreign Unseen—it was like a movie! No, there was too much material for that; their meeting was rich enough to support a twenty-episode drama.

He felt like a leading man again for the first time in years. So he tugged his mask down—Covid-19 didn't appear to pose the same risk to Unseen that it did to humans, and even if it did... He wanted her to see his face.

He sat next to her on the bench and reached forward to show her the small tab at the top which would tear the *onigiri* wrapper in half.

But their eyes met, and he forgot how to speak.

They were dark pools, like all Unseen, and yet they were like nothing he'd ever encountered.

They scorched him, and the flush on his cheeks spread to his whole body.

She stared at him. He thought he asked her name, but her only response was to grab the front of his t-shirt—the still wrapped *onigiri* fell to the pavilion's floor—and she pressed her lips against his.

The rose and leaf musk overwhelmed him in the best way, sweet with a hint of spice. His hands, seemingly of their own volition, settled around her waist. Her lips left his to make a burning path to his ear.

Kazuki gasped, "I don't think we should do this here."

He didn't let himself think too hard about what this was.

Maybe she didn't speak Japanese because she didn't seem to even register his words.

He stood up, and she followed him. He tried to disengage—he balked at the idea of leaving the *onigiri* on the pavilion floor—but her hands seemed to be everywhere.

That infamous woodcut, where a woman is making love with a squid, popped into his head. Only she was the squid.

Finally, he pressed her hard against one of the wooden pillars and kissed her so fiercely that their breaths became one.

She stayed there just long enough for him to collect their bags—and the rogue *onigiri*—and then she latched onto him again.

He no longer objected though.

Instead, he put a mask on both of them—he gave her a spare from his pocket, since he wasn't sure where hers was. Then he led her to the bus. The whole park seemed to blur around him, while she gained a sharpness, a vividness that was intoxicating.

He was vaguely surprised when he realized they were both seated on the bus that would bring them to his apartment—he didn't even remember swiping his pass.

In this moment of lucidity, he looked directly into her eyes and felt alarmed.

If he was having trouble keeping track of the rest of the world, she was even worse. *If I sleep with her like this, won't I be like one of those human scumbags who take advantage of drunk girls?*

But that thought fled as fast as it came; the only conviction he was able to hold onto was that they had to remain fully clothed on this bus, not kissing. He was grateful for the masks—they helped him remember that, even though the reason for waiting escaped him.

He pulled the masks off as soon as they exited the bus.

And then they were careening wildly on the rickety metal stairs that wrapped along the side of his building. He broke free from her to run—she followed, no worries about that—and he managed to key in his door code before she caught him. They practically tumbled over the threshold, and Kazuki kicked the door shut behind him. He heard it chime as it locked automatically, though if it had remained open to the world, he wouldn't have been able to bring himself to care.

While he focused on removing their shoes, she stripped off their shirts. Their pants, socks, and underthings all found their way to the floor before the two of them found their way to Kazuki's bed.

By the time they slammed into his soft futon, he couldn't have said where he ended and she began.

We're already binding to each other.

Kazuki stopped trying to think at all.

FOLLOWED

Finally!

At last.

Now we feast?

Yes!   Yes!

NOT QUITE.

What?
WHY?

YOU IDIOTS. THERE'S MORE OF THEM!

AND IT'S A BABY WE NEED.

But they...

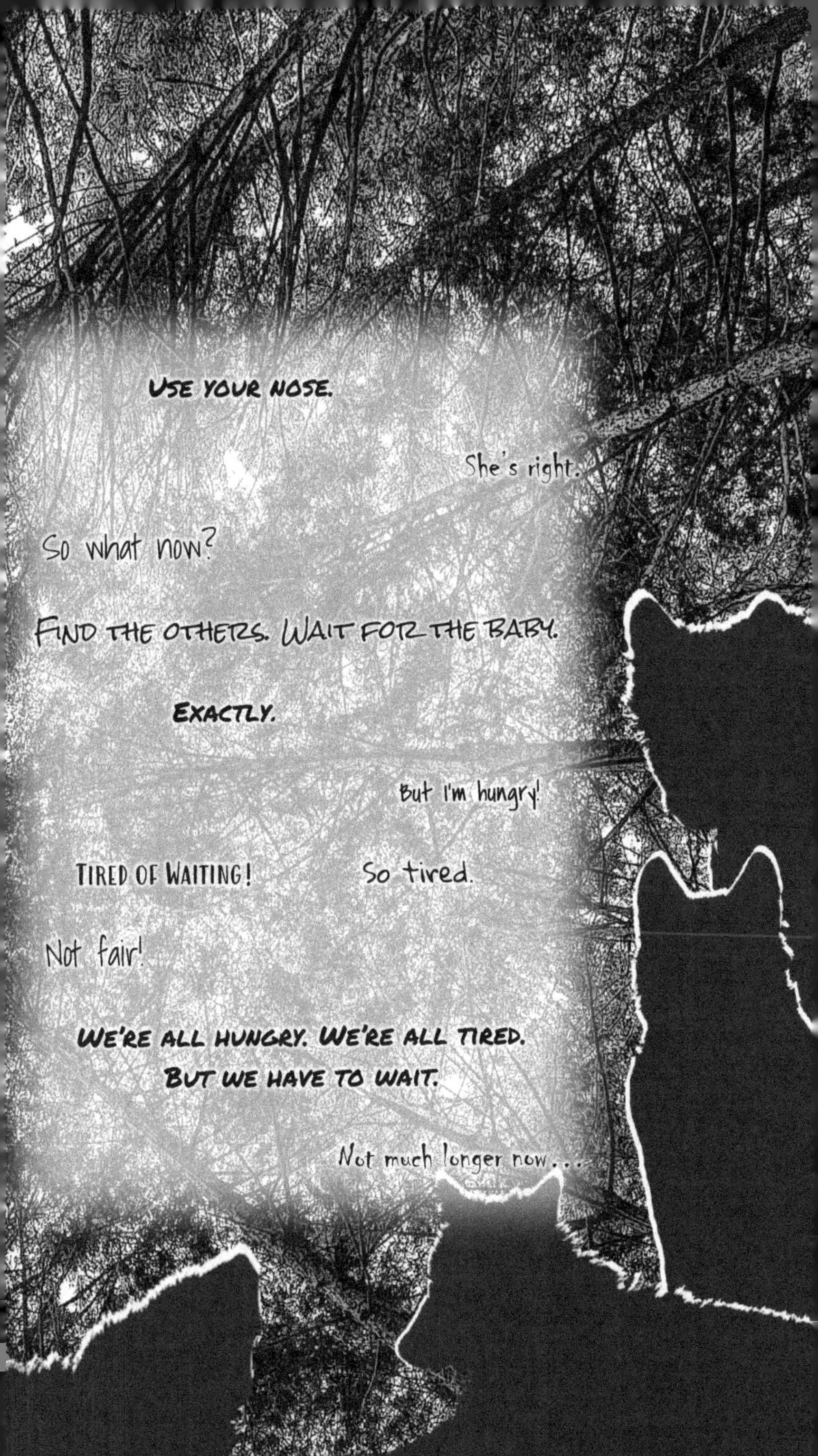

USE YOUR NOSE.
She's right.
So what now?
FIND THE OTHERS. WAIT FOR THE BABY.
EXACTLY.
But I'm hungry!
TIRED OF WAITING!
So tired.
Not fair!
WE'RE ALL HUNGRY. WE'RE ALL TIRED.
BUT WE HAVE TO WAIT.
Not much longer now . . .

2. BOUND

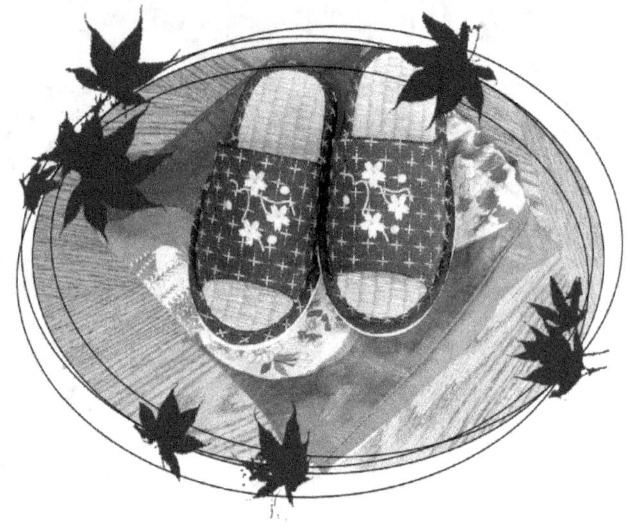

和希

KAZUKI woke, as he always did, a few minutes before his alarm. It was two hours or so past sunrise, but it was dim inside his apartment, indicating a cloudy day—indeed, when he listened intently, Kazuki heard raindrops against his window.

The laundry!

Kazuki tapped the top of his alarm clock to prevent its ringing and tried to sit up.

But something was pinning him to the bed.

Kazuki twisted and found himself face-to-face with a gorgeous Unseen who was using his arm as a pillow. Pale bangs crisscrossed fine, equally pale eyebrows. Her nose was narrow and small, with the faintest upturn at the tip. Her lips were a soft rose that complemented her flushed cheeks. She shifted, poking his bicep with her pointy chin.

The park. The foreigner. Kissing in the pavilion. The bus. Tumbling into his apartment. And...

"*Kuso!*" The swear slipped out before Kazuki could stop it. He froze. But his bedmate kept sleeping, apparently finding his bony arm comfortable.

In fact, he knew she did—he could feel it, pressing against her cheek, warm and softer than he'd have expected.

He could feel what she was feeling.

Relieved tears pricked his eyes, but Kazuki had no time for them. Finally, he'd been bound. At last, he'd reclaimed a leading role in his own life. He focused on her, on their binding, seeing how closely they'd been linked. Her toes were a little cold, exposed by the blanket. The knuckles of her right hand were pressed against something hot—his hip, he realized belatedly.

And, when he focused, there were flashes of riding a deer through Nara Park. *Her dream.*

Yesterday, the scent of roses and autumn leaves had summoned him from across the city—it had been a calling so intense that it boggled the mind.

And when he found her, he had barely been able to think. He had taken home a woman he had just met, and without even speaking to her, had sex three—or was it four?—times! When he'd never had sex before; never even felt sexual attraction.

Suddenly, he smirked. *Obā-chama*'s prediction, a strong binding that would enable him to lead the clan, had come true. He couldn't wait to tell everyone, to introduce his mate to the clan elders.

When they learned he was bound to a foreign Unseen... Even *Obā-chama* would be shocked by that.

And the binding would exceed all expectations—it was stronger than any he knew.

All bindings resulted in an empathic connection, an unusually keen insight into a partner's thoughts, but this was so much beyond that.

He had heard of this in stories. The *samurai* lovers of his clan who saved the *shōgun* in the early thirteenth century had supposedly been able to use each other's senses as their own, but... His sister had been bound for seven years, and her binding only let her know when her boyfriend was hungry or tired or how he felt—not much beyond a human couple that was sensitive to each other's needs.

When Kazuki had asked Yuriko if she'd ever shared a dream with her mate, she had denied it.

"Fairytales. The old folks say that bindings used to make our minds one, and that the magic is getting weak." Yuriko had rolled her eyes. "We all like to pretend we're something special—elves or *oni* or vampires." She had laughed at the last. "But in the end, we're just another kind of ape. A binding that lets you read your mate's mind, see through their eyes, experience their memories? Nonsense!"

Kazuki had thought she must be right, but he could see his mate's dream. *Feel what she was feeling.*

He'd like to stay with her all day and process their binding. Find out where she was from, and why she had come to Japan *now*—he wasn't sure of current protocols, but he did know that Covid-19 quarantines were still mandatory for international travelers.

He glanced at the clock again. He was supposed to meet some cousins at the library this morning, but he'd text them. They'd understand, especially…

Emiko.

Kazuki pressed his fist against his mouth.

Like Kazuki, Emiko had also never been called or bound. Most bindings were between Unseen of the same age, or a few years apart, and so *Obā-chama* had recently proposed the two of them should marry and mate. She had explained that if one or both of them ended up called later, as other clan members grew up, they would divorce. The calling and binding superseded all other arrangements.

Kazuki and Emiko had agreed—they were friends, they both wanted a family someday, and they were in the same year at school. Neither of them had wanted to end up perpetually alone, like two of their older cousins who had never been called.

So Emiko would understand the calling; it wasn't like he'd been unfaithful, not by Unseen standards…

But if the situation were reversed, he'd feel upset. Abandoned. He had better explain everything, in person, as soon as possible.

Reluctantly, he slipped his arm out from under his bed companion's head—she was still dreaming—and hurried to the shower. He dressed, brought in his wet laundry, and stuffed it in his combination washer-dryer. He glanced at the floor, where their clothes from yesterday were spread haphazardly. He grinned suddenly. He'd wash hers as well—wouldn't that be a thoughtful mate thing to do?

He popped their clothes in the machine, added detergent, and turned it on. Usually, he'd dry everything outside, but given the rain, and the fact she probably needed hers sooner rather than later, he set a drying cycle as well.

He checked on her and chuckled. She was a deep sleeper. Back to the kitchen. Normally he'd grab something from the Lawson for breakfast, but he wanted to cook for her. Not that there was a huge selection in his fridge—but some fresh fruit, rice, and *miso* soup should be enough, shouldn't it? He hoped she liked *miso*—he knew some foreigners disliked fermented soy. But it wasn't like *nattō*, which even some Japanese found overpowering.

Kazuki worked efficiently, starting the rice in the cooker first, then setting the water to boil. He dropped in a pinch of dried *wakame*, maybe more than he should have, and it began swelling to a generous serving. The green onions he sliced first, and he almost started peeling the apples with the same knife, but he stopped in time and washed it first. The water was boiling by the time he got the apples plated, so he turned down the heat and added a huge dollop of *miso*. He served hers the same time as his own—he wished he'd gotten her name; it was weird to think of his own mate as "the foreigner"—and sat down to eat. As he watched her soup cool, he flushed. Breakfast might be cold when she woke up.

When he finished eating, he checked on her again. She had shifted but was still sleeping. His hand hovered over her shoulder as he debated waking her. Just to announce that he was leaving though? He shook his head and grabbed a notepad featuring scarlet maple leaves.

He wrote her note—and then threw it away, realizing he'd written in Japanese. As far as he could tell, she didn't speak the language. Well, he'd aced his TOEFL, and he was even taking a class in English this semester.

But suddenly all those words he memorized wouldn't come to mind.

His note was terse. He hoped she wouldn't be offended. He set it on top of his spare robe and guest house slippers.

He hesitated, then pressed a kiss to her temple. Her fine, silky hair tickled his nose—the scent of roses and autumn that had led him to his destiny. He smiled as he left.

Kazuki carefully closed his apartment door behind him and breathed in the cool, damp autumn air—quite the contrast to yesterday, though it still echoed her scent. He pulled his umbrella from his messenger bag and discovered an unwelcome surprise—his *bentō* from yesterday. Well, that was a shame; he'd forgotten to refrigerate it. He hesitated—he didn't have time to separate the compost from the trash now, but he didn't want to carry it around all day. He'd drop the whole thing into the garbage behind the cafeteria—nobody would complain about it there.

He opened up his umbrella and started humming Anpanman's March from the kid's show. He couldn't help but do a little dance as he went down the ironwork stairs that led from his third-floor apartment to the sidewalk. When he was a few steps from the bottom, he sang the chorus aloud—*Go! Protect everyone's dream!*—and jumped the rest.

Today, he was indestructible.

He even felt optimistic about Emiko's reaction.

オーレリー

SILKY cotton slid across her limbs, luxuriously and sensuously, as Aurelie stretched. She smiled as she opened her eyes, a deep sense of well-being permeating her entire body.

And then she blinked in confusion. Where was she?

It was a large studio apartment—or a hotel room? No, definitely a studio, given the haphazard stacks of books along the walls, even though it was minimally furnished. She sat up and gaped at her own nakedness. She pulled up the duvet, a nice light blue color made from, she was pretty sure, coveted 500-hundred-thread-count cotton. Or maybe higher—it felt like rose petals. The mattress was on the floor, and she found slippers and a robe with a note on top set next to her.

Aurelie grabbed the note first.

> *Hello, my mate ♡*
>
> *You're still sleeping, but I must leave. (>_<)ʃ*
>
> *Let's talk soon! Wow! So much to say. I'll be home at 14:00. (^_^)*
>
> *My phone is...*

And there was a number, but it blurred before Aurelie's eyes. *He didn't even leave his name*, she huffed.

She touched the little heart drawn after "my mate." *My mate.*

She'd been *called.* When she closed her eyes, she could feel rain blowing against her face. No, his face.

They were *bound.*

Shit.

This couldn't be happening.

Oh, she remembered it alright, but up until thirty seconds ago, she thought all...that...had been a dream. A really good dream, but only good if it were a dream.

Aurelie knew exactly how much the call and binding could mess up a life—it didn't take much to conjure her aunt, hanging lifeless from a tree branch, to escape her binding.

Aurelie suddenly slapped her own face and then cradled it a moment.

Trite as it was, she was now certain that she was awake.

She pulled on the robe and shoved her feet into the slippers.

Okay, so if yesterday really happened, today was October third. The first day of term—Aurelie's eyes flew around the room, looking for a clock.

Eight-thirty.

Her office hours started at nine. She'd be a little late, but not terrible...except! Where was she?

Aurelie hurried to the window. An overcast sky was quietly drizzling, and it was the most beautiful sight she'd ever seen because it held her office! This apartment was even closer to campus than her own! She just needed to get dressed—she looked down at the blue bathrobe she was wearing. Where were her clothes?

She glanced around the apartment but saw no sign of them. There was, however, a soft rumbling sound coming from the kitchen that sounded like a dryer. She reached it in time to see her bright red bra strap slap the glass door. She laughed, so relieved that she didn't even care that her expensive lace bra was undoubtedly getting damaged by the machine. That was rather thoughtful of him, really, to wash her clothes. After all, she didn't have time to go back to her apartment, and it would have been terrible to wear dirty clothes on her first day of classes! Good thing she'd dressed nicely yesterday.

And then Aurelie noticed that there were *forty minutes* remaining on the dryer.

There was no way she'd make her office hours! Maybe she could borrow his clothes. They were easy enough to find, hung neatly behind some sliding closet doors, but despite their orderly presentation, they were anything but. Ripped jeans (fashionably, she supposed), oversized t-shirts with terrible English, and a couple of jackets that screamed grunge. She wrinkled her nose in distaste, trying to remember what he'd been wearing yesterday, but to her mortification, she couldn't even remember what he had looked like. If she walked past him in the street, she wouldn't even recognize him!

Well, unless she smelled him—that earthy spiciness seemed to be all around her.

Or if he touched her. Even now, her skin still bore the phantom weight of his fingers, the urgency of his mouth.

Which somehow made it that much worse that she didn't know his name, his face, or what responsibilities occupied him this morning.

He can't work an office job, she thought, *not with this closet. Unless he works for some hip tech company.*

She took a few deep breaths.

She wasn't going to make her office hours, but she should be able to make it to her class at ten. She needed to let someone know—her phone...

She found her bag, sitting on top of the shoe shelf by the door, and inside were her phone, wallet, a mask, and two *onigiri* from the day before. That was great—she could eat them today.

She texted her office neighbor Akido who agreed to put a note on her office door. Then, with great reluctance, Aurelie entered her unknown lover's phone number into her cell. She wasn't sure what to call him—he'd called her "mate," but the word had always felt like a sick joke to Aurelie.

Aurelie discovered breakfast next, and though her nerves had more or less destroyed her appetite, she sat down and tried to eat.

Despite being a bit cold, the soup was tasty, and she ended up finishing everything he had left her.

Since she still had fifteen minutes until the dryer finished, she made herself at home in his bathroom. It took her a little while to figure out how to switch between the bath and shower heads, but she managed to wash away the smell of sex and emerge as the dryer chimed.

As she left the apartment, Aurelie was aware that she was doing the infamous "walk of shame." Not that she cared about Christian notions of propriety, but she had given up hope of finding a sexual partner over a decade ago, so it was unnerving to have lost her virginity in a one-night stand (if she had her way) at thirty-six years old.

It felt like all eyes were on her as she crossed campus—and maybe they were. Aurelie's hair was unusual in the States, and here it was practically a beacon, even accounting for the fact some Japanese bleached their hair blonde.

At last, she reached the gray building that housed her English immersion lecture on Medieval Europe. Akido had warned her that the students would be taking it for language practice and probably wouldn't be particularly interested in the actual material.

Up a flight of stairs to room 202—she checked her phone to find she was only two minutes early rather than the ten she'd been advised to be, but still, given her morning, she felt pretty damn good about herself.

She swung open the solid wood door, and entered a room with old linoleum, wide windows (cracked to increase ventilation), ten long tables, an incongruously modern projector and interactive board. She had checked the room out yesterday, so it was vaguely familiar. Less familiar was the stream of rapid Japanese.

Oh, not directed at her—the students were talking

to each other.

But the weird thing was, she understood it all. Aurelie had been studying Japanese, and she could manage simple conversations, but this was fast and full of slang. So why was it as clear as if they were speaking English?

"I hate foreign professors," said a brash voice to her left. "She blew off her office hours the first day! I needed to get her to sign my drop form, but since she wasn't there, I had to come to this class, just so it wouldn't mess up my attendance!"

Hayashi University had a strict attendance policy that professors had to follow. Aurelie's face burned at the student's (valid) criticism. She walked down the narrow aisle and stopped behind the student to whom he was talking.

"I'm sorry about that, I had some extraordinary circumstances this morning. If you have your form now, I can sign it, and you don't have to stay for class." She said that in Japanese. Aurelie didn't know if she should feel proud or scared.

The student, who was still looking at his friend, jerked his head up at her spiel. "Oh—well, thanks."

He passed a form to his friend, who turned to hand it to Aurelie.

She looked down and met the eyes of her lover from the night before. She'd been an idiot to think she wouldn't recognize him; she would have known him even in a crowd of a hundred Unseen, all wearing masks.

林大学の後期

10月

日	月	火	水	木	金	土
					1	2
3	4	5	6	7	8	9
10	11	12	13	14	15	16
17	18	19	20	21	22	23
24	25	26	27	28	29	30
31						

11月

日	月	火	水	木	金	土
	1	2	3	4	5	6
7	8	9	10	11	12	13
14	15	16	17	18	19	20
21	22	23	24	25	26	27
28	29	30				

12月

日	月	火	水	木	金	土
			1	2	3	4
5	6	7	8	9	10	11
12	13	14	15	16	17	18
19	20	21	22	23	24	25
26	27	28	29			

1月

日	月	火	水	木	金	土
				5	6	7	8
9	10	11	12	13	14	15
16	17	18	19	20	21	22
23	24	25	26	27	28	29
30	31					

2月

日	月	火	水	木	金	土
		1	2	3	4	5
6	7	8	9	10	11	12
13	14	16	16	17	18	19
20	21	22	23	24	25	26
27	28					

3月

日	月	火	水	木	金	土
		1	2	3	4	5
6	7	8	9	10	11	12
13	14	15	16	17	18	19
20	21	22	23	24	25	26
27	28	29	30	31		

10月4日：授業開始
12月30日〜1月4日：冬季休業
1月24日〜2月4日：定期試験
3月25日：卒業式

3. SCHOOLED

THE tight, ripped jeans and oversized T-shirts looked a lot better on him than they did on his hangers. He was muscular for an Unseen (which meant he was more human supermodel than athlete). Deep black eyes were framed by ridiculous lashes, and slashing brows made him look surprised (or maybe he *was* surprised—she certainly was). She couldn't see his lips, but she *felt* them curl into a smile against the polyester of his mask.

At least she knew why his closet had looked like that of a jobless youth. He was a student.

Her student.

Fuckfuckfuckfuck.

No, that was what had gotten her into all this

trouble in the first place.

Aurelie swallowed a hysterical giggle and struggled to breathe while she had visions of Japanese police bursting into the room and arresting her.

No, surely, he wasn't a minor—he was a university student. Probably a junior or senior, so twenty or even twenty-one. The police wouldn't be called—just the university ethics review board. She'd be fired faster than she could write her name in *katakana* and sent back to the US in shame.

Maybe she'd never work as a professor again.

Panic rose up like a tsunami, but before it could make landfall and wash her away, a great calm swept through Aurelie.

It's going to be okay.

That was *not* her thought.

"Good morning, Dubois-*sensei*," said the man-child who'd dubbed her "my mate" a few hours earlier.

Well, he could be calm. Aurelie had only skimmed the policy regarding affairs with students because she had never expected to be tempted to break it, but she was pretty sure that the student was considered the victim and thus not punished.

But, she suddenly thought, he considered her his mate. Even before Aurelie knew he was her student, she had had no intention of accepting that role, but that meant he wouldn't want her to be fired and deported. He wasn't going to tell anyone. Could it be harder to hide this indiscretion than to hide the fact they weren't even human?

Aurelie forced herself to accept the drop form.

Their fingers brushed, and she wondered that the paper didn't incinerate from the heat that generated. It was a good thing they were in a room full of curious eyes—otherwise she might jump him. Again. His smile faded, and his eyes heated, responding to her lust.

Note to self: do not meet him alone. Ever.

She signed the paper, and she managed not to soak it with nervous sweat. She asked, "And your name is?"

"Hayashi Kazuki."

"Hayashi," she repeated. "That sounds like the university."

He chuckled. "It does."

A couple students laughed, as if Kazuki had made a hilarious joke.

Aurelie handed the page to the impatient student and walked on to the podium. She drummed her fingers on its scarred wooden surface as she opened up the attendance form on her phone. Her eyes lingered on Hayashi Kazuki's name. She didn't know if there were any homophones for Hayashi, but it didn't just sound like the university, it had the same character.

And as if from a great distance, a warning from Akido floated through her memory.

"Oh, you've got the son of one of the board members in Medieval Europe. Their family founded the university. Don't worry—he's a great student. But—do your best in that class. Just in case. You don't want him talking badly about you to his father."

Did—did that mean this university was founded by Unseen?

That Kazuki wasn't some anomaly, some lone

survivor like that French bastard, but in fact a member of larger Unseen clan that had somehow survived in Japan? No, not only survived, but thrived, if they were founding universities?

It couldn't be. Just because she'd been called didn't mean she'd start believing in fantasies.

和希

THIS was wonderful. She was his professor!

Well, it did make things a little awkward. The university said faculty weren't supposed to date students enrolled in their classes, but at least she wasn't a tourist!

While Keshi had been complaining about the professor missing office hours, Kazuki had been trying to figure out how to keep her in Japan—or follow her home when he graduated in March. But if she were a professor, she clearly had a work visa. Hopefully, she was planning on staying for a few years. If so, they'd have plenty of time to marry, and she could apply for permanent residency. Or something. He knew it was complicated to marry foreigners, but he didn't know the specifics. He never expected to, after all.

With a guilty start, he remembered Emiko. She had met his admission at the library with skepticism. In fact, she had all but said that he had slept with a human and deluded himself into thinking she was Unseen. She had forbidden him from telling the others, and she had sat on the opposite side of the room—*kuso*, she had this class, too.

Kazuki glanced at Emiko and was unnerved to find

her glaring at him.

She knows.

He looked away. He didn't blame her for being upset—how would he feel if the situation were reversed?—but it didn't change anything.

He focused on Aurelie's self-introduction. The other stuff could be sorted out later.

恵美子

COULD this day get any worse?

This morning, Emiko had greeted her boyfriend with a cup of tea, and he had told her that he'd slept with somebody else.

Okay, so Kazuki wasn't *exactly* her boyfriend. He was the only available option—the only male of her species who was A) her age and B) hadn't been called. They had made out exactly once and it had been so awkward that it was depressing, but Kazuki was the closest thing she had to a boyfriend. Even though they'd never discussed fidelity, she had assumed it wouldn't be a problem. Because of aforementioned A and B.

Yeah, there'd been an asterisk—if either one of them was called, maybe when a child of the clan reached puberty, their arrangement would end. But given that they were both twenty-two, and the biggest mate age-gap that Emiko could think of was six years (and that was unusual), that possibility had felt more and more unlikely.

So Kazuki's claim had been terrible and awkward, and the only redeeming part of this morning was when she realized that Kazuki must have slept with a human woman. There was no way that the clan would let that fly—twenty years ago an Unseen had tried to start a romantic relationship with a human, and they had been under unofficial house-arrest at the family estate ever since.

But he hadn't slept with a human. He had legitimately been called to a foreign Unseen and bound with her.

Emiko knew this because the jezebel who'd stolen her fiancé was now standing in Emiko's classroom as a *professor*.

Emiko wasn't sure how she knew that the foreigner was an Unseen. The professor's face was half-covered by a gray mask, and there were human women who were equally skinny and tall. Not many maybe, but some.

But she'd seen Kazuki unrobe the professor with his eyes when she stood in front of him, and she'd seen the way their eyes had met. The way their fingers had touched and lingered.

And she'd known, even though it would have been inconceivable yesterday, that an American Unseen was in Nara, and she was now teaching Emiko European history.

And she was doing a terrible job. This class was supposed to be taught in English.

Emiko shot her hand into the air—a missile taking off to decimate the American.

Alright, that was a little World War II of her, but seriously, she was *pissed.*

The professor called on her, and Emiko unleashed her fury.

"Excuse me, Professor Dubois, this class is supposed to be taught in English."

There. That was telling her.

オーレリー

AT least Aurelie only had to cover the administrative tasks today. She had even managed to still her fingers, thanks to Kazuki's continuous bolstering of her mood, but Aurelie didn't think she could manage higher order thinking.

It galled her to need help, but she was grateful to him. Left to her own, she might have fainted. She would definitely be babbling.

Instead, she was doing a decent job of her self-introduction. Of course, given the number of interviews she'd done in order to get a teaching position in Japan, she probably could have rattled off her credentials while hanging from her ankles. Which was how she felt—like the whole world was upside down.

One of the students' hands shot up.

"Yes? Morimoto-*san*?"

"Excuse me, Professor Dubois, this class is supposed to be taught in English."

Aurelie had thought she was speaking English. Her Japanese definitely wasn't good enough to have said all that she'd been saying.

She looked at Kazuki again. His elbow was on his desk, his chin balanced on his right fist insouciantly.

His eyes had been glued to her since their hands had touched—in fact, she could see herself if she focused.

And she looked beautiful, brilliant, and competent.

He was way too young for her, and he chose clothes that looked like they were falling apart, but...

She felt like she had finally come home.

That thought was terrifying.

She forced herself to look back at Morimoto. Very deliberately speaking English, Aurelie said, "Thank you for the reminder, Ms. Morimoto. As I was saying..."

和希

"AURELIE Dubois" sounded French to Kazuki, but she started her self-introduction by saying she was an American.

She had studied at the University of Vermont. Kazuki didn't know that state, but he would Google it later.

Emiko interrupted to point out that Aurelie was speaking Japanese—Kazuki hadn't noticed, but he was glad she was fluent after all. It must have been the strength of the calling yesterday that stopped her from speaking.

Aurelie resumed in English, and Kazuki was surprised that he followed effortlessly.

It's because we're bound, he realized with delight. Her own fluency was transferring to him. Well, wasn't that a handy side-effect?

Aurelie completed her graduate studies at Yale, and Kazuki felt as proud as if he'd been the one who'd gone to one of the best schools in the world.

Her voice hitched when she explained that she'd spent a few years teaching and researching in France. It seemed unlikely that Google could explain that hitch, so Kazuki decided to ask her about it later. After France, she ended up at Duke. She glanced away from the class, and her stress shifted into sadness. Through their binding, Kazuki pushed a little more reassurance.

How could such a gorgeous woman have so much sadness?

That was the word he kept linking to her—from that American pop song that his sister had been obsessed with back in high school. *Gorgeous.* Unattainable was what it meant.

Kind of strange for him to think of that, when he'd already attained her. Maybe it was the fact she was his professor. They would definitely have to be circumspect for a few months—Kazuki didn't think her job would be in danger, not with his father on the board, but rumors were never helpful.

"Are there any questions?" asked Aurelie.

He liked that name. It was Japanese-friendly, not that it mattered, but it was nice that her name wouldn't be butchered for the rest of her life. Americans with "th" names had to reconcile themselves to "s," but Aurelie would sound almost the same.

Kazuki raised his hand, glorying in the privilege of drawing his mate's attention.

Her white-blond eyebrows snapped together, and he could feel her suspicion. He sent her soothing thoughts.

"Yes, Mr. Hayashi?"

"What's your family like? How do they feel about you working in Japan?"

Across the room, Emiko added, "Are you married? Boyfriend?"

Kazuki turned to glare at her.

オ ー レ ッ ー

SHE'D been prepared for personal questions, but not for ones coming from Kazuki. Naturally, he wanted to know if there were other Unseen in America. He was probably as curious about her family as she was about his.

But the whole answers were too messy to share in front of a class. She was grateful for the obnoxious inquiry into her relationship status from the girl who'd corrected her for speaking English because it had an obvious rebuff.

She cocked one of her eyebrows and looked down her nose at the girl. "I don't see how that has any bearing on my credentials. Are there any questions that do relate to my work?"

The girl replied immediately. "Why did you choose to come to Japan?"

Because she had to go somewhere that French bastard couldn't go. And there had been those letters in France, which had made her think Japan held secrets of the Unseen.

She hadn't considered it might hold living Unseen.

"Most of my research is on folklore. Stories are a way that people pass on their values and make sense of compelling events around them. Recently, I became interested in Japanese folklore. I also was ready to live somewhere new." She shrugged. "So here I am."

"Wasn't it hard to move during the pandemic?" asked another student.

That had a nice technical answer that Aurelie threw herself into perhaps too enthusiastically. There were a few more questions, then she called up the class syllabus on the screen.

和希

KAZUKI was a little disappointed when Aurelie ended the self-introduction to go over the course syllabus. She explained they'd be writing five essays in English in addition to the final exam. This wasn't a slacker's class, but Kazuki mused it might become one for him. He had a sudden vision of lying in bed, Aurelie using him as a pillow while she proofed his paper. He was glad his mask covered his grin when Aurelie paused to look at him again.

Could she see his fantasy?

He forced himself to think about European history and grades for the rest of class.

But as soon as she dismissed them, he was on his feet and at her side.

"Can I carry your bag for you, Professor Dubois?" He reached for the strap as he spoke.

She jerked it out of his hands.

"I'm fine by myself, thanks." Her voice was brittle. Hard.

Fine by myself. Kazuki felt tension stretch between his shoulders. He tried to lean into the binding, only to find it harder than before. Could she be talking about more than the bag?

オーレリー

KAZUKI bounded up to her after class ended, his eyes two big heart emojis.

And inside those hearts were her. Or—not her, but an idealized version of her.

The woman in Kazuki's eyes was intelligent, well-bred, elegant, and confident.

That woman never gone days without bathing to avoid that French bastard; she hadn't passed her adolescence so cringingly grateful to a human stepfather that she also despised him; she hadn't contemplated finding a tree-branch like her aunt when she uncovered the sordid truth in France.

If Kazuki's family founded this university—

He would think her trash when he learned about her past.

Kazuki tried to carry her bag, like they were dating in high school.

She had to push him away.

She grabbed the bag and said, "I'm fine by myself, thanks."

He looked as if she'd slapped him.

And she suddenly realized that not only had he put her on a pedestal, he was happy about the calling. The binding. For her, this was a nightmare. For him, it was a dream come true.

Tears pricked her eyes, and she swept the room with her gaze, taking a moment to collect herself.

Most of the other students were filtering out the door rather than paying any attention to the drama unfolding between their classmate and professor. That meant it didn't look like drama.

She needed to keep it that way, while explaining to him that they couldn't be together.

And not just because she was a professor and he was a student, making a relationship between them beyond inappropriate.

"You asked about my family," she finally said. "I am not close to them. I have worked very hard, in fact, to put some distance between us. That was even part of my motivation for coming to Japan. I expect to—" she swallowed, finding the words harder to say than she expected, "—to focus on my studies here. I'm not here to make friends or—or anything else."

"I'm happy to hear that," came another voice, and Aurelie turned to find the girl who had corrected her. As Aurelie watched, she slipped her hand through Kazuki's elbow. "Professor Dubois, did Kazuki tell you that I'm his fiancée?"

Now it was Aurelie's turn to feel buffeted by a metaphorical blow. (Which was the opposite of how she should feel).

But a greater shock was yet to come. As Aurelie turned toward the "fiancée," the hair on the back of her neck stood up. She had been so focused on Kazuki that she hadn't even noticed the second Unseen among her students.

和希

KAZUKI swallowed. Aurelie really wasn't just talking about the bag.

She—as impossible as it seemed—intended to disregard the mate binding. To act like yesterday never happened.

He supposed he shouldn't be surprised. She was the most gorgeous—*kuso,* there was that word again—Unseen he had ever met, and she was obviously competent and self-reliant. The idea that she had achieved a professorship and travelled abroad as an Unseen without the support of her family...

Kazuki's whole life had been determined by the Hayashi clan. Her independence was as alluring to him as her scent; but his age and obvious dependence on his family must repulse her. Had he really joked about the university having the same name as his family?

He didn't have a chance to think of a reply though—Emiko came up and took his arm. Kazuki tried to pull away, but she held fast and introduced herself as his fiancée.

Aurelie gave Emiko a hard look. Kazuki could feel Aurelie's roiling emotions, even if they were oddly muted compared to before, but an outsider would think her unfazed. "How many of you are there?"

"Fiancées?" asked Emiko—choosing the most obnoxious interpretation, Kazuki was sure. "I'm not sure what you consider normal, but here we tend to prefer monogamous relationships. One man, one woman."

Aurelie's shoulders hitched, but she shook her head. Dropping her voice, she clarified, "How many Unseen are there?"

Emiko was too annoyed at Aurelie's lack of reaction to respond, so Kazuki seized the lead. He twitched his arm free from Emiko's hand and said, "There's about a thousand of us."

She swayed on her feet, and Kazuki caught her.

He could feel her overwhelming shock. He wished they could speak in private, but Emiko clearly wasn't going to leave.

So, despite Aurelie's recent withdrawal, he pushed on the mate binding.

4. REJECTED

恵美子

THEY'RE really bound. And it's a strong binding. Emiko suddenly felt petty and depressed.

She could see the two of them were communing silently, the way her grandparents did. Her parents didn't have that powerful of a connection. If the binding was fate as legend said, then Kazuki had never bound because he was waiting for this foreigner to show up, to strengthen the clan's magic once again.

But if Kazuki had found his fated mate, where did that leave her?

It was too mortifying to sit here and watch, as Kazuki and the professor did... whatever they were doing.

Emiko turned and walked away. She glanced back

once, at the door, but they hadn't even noticed her leave.

Despising herself, she lingered in the hallway—she didn't want the two of them to be interrupted by another student—but when she heard them approach the door, she quickly ducked into a restroom on her right.

Her heart was racing as she leaned back against the door. Taking a steadying breath, she went to the sink, pulled down her mask, and splashed her face with cold water.

She focused on the broad rectangular mirror in front of her.

Her face was slim, her nose a little too long, and her eyes dark. She had never thought of herself as pretty or not—she was Unseen—but she felt rather dowdy compared to the professor.

It had always sucked to not be called. It was lonely. But with Kazuki unbound, she hadn't been alone. She wrapped her arms around herself in a parody of a hug.

What was she going to do now?

If the calling was magic—*fate*—was she a dud destined for nothing?

オーレリー

KAZUKI'S sincerity, interest, and confidence pouring through the binding was like gorging on chocolate. Euphoric, but stomach churning. An intimacy that Aurelie craved but couldn't digest.

His apology made her heart ache. He blamed

himself for not stopping the call.

That would have been as impossible as stopping her monthly menstruation. It was simply an inconvenient element of their genetic makeup. And truth be told, if he had been as cognizant during it as it seemed—she had been nearly mindless herself—then she was the one to blame. The strength of the call was definitely her body's desperation to fulfill its biological purpose.

Producing a little Unseen to stop their species from going extinct.

And then came his practical worry.

He needed to tell his family about her. Even if she refused to marry him, to stay in Japan, how could he forget there were more Unseen in the world?

和希

AURELIE leaned into him, and Kazuki wrapped his arms around her. Tears were streaming from her eyes, and she was having trouble breathing. Kazuki pulled her mask, below her chin, but absently.

Most of his attention was on the images that flowed back through their bond. A wooden house that shook in a strong breeze. Bare feet stained green by grass and black by dirt.

Many blond women, many blond babies.

All girls.

Aurelie had thought their species was dying out. That their fear of discovery by humans had driven them to extinction.

That there might be more than a thousand Unseen in Japan...

Kazuki showed her family parties—New Year's, *Omizutori*, *Obon*, births, deaths, and *tsukimi*—reassuring her that the clan was strong and large. Her thoughts swirled too fast to follow, and suddenly she hugged Kazuki back. Her anguish changed to hope; her jagged breathing to a tremulous laugh.

All the tension left Kazuki's shoulders.

She wasn't against their binding—she wasn't against *him*—she had simply been unwilling to bring Unseen children into this world to die alone. She had been trying to take that burden upon herself.

As her laugh strengthened, turned jubilant, Kazuki laughed too. "Can we talk about the future now? Our future?"

Aurelie ripped herself from his arms.

She stared at him for a beat, then leapt to her feet and swiped at her eyes like they had personally offended her. Without so much as a goodbye, she scurried from the room.

The antagonism radiating off of her had been so intense that he hadn't dared call out to her, much less follow.

In fact, he was still sitting in the classroom, trying to make sense of it all when his cell chimed. He pulled out his iPhone and found the message.

This is Professor Dubois. You can call any time after 7 pm to discuss the project.

He stared at the mail for some time, and not just because it was in English and his miraculous fluency had left with Aurelie. There were so many things he wanted to send in return, and yet he got her unwritten message too because his family practiced it as well: you didn't record Unseen secrets. Not anywhere.

So his questions would have to wait until 19:00. He saved her as a contact (Dubois-*sensei*) and went to lunch.

オ ー レ リ ー

WHAT was wrong with her?

Despite all her resolutions, Aurelie had sobbed her eyes out *in his arms.*

Yes, it had been shocking to learn there were so many Unseen in the world. Both terrifying and wondrous. Overwhelming.

But couldn't she have waited until she had gotten back to her office to bawl? She had just finished putting up barriers between them!

She was so mad at herself. He was a kid—practically, anyway. She needed to be the adult, the responsible one. She was contemptible, jerking him around like that. Even if she hadn't intended to lean on him specifically. At that moment, if anyone had found her and wrapped her in a hug, Aurelie probably wouldn't have resisted.

Knowing she looked like she had sobbed her eyes out, Aurelie beelined to the bathroom to repair her appearance.

She stopped short inside the door.

"Hello," she said to Kazuki's fiancée.

The girl's face was bare, her mask under her chin, and water droplets clung to her cheeks. For a moment,

Aurelie thought she had been crying too, but then she realized she'd been washing her face.

"Hi," said the girl. Emiko, Morimoto Emiko.

Aurelie drummed her fingers against her thigh. "I didn't mean..." She flushed. *I didn't mean to sleep with your fiancé, who happens to be my student.* She would choke on those words.

"I know," said Emiko. "I'm sorry I was rude. It's been a weird morning. But Kazuki-*kun* and I were only engaged because neither of us had been called." She shifted her weight back and forth between her feet.

"Do you want to get lunch with me?" Emiko blurted.

Aurelie hesitated. Part of her wanted to run as fast as she could. But Emiko also represented information and was far less unsettling than Kazuki.

"Please," Aurelie said.

Fifteen minutes later, they were seated in a small on-campus café. Aurelie had a steaming bowl of soba before her, as well as a small dish of tempura veggies. Emiko had the same.

Aurelie fiddled with her chopsticks before forcing herself to look at Emiko. "So, how many, uh, family members do you have at this university?"

"*Ēto*, twenty-two are students." Emiko folded her chopstick wrapper into a holder with the efficiency of experience. "Not my entire family goes to this university, but most of them do. And there's also some on the faculty and staff. Maybe forty?"

"Wow," said Aurelie.

"How big is your—family—in America?"

Aurelie didn't actually know the answer. "The

family is dying out because there are no young men. My mother moved my sister and I far from the rest of them when I was ten."

"No young men," Emiko repeated.

Aurelie was surprised that was what interested Emiko, but then she understood. Emiko must be wondering if there was a mate for her in the US.

Aurelie tapped the table twice and then raised her eyes to Emiko's. "I'm sorry."

Emiko shrugged.

"So what are you majoring in?" asked Aurelie.

Emiko's brows raised at the abrupt change in subject, but then she smiled. "English, actually. Though I never expected to go abroad. The family forbids leaving the country, but there's enough foreign business that it's acceptable for a few of us to focus on it."

"The family dictates your major?"

"Not entirely, but all life decisions get discussed. And we meet with *Obā-chama* after important milestones, like high school graduation."

"*Obā-chama?*"

"Kazuki's great-grandmother. We all call her *Obā-chama.* She's the head of the family. Doesn't yours have a head?"

"The last one I knew of died before my mother took us from the clan. I don't know if anyone ever took her place," Aurelie admitted. She stuffed broccoli tempura into her mouth, lest she say more than she needed to.

Emiko blinked twice. "I can't imagine that. Or, maybe I can. I wouldn't mind a little less family expectation, though of course I am grateful for their support."

Aurelie nodded mechanically and tried the noodles. Slightly sweet, with a salty broth. She liked it.

"Just so you know," said Emiko, "a lot of modern soba noodles have wheat in them. Be sure to check if you buy it elsewhere."

This opened the floodgates; Aurelie seeking advice on the mundanities of life in Japan, and Emiko asking questions about how the US and France differed.

It was while they were laughing over Aurelie's confusion over the toilets at the airport (why were there so many buttons?) that Aurelie suddenly realized that she was enjoying herself. It didn't hurt that Emiko's English was excellent and that she was extremely polite, though every now and then Aurelie saw hints of strength and rebellion that made Aurelie feel she had found a friend.

Never had she made one so quickly before, but there was no binding with a friend. Maybe this was safe?

When Emiko slurped down the last of her soup, Aurelie impulsively suggested exchanging numbers.

There was a visible hesitation before Emiko nodded and smiled. "I wanted to hate you," Emiko admitted, "but a friend is better than an enemy."

"The thing you'd hate me over won't come to pass," Aurelie promised.

Emiko narrowed her eyes and then said, "Well, I wish it would. Kazuki-*kun* is a good person."

Aurelie flushed. "I know that."

And she thought about it as she braved a thick mist

back to her office. Kazuki was a good person, but bindings were dangerous. They gave someone else power over you; they clouded your judgment. Even if Kazuki seemed to be a good person, how could she trust him with herself? To expose her sister and mother to another male who might—no. No, she couldn't risk it.

In fact, she was even doubting that Japan was the sanctuary that she had imagined. The Hayashi clan seemed too good to be true, and Aurelie was uneasy about the whole thing.

和希

MOST of Kazuki's cousins sat at their usual outdoor picnic table when he arrived for lunch, though Emiko was noticeably absent.

He waited for someone to ask about Aurelie, but no one did, and he realized Emiko must have kept it a secret. He felt relieved and had to ask himself why.

Because you'll be the first Unseen in the history of the clan to be rejected after *a binding.*

If he could keep this secret for a little while he talked Aurelie around—well, that would be good.

Kazuki stuffed some sticky rice dotted with black sesame seeds into his mouth as he listened to his cousins dissect a new online game.

When they invited him to an internet café to try it out, he declined. He wanted to talk about Aurelie, but not with the guys. Instead, he walked to the roof of the film studies' building and called his sister.

"This is unusual," Yuriko said as she answered the

phone.

"Yeah. Well, something unusual happened."

"Okay," she replied. "I'll bite."

"I met an Unseen. In Nara."

"Yeah? Aren't there like fifty of you there?" She sounded bored.

"Not a relative. A *foreign* Unseen."

Silence. "Sorry, what?"

"I met an Unseen woman from America, and I was called to her."

Yuriko burst out laughing. It was a few minutes before Kazuki was even able to make himself heard.

"*Onē-chan. Onē-chan!* I'm not joking!"

"Yeah, okay, I'm not an idiot."

"Her name is Aurelie Dubois! She's an exchange professor!"

"Oh, yeah? And why are you just meeting her now? Are you trying to tell me that you missed her all last semester?"

"No—you know American schools don't follow the same academic calendar. I guess she was only hired for the second semester. She's teaching Medieval Europe."

"Riiiight. And so you strolled into your history class, and boom! Bound with your professor?"

"No, I didn't meet her in class. I met her yesterday."

"So why didn't you call me yesterday?"

"Because I was called! All last night we—well, we were...binding."

"Binding? Wait, you mean...

"Hayashi Kazuki! Did you have sex with a human?"

Kazuki considered kneeling on the roof and

smashing his head against the concrete a few times. That would undoubtedly be more productive than this conversation. "No! I told you, she's an Unseen."

"That's impossible. Wait, so you did have sex with her?"

Kazuki let out a groan. "Hayashi Yuriko!" he said, since she had busted out his full name. "You are missing the most important part. I am sure—completely sure—that she is an Unseen. She says there are more—but not many more—in America."

Yuriko was quiet for a long time. "Really?"

"Yes."

She checked three more times, before saying, "Okay. Okay. I believe you. If you're sure..."

"I'm sure!"

"Wow. Wow. I don't know what to say. Yes, I do. Congratulations! You were called."

"Well, don't congratulate me yet."

"Why not?"

"She, umm, she wants to ignore the binding."

Although Kazuki couldn't see her, he imagined Yuriko cocking her head, the way she always did when she was thinking hard.

"Why?" The word was drawn out, heavy with confusion.

"Well, I guess there's the fact I'm a student and she's a professor. And she's a lot older than me." Kazuki had done some math based on her college graduation year and realized she was close to forty. That was weird to think about, but it obviously hadn't been a problem last night, so...

"Okay, it's a *binding*. All of that means nothing next to it. There's got to be another reason."

"Maybe she doesn't want to live in Japan for the rest of her life." But Kazuki didn't buy that either. Now that Yuriko had said it, he was sure there was something else bothering Aurelie. Some reason she didn't like bindings.

"Wait, if she's rejecting the binding—you want the binding?"

"Yes, obviously."

"Then you'd better not tell the family."

"Why?" He had already decided not to tell until Aurelie accepted their binding, but he didn't think Yuriko cared about his pride.

"I just realized—don't you think Kento-*san* or Shigeru-*san* would be very interested in meeting her?"

Yuriko had named the uncalled male Unseen in the family, both of whom were ten to twenty years older than Kazuki.

Making them Aurelie's age.

It was all too easy to imagine what she was suggesting, but it wasn't as if they would be called to her—she was already bound to him.

Kazuki thought about the way Aurelie had rejected him. Her determination to put some distance between them.

He was a college student—her college student. Would she be so fast to reject Shigeru, who ran his own company and turned a tidy profit year after year? Or Kento, who managed the family investments and owned four cars?

They would be all too eager to woo Aurelie even without a calling, and they'd be far better at it then Kazuki.

"Okay, so I need to get this binding figured out before the family finds out," Kazuki said.

"Yeah. Do your classmates know?"

"Only Emiko-*san*."

"Oof. How'd she take it?" Yuriko asked.

Kazuki sighed.

"That well, huh?"

"At least she's not eager to spread the news around," said Kazuki. "Hey, *Onē-chan*, I'm supposed to call Aurelie-*san* tonight. What do you advise?"

"Advise?"

"I mean—if Takeshi-*san* wanted you to do something you didn't want to do, what would be effective?"

Yuriko burst out laughing.

5. ANSWERED

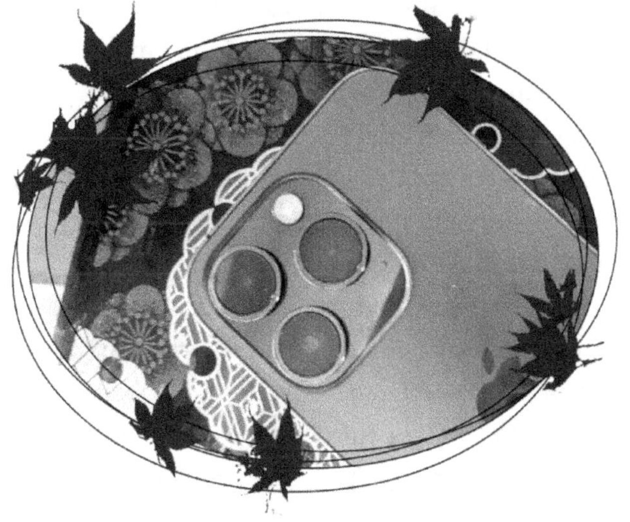

AFTER lunch, Aurelie had two hours before her afternoon lecture. She traded her rather damp mask for a spare from her desk and pulled up Kazuki's student record. Twenty-two years old as of July. Film studies major. If that didn't scream what's-a-job rich... He had a high GPA though, even in tough, out-of-major classes. Why was he taking Medieval Europe anyway? The English credit?

After staring at his student photo longer than she intended (Aurelie didn't look that good on any of her photo IDs), she brought up her class list for Colonialism in the Americas. She didn't want to be surprised by another of Kazuki's cousins.

Both Hayashi and Morimoto had *kanji* for trees in

their names. "Dubois" meant "of wood" in French. So Aurelie looked for family names with similar meanings.

There were many—Kimura, Kobayashi, Suzuki...

Okay, well, half the students in the university were not Unseen.

She Googled the most common last names in Japan (she'd met plenty of Dubois's in France, and all of them had been human), and sure enough, tree-*kanji* were sprinkled throughout them.

She rubbed her temples. She did sort of want to meet more Unseen—maybe they had answers to some of her questions—but she also didn't like being caught off-guard. But unless she was going to beg Kazuki or Emiko to sort through her class list, she was going to have to wing it.

Seeking distraction, she pulled up her email and found, among beginning of the semester reminders, a note from her sister.

Hi Au –

Went to call you and but realized it was 3 am before I hit dial! Aren't you lucky?

Aurelie snorted.

Dan fell this morning when he was feeding the animals.

Aurelie frowned. *Fell*? Dan was the epitome of a Yankee farmer; he went walking in all weather and threw hay bales around for fun. Though—was he going to be eighty this year?

Mom found him really confused and bleeding, so

she took him to UVM.

Oh, no. Her mother *hated* hospitals and doctor's offices. She said the antibacterial wipes they used made her skin itch.

> The doctors say he was lucky so far as the fall goes, but they think he had a seizure. So they are doing a lot of tests.

That didn't sound so bad—if Aurelie were home, she'd do the paperwork for her mother, but of course her mom had been handling all of that herself for years now. (Years—had it been four years since Aurelie had been home? Yes, not since France...)

> I wasn't sure if I should tell you, since there isn't anything you can do, but then I realized I will have to cancel our video call since I have to do Dan's chores tonight.
>
> Anyway, if my timeline is right, you are out of quarantine and maybe even teaching already?! So exciting. I hope Japan is as beautiful as the photos. Send me some!
>
> Lis

Aurelie hit reply, but her fingers twitched above the keyboard, unable to decide which keys they needed. Should she mention Kazuki and the other Unseen? She could do it without saying anything incriminating, and Lisette ought to know but...

Where to start? What to say?

And would it sound like bragging when Lisette was obviously overwhelmed and alone?

Lisette had moved back in with their mother and

stepfather after her marriage ended. She was a vet, and there was plenty of work among the dairy farms near their home, but (and maybe Aurelie was just projecting her own values), it seemed like settling. Giving up.

In the end, Aurelie expressed her regrets about her stepfather and attached the few pics she took in the park before the calling. After a moment, she texted her mother, too. There was no reply—since it was now the middle of the night in Vermont, that was hardly surprising.

She then turned to work and by the time she walked into her afternoon lecture (Colonialism in the Americas) she was once again projecting cool detachment. She did scan the stadium seats for Unseen eyes, but either there weren't any or they were all too good at passing for human.

This class wasn't cross-listed as an English credit (though the students knew many of the readings were in English), so Aurelie made an effort to do her self-introduction and even part of the syllabus presentation in Japanese. She felt awkward without Kazuki's skill extending to her, but the students all clapped and said how skilled she was.

Of course, it was the same condescending tone Akido had adopted when Aurelie had managed to fill out her own residency registration form with Japanese characters, so she thought the praise said more about their need to be polite than her actual proficiency, but she'd take it.

When she headed home in the evening, it was raining again. Aurelie would have ignored the soft drizzle, but Akido happened to be leaving at the same time and was overly concerned.

"I'll drive you," said Akido.

"Oh, no, don't worry about it!" Aurelie protested. "I want to stop at the supermarket anyway—"

"Then I'll take you there. You don't know Japanese food yet; I will help."

Aurelie wanted to protest that meat, rice, and vegetables weren't that different world over (not to mention she had already successfully shopped on her own on Saturday), but she didn't want to offend Akido. He had been generous with his time so far, helping her translate her schedules to English and her syllabi to Japanese, and she was sure she would continue to need his help.

The grocery trip took longer than it would have taken Aurelie alone because Akido kept trying to get her to buy "American" foods—particularly bread, which Aurelie never ate, since she (like all Unseen, so far as she knew) couldn't digest gluten. She finally accepted the bread so Akido would let her check out and resolved to come back tomorrow for the things she wanted.

But she ended up being grateful for his company after all because he registered her for the store's rewards program during checkout. Aurelie had a tight budget, because she felt obliged to send money home, and every little bit helped.

"You'll save so much money that you can pay for your welcome dinner this weekend," Akido joked, and then hurried to add, "I'll pay though. You must save for marriage and children."

Aurelie hunched her shoulders. "I'm a bit old to have children."

"Nonsense! Everyone gets started later these days."

Aurelie snorted. "Right, that's why you're a grandpa at fifty."

Akido laughed happily. "My son and I found our wives early!"

He dropped her off a few minutes later, and Aurelie met her neighbor going into the building, so she offered her the bread.

"Oh, yum! Thank you so much!" the woman said in Japanese.

"Don't mention it!" Aurelie responded. "I'm allergic. Please enjoy." They bowed to each other what seemed an excessive number of times, before Aurelie made it inside her apartment.

She locked the metal door and sagged against it.

She scanned the apartment. It was too large for her (two bedrooms, a living room, dine-in kitchen, and the bath area), and yet felt a little cramped to Aurelie because the ceiling was low (the light fixtures all dangled at eye level). It didn't feel nearly as comfortable as Kazuki's studio.

Which had nothing to do with Kazuki! He just had a nice apartment, even if it could use a few more pieces of furniture. Like a loveseat or at least an armchair.

She kicked off her shoes and stepped up onto the tatami floor (the entryway was about four inches lower than the rest of the apartment to separate the shoe area from the no-shoe area). She tried to ignore her shoes, lying haphazardly behind her, but she only went two steps before turning back and turning them so their toes pointed to the door (apparently it was bad luck to leave them pointing into the house, as if you'd never leave again).

She went to her bedroom first, to change into pajamas and check the time.

18:46, her alarm clock read. Subtract twelve, that made it quarter till seven. (Would she ever adjust to a 24-hour clock?)

She sat on the bed, pulled out her phone, and waited for Kazuki to call.

That lasted all of thirty seconds before she realized what she was doing.

She dropped the phone on the bed and returned to the entryway for her groceries. Some of them should be refrigerated, so...

At five of, she once again caught herself holding her phone. She slammed it against the mattress in disgust, only to pick it up an instant later.

Kazuki was going to call soon, after all.

She took it with her to the kitchen and started tea.

No sooner did the phone start vibrating in her pocket than she had it pressed to her ear.

"Hello?" Did she sound breathless? She shouldn't be breathless—it wasn't like she'd been doing anything.

"*Hai, Hayashi Kazuki desu.*"

"What?" A beat later Aurelie realized he had introduced himself. "Oh, yes, Kazuki-*san*. I mean, Hayashi-*san*."

He said something else.

"I'm sorry? Could you say that again?"

"Should I speak English?"

"Oh—" She was embarrassed. Now that he'd said it—in English—she realized that he asked that in Japanese first. If she said that Japanese was fine, when she hadn't even managed that much, wouldn't she look vain and stupid? But it did chafe at her pride, that they were in his country yet he was adopting her language.

Lamely, she replied, "That would be very kind of you. Thank you." She cleared her throat. "You are quite fluent, I suppose, what with taking Medieval Europe for English credit."

He hesitated. "Sorry? What did you say?"

She had babbled, fast and incoherently. "Oh, sorry, nothing important." Aurelie suddenly recalled how she had always asked her neighbor in France to help her with service calls even though she was fluent in French. Actually, it was always harder to understand disembodied voices than when you had expressions and surroundings for context, and when speaking a foreign language...

If they were in person, they'd be able to understand each other perfectly.

But if they were in person, Aurelie wasn't sure they wouldn't fall into bed together again.

"Do you have an iPhone?" he asked suddenly.

"Uh—yes. Do you?" Not because she was curious, but because it was the automatic response.

"Yes. Let's Facetime." And he hung up.

Facetime?

Aurelie glanced down her worn flannel pajamas in dismay. Only the large size had been long enough to cover her arms, but it left her drowning in fabric. Of course, she didn't care if she looked attractive to him, but she was his professor after all. She ought to at least look professional, right?

Her phone was vibrating again—this time for a video call.

It would be worse to have to explain why she had delayed than to let him see her pajamas.

She regretted her decision a moment later, when she saw him sprawled on his bed, hair artfully brushed back from his face.

He could at least be sitting at the table, even if he didn't have any other furniture in his apartment.

Although—maybe seeing what the mask had hidden was worth her discomfort because, *damn*, those cheekbones! How could she have forgotten them?

His full lips (lips she would never touch again) were quirked in such a sweet smile that Aurelie's tummy did a somersault.

和希

AURELIE made over-sized pajamas look like high fashion. The pink and blue plaid made her look younger than her flowy blouses. The fluorescent lights of her apartment cast harsh shadows on her face, highlighting the hollows of her cheeks and the point of her chin. Her face was serene, her eyes fathomless.

Then she fidgeted with her hair, her lips briefly folding inward, and he realized she was nervous.

That was good. It meant she wasn't as unmoved by their binding as she pretended.

"So.." she hesitated, "what can you tell me about your clan? Did they really found the university?"

"Yes," said Kazuki, "because they wanted a school that they knew would protect Unseen students. That drives a lot of our ventures. I guess we're pretty insular. There're even several big estates that many of us live at. The Forest-Heart Home, about an hour northeast of Nara, is where the elders of the main branch live. And my parents." He cleared his throat, not sure if his next admission would put her off. "I'm a direct descendant of the current matriarch."

Aurelie didn't seem surprised by this; he tried to reach for her through the binding, but he couldn't tell more than that she was physically well.

"Of the subsidiary estates, the biggest is the Morimoto—that's Emiko-*san*'s family—branch near Nagasaki, and next is the Kobayashi's in Iwate."

Her eyes were starting to glaze over, and Kazuki supposed he had rattled off too many names.

"The family says we came to Japan with *kanji*, in the fifth century,"

Aurelie perked up. "Came from where?"

Kazuki shrugged. "*Kanji* came from China, so..."

Aurelie smiled slightly. "True, but..." She shrugged as well.

"Family records are spotty before the seventeenth century," Kazuki admitted. "That's when we gained some prestige as a samurai clan that supported the Tokugawa shogunate. We developed business interests after Japan opened in the nineteenth century and founded the university in 1903."

Aurelie asked a lot of specific questions that taxed Kazuki's own knowledge before asking, "Morimoto-*san* said not all of your family goes to Hayashi University?"

"No—wait, you talked to Emiko-*san*?"

Aurelie flushed.

"We had lunch together."

Kazuki nodded slowly, not sure how he should feel about that. He wished he could feel her as well as he could this morning.

Their binding seemed to have weakened over the course of the day, though if someone had asked where she was, Kazuki could have pointed straight towards her. He was certain that he could find her anywhere— well, in Nara, at least. He wasn't confident about the range of this odd sense.

He cleared his throat. "What about you? I saw that you were worried your family was dying out. How many are there? How did you get to this point?"

She shrugged one shoulder. "Last I knew, there were twenty-four of them."

"Twenty-four? *Nijyuyonnin?*" He repeated in Japanese, doubting that he had heard correctly.

Her lips twisted, and she confirmed in the same language. "*Hai. Nijyuyon.*" She looked at something he couldn't see—he suspected she was lost in memory.

"In the fifties, there were several dozen families. All cousins, but I guess the community was fairly stable. But one family took in a human hiker that they found collapsed in the woods. I suppose they thought it was dehydration or hypothermia, but it was illness. The hiker died after a few days, but the fever spread through the community and proved deadly. By the sixties, only my mother's family remained. And in my generation, there were only girls born."

"So none of them could have children," Kazuki realized.

She looked away.

He hesitated, and then said, "Earlier, you said, 'last you knew.' Have you lost contact with the community?" That final word tried to tangle his tongue; it wasn't one he'd used often (ever?), and he suddenly thought it strange that she didn't say "family." But then maybe he didn't understand the subtleties.

It ought to have been a simple question, but Aurelie went so still that Kazuki thought the image had frozen.

"Au—Dubois-*sensei*?" he asked, to see if they were still connected.

She said, "I grew up in Appalachia—a mountainous wilderness. But when I was ten, my mother took my sister and I to live among humans. She eventually married a man—a human man—in Vermont, and my sister and I went to American public schools from that point on. I am still in touch with them, but the rest..."

Again, the lopsided shrug.

She wasn't in an expansive mood.

That was fine. Kazuki was planning on the long game—he could wait for the answers.

But there was something that he had to say today.

"Dubois-*sensei*," he said again, though the formality

galled him, "I haven't told my family that you are here yet. Only Emiko-*san* knows."

Her brows lifted in surprise. "Why?"

He had decided to be forthright. Even though he only knew her through their strange binding, he knew he needed to earn her trust and Yuriko said the best way to do that was to show his sincerity, to make his thoughts transparent.

"Because there's uncalled males among my cousins who would all come to Nara to try to convince you to be their wife if they knew you were here."

Surprise shifted to shock. "Well. Thank you. I have no desire to wed."

He nodded. "I know. But it's not for you. It's for me. Because I don't want the competition."

Being a coward, he ended the call before she could respond.

6. CHALLENGED

オーレリー

SATURDAY morning was Aurelie's first Zoom call with her family, and she had spent the five days leading up to it rehearsing her story. But she was a coward to the core, and as soon as she saw Lisette and her mother, Deborah, she forgot her script. (Should she have written it down?)

She blurted, "How's Dan?"

"Hello to you, too," muttered Lisette.

"He's doing as well as can be expected," said Deborah. "Which is to say, not very well at all."

"Damn, I'm sorry, Mom."

The Zoom call wasn't sharp enough to reveal the details of her family's expressions—the Internet at the farm was lousy—but Aurelie saw Deborah nod and shrug. Aurelie felt guilty that she couldn't give her mother a hug—and even guiltier that she thought her mother was close to being free of her marriage. (Dan was kind and generous, but she knew her mother had married him so that her daughters had a house to live in).

"You're acting weird," said Lisette.

"Am not!" Aurelie realized her fingers were fluttering against her forearm; she stilled them.

"Yeah, you are. You're acting guilty."

"I'm not guilty!"

"Is there something you wanted to talk about?" put in Deborah, doing her best (as always) to keep peace between her (very different) daughters.

"Yes. I, um, well, I met someone."

Lisette was so still that Aurelie wondered if the call had frozen.

"No fucking way. After all the shit you gave me and Mom about marrying humans?"

"He's not human."

Lisette laughed.

But Deborah asked, "You were called? There are Unseen in Japan?"

Lisette stopped laughing. "For real?"

"Yeah," said Aurelie. "They've got a network here. About a thousand of them."

"Whoa," said Lisette. Deborah pressed her fist against her mouth.

"I... I'm sorry," Lisette continued, "I can't process what you are saying. Wait, are you high?"

"Pot is illegal in Japan. And I don't do drugs."

"True. Not even caffeine." Lisette pulled off her baseball cap (the one that said "Bunny's Beer is the Hoppiest") and ran her fingers through her hair.

Deborah nodded silently.

"Pictures or it didn't happen," Lisette added.

Aurelie flushed. She hadn't taken a picture of Kazuki. She had wanted to (so much so that it was unsettling), but she hadn't.

"I don't have any."

Lisette rolled her eyes. "Then it didn't happen."

"Wait," protested Aurelie. "I'll get one." She pulled out her phone to text Kazuki and hesitated. What would he think?

Her eyes darted between Lisette and her mother. "Do I have to show you a picture?"

"Yes. Hell, yes."

She couldn't ask Kazuki for a picture of himself. But she could ask Emiko.

> I told my family about recent events, and they are skeptical. Do you have a family pic you could send me?

There was no reply.

"It's early for college students," she told Lisette.

A second later, a photo came and Aurelie choked on air.

"What? Let me see!" demanded Lisette.

Even though she had texted Emiko, it was Kazuki who had replied. (Why were they together at eight in the morning? Or had Emiko texted him?) Moreover, Kazuki had not sent a "family pic" but a thirst trap.

This definitely violated their (implied) text discretion rules. Aurelie hesitated, then forwarded it to Lisette. She saw her sister pull out a phone that was more Otterbox than device. A necessary evil when one spent all day working with massive animals.

Lisette stared silently. "Okay," she said, "he's hot as fuck, but he *could* be human."

"He's an Unseen, Lis. He—I was called to him, okay? We're bound. Right now, he's still in bed—"

"I know he's in bed, I saw the picture."

"—stretching. He's hungry and he has to pee. He's getting up, now he's p—" Aurelie cut herself off and retreated from the binding and the TMI that she wasn't ready for. (Damn, but she hoped he had never felt her bodily functions...)

"When did this happen?" Deborah at last broke her silence and set down Lisette's phone.

"Sunday afternoon—"

Lisette, arms crossed: "And you're just telling us *now*?"

"This will go faster if you don't interrupt." That was asking too much, but Aurelie eventually got the whole story out despite Lisette's snarky and incredulous observations.

Suddenly Lisette slapped their table, hard enough that the webcam bounced.

"You didn't explain why you kept this a secret for a week."

"Because!" said Aurelie. She drummed her fingers on the table. "I was embarrassed! And—I don't know! I didn't know how to talk about it."

"I can't blame you for that," put in Deborah. She smiled, but her shoulders hunched with emotion.

"I'm sorry, Mom," Aurelie added.

"It's okay," Deborah said again. Then she stood, "I need to get some sleep. You girls talk."

As Deborah walked away, Lisette repeated her tic: baseball cap off, fingers through hair, cap back on.

"Okay," said Lisette. "Okay, I get it. It's not like I could hop on a plane to Japan right now to get some action of my own. I'm not even sure I would if I could."

"Is Mom mad at me?" asked Aurelie.

"At you? The golden child? I don't think that's possible."

Aurelie bit her lip because Deborah had definitely been upset, even if Lisette hadn't noticed. Lisette had already moved on though.

"Let's discuss the elephant in the room."

"What are you talking about?" asked Aurelie.

"You *like* this kid."

デボラ

DEBORAH went to bed, but she didn't go to sleep. How could she when her baby had been bound on the other side of the world?

It didn't take a genius to know how those Japanese Unseen would see her daughter—as a brood mare. It was positively gothic.

Or positively Unseen.

Deborah pulled the old cotton quilt over her head, trying to hide from her past, but unfortunately blankets don't block out memories.

Deborah had been nine when her sister Emily had become the matriarch of their family. The epidemic had wiped out most of their community, and at nineteen, Emily hadn't been ready to take responsibility for everyone.

But she had anyway and had headed to Europe to seek out others of their kind.

When she had returned with Robert—oh, how happy they had been!

Robert had been a little funny looking—his eyes seemed perpetually crossed and his pale skin verged on sallow—but he had been the future. His and Emily's binding had been strong, bringing power to the clan that everyone had dismissed as legend. He had held an odd sway over all of them. As the years passed, he offered to give her sisters babies as well. All of them had accepted with gratitude.

Except Deborah. At fifteen, she had absolutely no interest in her twenty-seven-year-old brother-in-law.

She had gone to Emily after, bitter and fierce over what she called a rape. (Because it had been).

Emily had slapped her and said that Robert didn't enjoy it. That he had to do this to ensure their species would survive.

Deborah had cradled her stinging cheek and realized that her brother-in-law's infidelity hurt Emily. And that Emily deluded herself that Robert didn't enjoy the authority he had taken on—the harem of women he had assembled.

Deborah wished she had left then. Oh, how she wished it!

But she'd been young and trapped.

Trapped like Aurelie was now?

She threw the quilt off and jumped out of bed.

She paced the floor back and forth and wished she could talk to Dan.

Dan, who had found a young mother living in a homeless shelter with her two daughters and offered them his home.

They hadn't been in love—they still weren't—but there had been gratitude and fondness and mutual support. After Dan lost his wife and young son in a car accident, he had needed someone to save him from his empty house as much as Deborah had needed someone to save her from the streets.

But Dan was dying. And he didn't know what an Unseen was, though he seemed to know there was something odd about Deborah and her daughters. (His fair folk, he called them).

Deborah had managed to do the bare minimum for her daughters—provide them a safe place to grow up— but she knew they deserved more.

She wanted to believe that Aurelie would find more, in Japan, but she couldn't.

If she had a passport, she'd fly to Japan tomorrow.

Bureaucracy or no, it was time to get one.

和希

AURELIE didn't respond to Kazuki's selfie—maybe he should have put on a shirt—and he decided he had to do more.

After showering, he grabbed some *oden* from the

Lawson and headed to the *hyaku-yen* shop. Seria was a little smaller than Daiso, but it was also closer, so Kazuki went there—its stationary selection was ample. Translucent paper in a spectrum of pastels and shimmering flower petals, pink heart sticky notes with Hello Kitty, and cards with red foxes cavorting though the seasons all went in his basket. Then he went to the market—salty, traditional *senbai*, a variety of chocolate-covered nuts, and deer cookies meant for tourists. For the next week, he left a note and a treat in Aurelie's mailbox each morning.

He also set his schedule using his uncanny awareness of her location. His new running route was in the periphery of Aurelie's. He had originally intended on running with her, but the first time she had encountered him, she had been so startled and uneasy that he satisfied himself with running *near* her.

He also renounced intramurals for the semester so that he could study in the lecture hall next to hers on Monday and Wednesday afternoons. He wasn't quite sure if this was for his benefit or hers—being close strengthened the binding and their foreign language fluency. So he did his English reading and made her Japanese lectures a little easier.

Unfortunately, he didn't think he was getting credit for any of this—and Emiko said that if Aurelie knew, she'd call him a stalker. In fact, Emiko asked him if he didn't feel pathetic for his efforts.

"She eats the snacks," he told her. "I can taste it when she eats them. She likes it, and she thinks of me, and I figure that's a pretty good start."

And so he continued to run at the same time, and study next to her lectures, and leave her gifts. His wooing might be as gradual as a river wearing away the shore, but he had a lifetime for it.

惠美子

DESPITE their surprisingly amiable conversation on the first day of school, Emiko and her professor had not repeated the experience, so Emiko was startled when her phone identified Dubois-*sensei* as its caller two weeks after the start of term.

She was at home, in the living room of the large home kept by the Hayashi clan, trying to study.

Trying because she shared the house with four cousins, two of whom were cuddling on the couch in an exuberant and irritating way.

Last semester, she would have headed to Kazuki's to study. Even though his apartment lacked a couch, it also lacked cousins, making it the better option. But she didn't quite feel comfortable doing that anymore.

She held the phone in her hand a moment, debating hanging up. But if she was living in a foreign country and had an emergency as an Unseen...

Emiko strode towards her bedroom even as she answered the phone. "*Moshi-moshi?* You've reached Morimoto Emiko."

"Yes, hello, Morimoto-*san*. It's Aurelie Dubois. I—I'm sorry to bother you, I just, I can't seem to find—I need to wash my hair. I mean, I have washed my hair, but the shampoo leaves it so greasy. I've been reading the bottles, and I don't understand..."

Emiko was shocked and then amused. Such a simple thing—but she also remembered freshman year, when she had bought shampoo for the first time, and it had completely ruined her hair care. Her hair was a lot finer and, seemingly, oilier than the average Japanese human's—it seemed this might be true of all Unseen. Most of the shampoos and conditioners on the shelf didn't cut it, and now Emiko ordered hers online.

"You probably won't find what you want at the store," Emiko said. "I'll give you some and then you can order the right brand. *Ēto*, where are you now?"

"I'm at the pharmacy near my apartment."

"Why don't I come to your apartment? Will you send me the address?"

"Oh—well, sure, I can do that, but I feel bad. Do you want me to come to you?"

Emiko considered her cousins' PDA downstairs and Kazuki's desire to keep Aurelie secret.

"No, I'll come to you," Emiko said, "if that's alright?"

"Yes, yes, of course. Thank you."

"You're welcome."

Since Emiko only had one bottle each of shampoo and conditioner, she had to split them before heading out. All told, it took her about an hour before she pushed the yellowing doorbell in front of Aurelie's apartment.

The door opened quickly, revealing a polished Aurelie. Emiko was wearing a pair of gray joggers and pink sweatshirt that said "I feel PRETTY," but compared to Aurelie's classic linen trousers and white lace blouse, she felt messy and childish.

But even though Aurelie looked beautiful, she seemed far less confident than Emiko—she immediately started apologizing for the trouble again. When she offered Emiko a pair of brand new, embroidered house slippers, Emiko saw her hands were shaking a little bit.

Emiko took the slippers, and, because a hug was too presumptuous, she caught Aurelie's hand and pressed it warmly. Aurelie gently squeezed Emiko's back—MacArthur and Emperor Hirohito shaking hands to end WWII. Except, you know, Aurelie didn't tower over Emiko. Maybe Emiko was MacArthur—she certainly felt like the one in power.

You need to get out more. Read some books from this century, Emiko told herself.

"I was happy to come," Emiko said, "And I'm always grateful for the opportunity to practice English."

Aurelie blinked. "You are?"

Emiko laughed. "I'm an English major who can't go abroad, remember?"

Aurelie grimaced. "That's right. If you ever want help proofreading or—or *anything!*"

Aurelie's desperation for a connection couldn't be ignored—and Emiko could admit that despite Aurelie's arrival wreaking havoc in Emiko's plans, she did like the older Unseen. It was time to make a stronger overture, even if it was a little brash and rude. Aurelie was an American after all—she probably wouldn't be offended.

"What I really want is a place to study," Emiko said.

Aurelie's whole face lit up, and she started assuring Emiko that she was always welcome.

Emiko laughed and suggested they shop first. But after Aurelie had added Emiko's toiletry recommendations to her Amazon cart, Emiko did stay and study. She had brought her books with the intention of going to the library, but this was better. Despite their difference in age and position, despite the fact that Aurelie had stolen (sort of) Emiko's fiancée, Emiko knew that Aurelie wanted a friend. And Emiko wanted one, too.

7. FEVERED

和希

IT was Christmas Eve, and the Hayashi Guest House was covered in bright lights and overly cute plushies, thanks to Emiko and Kano. It looked very festive, but Kazuki felt like the Grinch.

Usually Christmas was the big date night before everyone headed home for the family New Year's celebrations, and even though hanging out with a bunch of bound Unseen couples was an exercise in patience, usually Kazuki enjoyed it. He liked to socialize, catch up on news, play games, and sing *karaoke*.

This year, he kept wishing Aurelie was here; if this was a drama, the scene would be interspersed with flashbacks of the two of them, that's how much of his mental energy she was consuming. When Ryōta snagged Kano around the waist to press a kiss under the "mistletoe," Kazuki wondered if Aurelie would ever let him do that. His cousin Masahi was sick, and his mate spent the whole night pressing tea and cough drops on him.

Kazuki growled that Masahi should have stayed home rather than expose the rest of them to his cold. Kano had rolled her eyes and told Kazuki to go make out with Emiko until he was in a better mood.

To Kazuki's shock, Emiko grabbed his hand and dragged him to her bedroom.

She pushed him onto her bed, but before Kazuki could object, she said, "Aurelie-*sensei* is still ignoring you?"

"More or less."

Emiko paced back and forth—she could manage twelve steps before she had to turn.

"I don't get her attitude about this," Emiko admitted. "I tried to talk to her about it couple times, but she always changes the subject. Maybe I should bring it up again—it's been a month."

Kazuki threw himself back on the bed. "I appreciate the thought, but it doesn't even matter. She never expected to get a binding, and she doesn't value it like we do."

"I'm not sure that's true," said Emiko. "She's lonely. She has only her mother and her sister—and she's got a stack of romance novels in her closet."

For some reason, that pissed Kazuki off more.

Maybe because it implied *he* was the problem. He jumped off the bed.

"I'm gonna get drunk," he said and stomped back downstairs.

He and Masahi tried to drink each other under the table—Kazuki's apology for scolding him earlier—but it didn't improve things. In fact, it made things much worse when Kazuki helped Masahi and his mate home, and Masahi spewed sake and Christmas cake all over Kazuki's pants.

With his current luck, he'd probably catch Masahi's cold, too.

オ ー レ リ ー

AURELIE reached her hand into her staff mailbox. Feeling nothing but smooth metal, she groped around for a few moments, then peered inside in frustration.

Seeing that it really was empty, she let out an involuntary sigh of disappointment.

"What it is?" asked Akido absently.

"Nothing," Aurelie hurried to reassure him, but her eagerness focused his attention more sharply on her.

Akido cleared the fog from his thin-rimmed glasses (the joys of continuous mask wearing) and glanced from Aurelie's mailbox to her empty hands. "What's this?" he laughed, "Your secret admirer..." The end of his sentence was obscured by rapid Japanese, but she knew what he was saying. *Your secret admirer has forsaken you? Has given up already?*

It was embarrassing that she even knew the words "secret admirer," but she had heard them regularly for the past three months—ever since Kazuki had started leaving snacks and trinkets in her mailbox.

Not that he had ever signed the accompanying notes, but she was sure it was him because she had compared the handwriting to the note he had left the first day of classes. (She had kept it in case she ever needed his phone number again—no other reason).

Aurelie could feel the blood in her cheeks and resented it. Akido was a gossip; undoubtedly he'd tell all the other professors in the department and everyone would be offering her their condolences all day, while laughing behind their hands. It wasn't malicious—Aurelie might have found it amusing, too, if only she hadn't known the identity of the sender.

Every time she read a note, she remembered Kazuki's expression when he told her he wasn't giving up on their mate binding.

Secretly, Aurelie had been glad, even though it was despicable. But that night she had learned there was still a little part of her that wished for marriage and children. That part hoped that Kazuki was different from the French bastard—that she could trust him.

And that part had gotten bigger every time she ate one of the chocolates or mochi or shrimp chips that he left in her mailbox. Emiko's blatant confusion over Aurelie's reluctance also made Aurelie reconsider her stance, though she often wondered if Emiko would understand if Aurelie explained (but she couldn't bear it if Emiko looked at her differently after).

She gave Akido a head bow as they reached his office and then continued one door down to her own.

She set down her bag and took off her hat and scarf—she left on her tweed coat though. The history department offices didn't have central heating and though it wasn't nearly as cold in Nara as it would have been in Vermont, it was cold enough to turn on the little kerosene heater in her office. However, Aurelie was intimidated by it, so she just kept wearing her coat. (She knew she should ask Akido to teach her, but she accidentally left him with the impression that she had figured it out so she was too embarrassed to admit she hadn't).

Aurelie had left her door ajar as she had office hours now, but no students poked their heads in. That wasn't surprising—mentally, everyone was already on winter break. (Except Aurelie, who had made no plans for New Year's—Emiko said Aurelie should come home with her as keeping her existence secret had taken on a ludicrous quality, but Aurelie had continued to demur).

Aurelie opened up her laptop and accessed the Hayashi University research portal. She found her last saved search and began scrolling through entries.

Then her hand crept down to the bottom left drawer of her desk.

One of those massive metal monstrosities that Aurelie associated with turn-of-the-century factories, Aurelie's desk was only half full. So the only thing in this drawer were notes. (Fifty-five, to be precise).

She selected Kazuki's most recent one—it was a delicate pink that had been folded into a heart.

Some of Kazuki's letters were in Japanese, but this

was an acrostic poem written in English.

Academic

Unbending

Ravishing

Elegant

Lovely

Intelligent

Everything I want.

♡ (^_^)♡

She blushed as she read it. It was so cringey, and she was sure he must have looked up half the words—were acrostic poems even a thing in Japan? But it had made her cry. Even now her eyes were feeling full, so she blinked to clear them.

She refolded the heart meticulously and set it back in the drawer. She had almost called him after this one, especially when Akido explained to her that young Japanese commonly celebrated Christmas as a big date night, similar to Valentine's. Aurelie wasn't Christian, but she was American enough to find that odd—she'd been celebrating Christmas since Dan had married her mother. In fact, she had tried to celebrate Christmas with Lisette, Deborah, and Dan via Zoom, only Dan had choked on sparkling cider and had yet another seizure. She felt guilty that she couldn't help and extra lonely when they ended the call to go to the emergency room. Surely Kazuki's Christmas hadn't been that bad—yet it hurt her to think he might have been alone too. Maybe she had been too cold, and he'd given up on her.

She shook herself.

It was good if he had given up, and she should be reading about *oni*, Japanese demons. Her hands returned to the laptop keyboard.

Maybe he was planning something else today. Maybe an invitation to meet his family for New Year's.

Her stomach flipflopped, and her heart rose to her throat.

She closed her eyes, and tentatively reached through the mate binding.

He was asleep.

She was disappointed.

But maybe that meant he hadn't given up—maybe he was extra tired this morning. Late night studying or drinking or whatever kept students out at all hours.

Aurelie chose a folktale and, armed with a translation app, started reading.

She'd see him in class soon enough.

オーレリー

ONLY Kazuki wasn't in class. Aurelie noticed his absence as soon as she walked into the second-floor classroom, but she called his name anyway during attendance. (She didn't want to pay him any more attention than any other student).

"He's sick," said Emiko. (Aurelie was *not* jealous that Kazuki had told Emiko instead of her).

"Sick?" Aurelie asked before she could stop herself. "How sick?" Her voice came out all worried, so she made an effort to project annoyed-college-professor and said, "He didn't send me an email."

"Uh—pretty sick. He has a fever and a cough."

Emiko glanced around the class, which had tensed up. "But he tested negative." The shoulders relaxed.

"Oh," said Aurelie. She finished taking attendance and started her slides on Charlemagne.

She pulled out her phone to text him after class, then slipped it back into her pocket without sending anything. She pulled it out three steps later, and forwarded him a link to the days' presentation and a short text:

Let me know if you have questions.

There, that was totally appropriate.

和希

TEETH sank into Kazuki's forearm and dragged him to the ground. He tried to grab something to anchor himself and cut his hand on the metal corner of the trash cage. He wrapped his fingers around the grate, but the animal ripped him away. Kazuki was surprised and scared—it was rare that he was overpowered physically.

"Let go!" he snarled and was shocked when he sounded like Aurelie.

Or was he Aurelie?

That didn't make any sense.

"Drop it!" he/she demanded, coldly, at complete odds with Kazuki's pounding heart, as if to dominate the—dog?

Kazuki glared into the shadowy form of animal. Not shadowed but shadowy—a street lamp lit the pavement next to the apartment building, but the animal biting him was like black smoke, thick and opaque.

Kazuki tried to kick the smoke, to dislodge the beast, but as soon as it released his arm, its teeth snapped shut on his leg. Blood gushed everywhere...

Kazuki sat up in his bed. A dream? Caused by those horror movies shown in his special effects course?

His heart was pounding, and his face was cold with sweat. In fact, his teeth chattered.

He wiped his face with his arm and glanced at his alarm clock.

It was already dinnertime; he must have slept all day.

It seemed he had caught Masahi's cold—what a wonderful Christmas present. It had hit him like a bullet train, which was typical. For some reason, no matter how healthy he thought himself, Kazuki always seemed to get sicker than his cousins. His grandmother had once told him it was because he was unbound—surely that was propaganda. Still, the coughing had been so bad last night that he had wondered if he might be the first Covid-19 Unseen case, but the test had been negative.

He blew his nose, quickly filling one tissue, and took a sip of water beside his bed. He knew he should drink more, but his throat hurt too much.

He lay back down, grimacing at the sweat-damp sheets and closed his eyes.

And heard a growl in his ear.

He opened his eyes again. He couldn't shake the feeling that Aurelie was in danger, even though it had been a dream.

He pulled out his phone and called her. She didn't answer.

He'd text.

大丈夫ですか?

Ugh. He should have written in English—his head was too foggy.

You OK?

There was no reply for five minutes—and that was as long as he was willing to wait.

Their binding seemed stronger than usual—Kazuki often had the impression of a blurry cord, but today he could see it. A red string tying him to Aurelie.

He dressed quickly. Well, he tried to. He had to sit down in the middle and breathe a few times because the room was spinning.

He grabbed a medical mask from the box he kept next to his shoes and made it out the door.

The sun had set about an hour ago, and it was windy, so Kazuki couldn't stop shivering. Luckily, his red string led him to a bus stop, and he only had to wait about a minute before a green and white bus, with deer leaping on its sides, pulled up. When he hopped on and felt the hot air blowing down on him inside the door, he sighed in relief. He tapped his bus card and took a seat by the exit. He didn't know where he was going, so he focused on the red string, trusting it to tell him which stop was the right one.

It was then that he realized what he was doing. He'd left his bed while running a fever to follow a red thread because he thought a woman was in danger on the other end. He started laughing, which soon turned into a coughing fit. Probably everyone on the bus was giving him the side-eye, but he was too preoccupied with the string to care. He almost thought he was still dreaming, but he was so uncomfortable that it seemed unlikely.

The red string went taut, so Kazuki got off at the next stop. It led him to an older apartment building, with poured cement walls and bars over all its windows. Kazuki liked that—a woman alone should have a secure apartment. His cord led him around a corner, and he saw Aurelie opening the trash cage from his fever-dream.

A low growl lifted the hairs on the back of his neck.

オーレリー

THE broth was quietly bubbling on Aurelie's small stovetop. She bent over and inhaled the steam deeply— ah, that rich scent that came only from boiling the chicken carcass.

Aurelie was making soup, the recipe that her mother always followed when either she or her sister was feeling poorly.

She wasn't sure why, given that she didn't have a cold and she had no intention of bringing it to Kazuki, but she had felt compelled to cook it tonight.

Aurelie poured in the chopped carrots and then added the already cooked rice.

She turned the soup to a low simmer.

Her eyes fell on the chicken carcass that had already

served its purpose and started bagging it along with the boiled carrot peel and onion skin. Trash would get picked up tomorrow morning, and she didn't want these sitting in the fridge for another week.

She took the bag to the entry and leaned it against the door to pull on her gray suede loafers but didn't bother grabbing a jacket. (Honestly, in the US, she probably would have run out in her slippers, but she was leery of causing heart failure among her neighbors).

She regretted leaving her jacket behind once she made it outside—the late December wind was fierce. She realized she had forgotten a mask as well and ducked her head to charge into the wind. The bag full of chicken bones bumped her leg repeatedly during her mad dash to the disposal station. This setup had been overwhelming at first, but now she went without hesitating to the white cage that housed burnables (it was already full in anticipation of the early morning pick up) and deftly undid the latch with one hand. She was vaguely aware of some noise to her left, but she was focused on her task.

Something she regretted when hands seized her and pulled her backward, moments before something dark and massive slammed into the cage, rattling the metal.

The *thing* snarled and lunged toward her again.

8. TENDED

和希

KAZUKI grabbed the garbage bag out of Aurelie's hand and heaved it at the—

At the—

What was that thing? A dog? What could it be but a dog, albeit one the size of a motorcycle?

However, whatever-it-was had no interest in the garbage bag. Instead, it lunged at Aurelie.

No, at the red string. The one that Kazuki had followed here. Though now it was as thick as Kazuki's forearm.

Kazuki pushed Aurelie behind him and, completely disregarding every animal rights speech he had ever heard, wrapped the red rope around the thing's neck. To his surprise, it went limp immediately.

Aurelie grabbed his arm and hauled him backward. He made a token effort to detangle the red rope, but it wasn't necessary. It was just string again, the diameter of his little finger, and it stretched taut between Aurelie and him.

Kazuki didn't have time to process this though because Aurelie hauled him into her apartment building and slammed the wide metal door shut behind him.

"What's the emergency number again?" she panted. "Not 911—or maybe we need to call animal control? But that thing needs tranquilizers!"

Kazuki looked through the narrow glass window to the left of the door.

"It's gone," he said.

"What?" Aurelie exclaimed. She pressed tight against him to look out the window as well.

He felt her body relax as she took in the empty stretch of cement between them and the garbage sorting station.

"Well. We should still report it to someone."

"Is this really happening?" he asked. "Was there really a massive dog out there? Or did I imagine it?" Now that his adrenaline rush was fading, Kazuki felt distinctly foggy.

To his surprise, a cool hand settled on his forehead.

"You're way too hot," she said. "How did you even get here? No, don't answer that." She cleared her throat uncomfortably, and Kazuki wondered if her throat was sore as well. "Let's get you upstairs first, and then I'll look up a number for animal control."

Kazuki let her lead him up a flight of stairs while he thought about what had happened. As impossible as it seemed, he had somehow seen this before it happened. The binding had warned him so that he could protect his mate.

He swallowed, not sure whether he should blame the lump in his throat on his swollen tonsils or his fear for Aurelie. If he hadn't arrived when he had...

Kazuki was surprised to find himself sitting on a bed. He half-rose, only for Aurelie to push him back down.

"Stay there," she told him.

"I'm so confused," he admitted.

Aurelie smiled at him, and the room spun. "That's because you are at least three degrees hotter than you should be. Come on, you need to eat and get to bed."

オ ー レ リ ー

NOW that Kazuki was in her apartment, it was hard for Aurelie to shake the feeling that she had been cooking for him the whole time.

Questions (How had he shown up just then? Had he followed her home?) were knocking on her teeth, but she swallowed them. The answers didn't feel as important as they should have while he was so feverish. She finally admitted that she had been worried about him all day. She didn't want to send him home; she was glad he was here where she could take care of him.

His consideration the morning after their binding had left an impression on her. Washing her clothes, setting out the bathrobe, making her breakfast. She couldn't recall the last time someone had taken care of her like that—maybe it had never happened. For the big, crisis-like moments, her mother had been the best. For the everyday, maternal stuff... Well, she had a lot of her own issues to work through.

Aurelie settled Kazuki on her bed, propping her pillow against the headboard and tucked her duvet around him.

"Sorry it's not blue."

He snorted weakly. "I like other colors, too."

"Don't talk," she ordered him, "I can feel how sore your throat is!" She rubbed her own self-consciously, before going to the kitchen to get a bowl of soup for him.

He was frowning at her when she returned.

You think of me as a child. His accusation was loud and clear through their binding.

Aurelie didn't respond the same way. Her lapse this morning notwithstanding, it seemed easier to hold her thoughts apart from him when she ignored the binding. And she didn't want him to know that while she *should* think of him as a child, she couldn't help but see him as an attractive mate.

She sat on the edge of the bed and collected a spoonful of broth even as she collected her thoughts. Both had to be fed to him with great care.

"I'm taking care of you like this because you're sick," Aurelie told him. "I don't know a different way to do it, child or man." Had her voice deepened on the word man? Please let that have been her imagination. Kazuki didn't seem to notice, thank his fever.

He swallowed the broth, and let her feed him half the bowl of soup before asking, "Did you make this for me?"

Aurelie froze, the spoon halfway between the bowl and Kazuki's mouth. He leaned forward and slurped up the broth, surprising her into a guffaw.

"Of course I didn't make this for you. I didn't even expect to see you tonight."

"Maybe you did though," he said, "maybe the binding guided you, like it guided me."

"What are you mumbling about?"

"I found you tonight following a red string. The string of fate, tying us together."

Aurelie knew what he was referencing; she did after all specialize in folklore. Legends in Japan—and much of Asia, for that matter—said that a man in the moon (sometimes a god) tied a red string between two people who were fated to meet. Lovers, in most stories.

"The binding isn't magic," she told him. "It's biology; a biological imperative. My stepfather had a dog. When she went into heat, all the male dogs from the neighborhood came to our yard, fighting for the chance to mate with her. They could smell her from miles away. I looked it up after—did you know a dog can smell up to eleven miles away? Oh—sorry," she felt his confusion, though his expression remained opaque, "that's um, I'm not sure, twenty kilometers? Anyway, the point is, that's what happened with us. We aren't like humans. You smelled me, tracked me to the park, and then we couldn't resist the urge to mate." She swallowed and realized that it would be all too easy to cry. "It's not love."

Did she want it to be love? How utterly absurd.

He lifted a hand and touched her cheek. His fingers were like a brand (the fever again), and she was so distracted that it took her a few moments to register the tear drop he had collected on his index finger.

"I have a younger sister," she reminded him again. "If you had met her instead of me, she'd be the one you were called to."

"If that's true, then why wasn't I called to Emiko all these years?" he asked. "It's different between you and me. You're special. Our binding is special. I can see what you see, feel what you feel."

She scoffed. "Insects communicate complex ideas through pheromones—I'm sure we release similar ones, if we had the capability to study it. You mustn't go thinking it's magic. We're not fated to be together."

He shook his head, and Aurelie felt doubt coat his confidence, like oil on water. She was the villain of an unrequited love song—this handsome, thoughtful, favored son knew that he tempted her. But he was overwhelmed and intimidated by her. It didn't make her feel powerful or sexy—it made her feel ashamed.

Her hand reached out, as if it were someone else's, and laid itself on his forehead. He was still burning up. "Let me get you a cool cloth."

和希

KAZUKI was sensitive enough to understand that Aurelie thought his "red string" was a delusion induced by fever. He might have agreed with her if it wasn't for the fact he could still see it.

It was flickering, like it might disappear again, but for now that red cord stretched from his chest to hers, lengthening and shortening naturally as she stepped toward and away from him.

Kazuki tangled his fingers in the cord—he could feel its silken threads—and tried to pull her closer as she walked away. The cord lengthened even more in response.

Maybe she was right, and they should save the conversation for tomorrow. Now that his adrenaline high was fading, he felt pretty terrible. He certainly wasn't up for an argument, and he was pretty sure that despite her kindness, her obvious yearning for him, she wasn't ready to accept that they were bound.

It's just biology, she had said. *It's not love.*

She might be right, but Kazuki didn't think it was a biological imperative. Yes, he felt the pressure as well, the sense that this choice had not been theirs. But, even though he had never believed in it before, he thought it was magic. If an imperative had driven them, surely it was a magical one.

Sick or not, maybe he should grab a bus home. He could rarely sense more than physical sensations from Aurelie lately, and he wasn't sure if he was welcome here or not. His head throbbed so badly, a pressure at his temples, that he shut his eyes for a moment. Well, he intended on a moment, but it was such a relief that he impulsively decided to stay after all. Maybe tomorrow he'd be clever enough to woo her. Tonight, he'd sleep.

When she returned, he kept his eyes closed tight even though he was embarrassingly aware of her. Let her walk away. He heard her shuffle her feet though, and then a blessedly cool cloth settled on his forehead. Her fingers, feeling almost as cold, drifted to his temples and rubbed them, oh so gently. How did she know that was exactly what he needed?

He tangled his fingers in the red cord, felt but not seen, and accepted her comfort.

オーレリー

WHEN Aurelie returned with the towel he was feigning sleep—feigning because she could still feel his roiling emotions through the binding. Grateful for his pretense, she dabbed his forehead and massaged his temples until he fell into a deeper relaxation and true sleep.

She lingered for a little while before looking up emergency numbers (110 for the police, 119 for other emergencies) and eventually had a short awkward exchange with an animal control operator who clearly didn't believe that a dog the size of a bear had attacked her.

She had to admit, looking at the empty alley, the whole encounter did feel imagined.

It must have been real though—Aurelie always lived in reality, not fantasy.

9. KISSED

和希

MORNING sunlight woke Kazuki—Aurelie didn't have curtains. He was alarmed to find his hand empty, though he couldn't immediately remember what had been in it.

Our cord. The binding.

He sat up in a hurry, but the brilliant red string was gone.

He pushed back Aurelie's white duvet and swung his feet to the floor.

Correction: he swung them into Aurelie's stomach, for she was sleeping on the tatami next to the bed, in a makeshift nest of pillows and blankets.

She grunted when his feet collided with her gut, and

her eyes flew open.

"I'm sorry," Kazuki said. It was all he could do to not pull the blanket over his head and hide his face. Belatedly, he jerked his feet back.

She blinked at him. "That's alright." Suddenly she turned bright red and sat up. "I'll make breakfast."

She practically ran from the room—Kazuki recognized her plaid pink and blue pajamas from their video call. They looked even bigger in person—he thought three Aurelies could have squeezed inside them. He rubbed his lip in amusement and abruptly realized he felt much healthier. That soup—or her tender ministrations—really had helped.

She had a box of tissues next to the bed, so he blew his nose.

What was that terrible smell, sweaty socks stuffed with broccoli? When had she last washed—*kuso*. That stench was him. He needed to shower yesterday.

He stuck his head through the door—*not* his whole body, lest the reek reach her, though logically he supposed she had already been exposed—and called, "May I use your bath?"

Her own head popped through another doorway, and she bit her lip. "Oh, I don't think—" Then she shook her head. "I'm sorry, of course, go ahead." An arm appeared and pointed to some cloudy glass doors that Kazuki hadn't needed her to identify as the bathing room since the sink was on the outside wall.

"There're towels in the closet."

He grabbed two, both fluffy and white, and entered the bath.

As might be expected of such an old apartment building, it had a traditional style bath, with a massive steel soaking tub and hose for prewashing. He wanted a shower though, so that the hot steam would clear up the remnants of his cold. Although it was less than ideal, he put the hose in its highest position, which was in the vicinity of his chest. How did Aurelie stand this every day? Or maybe she liked the bath.

He turned the faucet, and icy water blasted his chest—he yelped.

Aurelie called, "Oh—you have to turn on—"

"Yup, got it!" Kazuki hollered back. He didn't want her coming in here now—even if being naked with Aurelie had been his favorite fantasy over the past few weeks, he had always imagined himself clean in it. He squatted and figured out the water heater—yup, the little blue flame was on. Fortunately, on-demand heaters worked fast.

Soon hot water was coursing down his back, steam was clearing his sinuses, and he was experiencing that odd intimacy of using another person's toiletries.

He hadn't realized that Aurelie's rose scent was at all tied to her choice of soap until this moment, as the sweetly cloying fragrance surrounded him—when he closed his eyes, it was as if *she* were all around him. He took advantage of his clear nose to inhale more deeply. Maybe he should tell her he needed help with the heater after all...

A glance downward told him that he had better change the direction of his thoughts.

He turned his mind to his odd vision of the smoke

monster. In the day, with a clear head, the red string was hard to believe in. Maybe Aurelie was right, and his vision had been some fever dream?

And yet...

His blood settled, even as his mind began to race.

オ ー レ リ ー

ALTHOUGH there was a short bar in the kitchen for eating, it only had one stool at present, so Aurelie set the low table in her living room (at least she had dishes for two). It wasn't a fantastic spread—Kazuki's homemade meal put this one to shame—but she normally just had some fruit and yogurt in the mornings. To that, she had added some hardboiled eggs and some pickled lotus root and daikon. (Those last were strange to her, but the hotel had served breakfast pickles every day during her quarantine).

Aurelie grabbed the flat *zabuton* that she had slept on last night and set one on either side of the low table. That looked respectable, didn't it?

She ran her hand through her hair absently, and realized that while the table passed inspection, she definitely didn't.

She couldn't shower, but she could wash her face and get dressed. Except the sink was next to the shower. She peered around the door frame at the cloudy glass doors. They were even harder to see into than usual (the steam from Kazuki's shower), but Aurelie could still hear Kazuki moving inside and even see his blurry silhouette.

Her mouth went dry.

Think of him as a patient. As a child.

Nope, she remembered the bold way his hand had painted the side of her body, the way he had squeezed her thighs while his teeth and tongue had teased her nipple.

This is why people shouldn't wait until almost forty to lose their virginity, she scolded herself. *You're obsessed.*

But she was secretly sure that she would be even more obsessed with Kazuki if she were twenty.

Now that the thought had occurred to her, she couldn't quite let go of it. If she'd met him at twenty...

Well, her aunt would still be dead, her mother would still be married to a human, and the French bastard wouldn't be any less of a creep. But...

Yeah. She wouldn't have been able to resist. At eighteen, she'd read about two-hundred romance novels, each as contrived and saccharine as the last. She had still cherished the idea that, even though she knew better, a handsome Unseen man would find her and they'd ride off into the sunset. If she had known she needed to fly into a sunrise (in the land of the rising sun, that is), she would have booked a ticket to Japan more eagerly than she'd applied to college.

But she had given up on those dreams in France. That tawdry little house—that terrible truth—those had killed the romantic in her. Now her dreams were dried up and crumbled to dust. And she knew better than to pour water on something already dead. She'd tried that with a houseplant once, and it had made a horrible mess.

She washed her face at the kitchen sink and rinsed

her mouth, doing without her facewash and toothpaste. And she did *not* take extra consideration dressing.

Purple looked good on her though, and not everyone could pull off the starkly white palazzo pants that she paired her blouse with. Maybe a little makeup—no! Absolutely not! Besides, it was in the bath area, where Kazuki would be emerging any minute, wrapped in nothing but a towel.

It took Aurelie a moment to find her voice after that image seared her brain, but she called, "Can I set some clothes out for you?"

Kazuki didn't reply right away, and she thought maybe he hadn't heard her over the shower. But then, "Sure, if you have anything that would fit. Besides those pajamas—I am confident in myself, but I don't think I could bring myself to go out in those."

Aurelie's face was surely beet red. But she did have one loose t-shirt that was his style, and maybe her leather jacket would fit. She shook it out twice, as if that would stretch it. Kazuki would look great in leather.

As for pants—well, he'd need something with an elastic waist. Her navy joggers would probably work, though they might be capris on him. She set them all in a neat pile on her bed. "You can change in the bedroom," she told him before fleeing to the living room, sliding the ivory and forest green door shut behind her. A little too enthusiastically—the sound of it colliding with the door frame echoed in her apartment.

Aurelie was too nervous to sit down, so she started

boiling water for tea. She hoped he liked raspberry hibiscus—she was too sensitive to caffeine to have green, and it was the only flavor in the house.

Less than ten minutes later, he emerged from her bedroom, and Aurelie had been right—Kazuki looked great in leather.

"I like this coat," Kazuki said as he sat, stroking the supple hide of the sleeve. Aurelie had to resist the urge to do the same. It was surprising how well it fit him.

"You can have it," she blurted. Which was a weird thing to say, really.

"Oh, I didn't mean—"

"I know," she said, unable to resist digging the hole deeper, "but it looks better on you than on me."

His eyes widened in surprise, and then he smirked. Damn it, a crinkled cheek shouldn't be sexy, but it was. Oh, yes, it was.

Kazuki reached out and tucked her hair behind her ear. Aurelie found herself leaning forward, as if for a kiss.

She sat back so fast, she got whiplash.

"Last night you were a little confused," she told him, "talking about red strings. But it was just sex, Kazuki. Not love, not fate. A physical release that yes, left us with an odd connection to each other, but I am confident that if we both ignore it, it will dim with time."

Kazuki's smile tightened, but instead of retreating, he came around the table.

His hand slid to her jaw, tilted it up, and his lips met hers.

Cardamom overwhelmed her, and her nipples puckered against her bra.

His lips moved from hers to her neck. She arched back and moaned.

For shame.

Aurelie reached for her fears and used them to push Kazuki back.

Thank God that he didn't resist, otherwise she might not have been able to keep her resolve.

Her shredded self-control was not sufficient to keep them from falling into bed together. She needed someone who found their relationship as appalling as she ought to.

"I want to meet the rest of your clan," she declared.

和希

KAZUKI was shocked.

Aurelie had been carefully keeping her distance from all the Unseen except Emiko on campus. And he'd abided by her decision because how could he tell everyone that he was bound but his mate had rejected him?

But now, between the couples' Christmas party, the desire in her eyes, and the red string last night, exposing their binding to the family sounded pretty good. Finally, she was ready to move past the first act, and all it had taken was a kiss. Maybe Hollywood was right about kisses after all—they were the answer to everything.

He grinned. "Good idea. My father is visiting the university today and tomorrow anyway."

Aurelie gaped at him. "He is?"

Kazuki nodded. "Why don't I bring him to your office this afternoon?"

Aurelie shook her head. "I'd prefer to meet him alone. If you'd give me his number..."

Kazuki shook his head. He needed to broker the meeting.

"I'm your professor," she told him.

"Who just kissed me."

"*You* kissed *me*."

Kazuki smirked. "What time are you available?"

She crossed her arms and then said, "Any time after one is fine." She jumped to her feet. "Take your time and lock the door when you leave."

"What?" he said in surprise, but her only response was to scurry out the door. An unfortunately familiar scene.

He waited a few minutes after the door shut behind her, then pulled out his phone to text his father.

You're at the guesthouse, right?

Five of Kazuki's cousins, including Emiko, lived there, but at least one bedroom was always reserved for visiting clan elders—usually Kazuki's father in his position as a university board member.

Yes. What's going on? You feeling better?

Yeah. I'm going to come over.

I can come to you.

No. I'm already out.

Okay. See you soon.

Kazuki gathered up his clothes in a plastic shopping bag he'd found under the sink, but then he imagined explaining the bag to his father. He left it by the door, with a note that he'd collect it later.

The sun was muted by clouds this morning and the faintest dusting of snow clung to the shadows. It would be gone by lunch, but it was cool enough that he zipped Aurelie's black leather jacket against the chill—a pleasant one, now that his nose was clear—and inhaled deeply.

The smell of wet fur and rotting meat tinged the crisp air, and Kazuki jerked his head to the left, seeking the source of the offensive odor.

For a moment, he thought the massive dog from last night had returned. Kazuki pulled out his phone as it straightened and became a man.

Kazuki twitched in surprise. The guy was wearing a shaggy polyester fleece. Quite tacky, and Kazuki was embarrassed to have mistaken it for real fur. The man stood by the white garbage cage—he'd probably been throwing away bones.

The man turned and met Kazuki's eyes. He cocked his head questioningly and smacked his lips in a rather weird way.

Mortified to be caught staring, Kazuki bobbed his head in apology. He almost said something about double-bagging that chicken or whatever it was, but then decided to just be grateful than his keen sense of smell had returned and walked on.

Aurelie's soup had worked magic, he felt so much better. The thought made him stumble. More magic?

Then he rolled his eyes. He'd drive Aurelie crazy if he kept thinking everything was supernatural—though he really did think he'd followed a red string last night, even if it had disappeared. Despite her explanation, he didn't believe that he was smelling her scent halfway across the city—besides, what about that weird vision? He had known a dog was going to attack her when she put out her garbage.

Kazuki waited with a small crowd at the bus stop (most people were heading to work at this hour), and, after several people threw him odd looks, he realized he was humming *Butter* by BTS. He tried to stop, but it kept playing on loop in his head.

The two-story Hayashi Guest House was a five-minute walk from the closest bus stop. It was already warm enough that all trace of snow was gone and the sidewalk was littered with rich yellow leaves from a late-turning tree, so Kazuki enjoyed stretching his legs. When he reached the beige outer wall, he keyed in *Obā-chama*'s birthday, and the door unlocked with a sweet chime.

Kazuki's father apparently agreed with him about the fresh air because he was waiting in the courtyard, tea in one hand and his iPhone in the other. He had probably been reading the news.

He slipped his iPhone into the pocket of his black pea coat.

Kazuki bowed and took a seat on the stone stool across from his father.

Kazuki's father waited patiently for him to speak.

"I was called. I've been bound."

His father's brows climbed the middle of his forehead, two black caterpillars reaching for each other. "To whom?"

"An American professor."

His father said nothing for a moment. Then, "Sorry, what did you say?"

Once again, Kazuki told his story to an incredulous audience, though at least his father didn't laugh like Yuriko had, nor grow angry like Emiko.

"Why didn't you tell me this three months ago?"

Reluctantly, Kazuki admitted how unhappy Aurelie was about the binding.

His father rubbed his chin thoughtfully.

"She wants to meet you this afternoon. Will you go?"

"Of course," said his father, "and I will make sure that she comes to the estate for New Year's."

"I'll come with you," said Kazuki.

"No, I don't think that's a good idea."

"Our binding is valid." Kazuki knew that his chin was jutting aggressively, but he couldn't help it.

"I didn't say it wasn't," his father said mildly, "But you might not like my invitation style."

"Oh." Kazuki didn't know what to say. He didn't want Aurelie to be bullied, but he also knew she was stubborn. Maybe it wouldn't be such a bad thing if his father pushed her a little?

"Will the family approve?" Kazuki asked after a moment.

His father smiled. "Of course! You've been bound. Everyone will want to celebrate with you."

Kazuki tried to smile back, but he suddenly felt

uneasy about New Year's.

オーレリー

AURELIE stood before the gunmetal kerosene heater in her office. There'd been some snow on the ground this morning; the time had come. Up to now, she had brazened out the cold and let students think she was an odd foreigner (she was used to being thought odd, after all).

But to subject Kazuki's father to the too-cold air of her office would be worse than telling Akido that she couldn't figure out how to operate the heater.

Actually, the diagrams seemed pretty clear, but Aurelie had seen the liquid kerosene get poured in by the college's maintenance woman. What if she messed up and set the whole contraption ablaze?

So she sheepishly trotted the few steps to Akido's office.

Akido's eyes crinkled in a smile at Aurelie as soon as she entered. She had a sudden rush of fondness for the older man because he was just so nice (if gossipy), and she wondered yet again how she could ever repay him for all his small kindnesses since she had come to Japan.

"What's on your mind?" he asked, coming to his feet.

A few minutes later, he was alternating between showing Aurelie how to operate the heater and scolding her for not asking sooner.

"Turn it off here when you leave for the night," he said. "Oh—and don't put your coat on it or anything flammable."

"Thank you," said Aurelie sincerely. (No need to tell him she was too afraid to stand close, never mind hang a coat on it!)

"Anything else I can help with?"

Aurelie hesitated as a couple explanations tangled in her mind before she decided to be as honest as possible. "Director Hayashi asked if he could meet me this afternoon. I don't think I am in trouble, but I am nervous. Do you have any advice?"

Akido's eyes widened in surprise. "Prepare snacks and tea. But don't be offended if he declines. Some people won't remove their masks around strangers at all. But it's good to offer anyway."

"How do I address him?" asked Aurelie.

"Hayashi-*san* will be fine," he told her and then patted her gently on the shoulder. "Don't worry. He's mild-mannered. You'll do great."

Aurelie collected the refreshments after walking Akido back to his office, but then the afternoon threatened to stretch interminably before her. (Kazuki had said his father was coming, but not when).

She opened up her research portal to distract herself from Mr. Hayashi's impending visit, but she searched for the red string of fate instead of *oni*.

The first few results were retellings of the most famous story, that of a youth who met the old man in the moon, but the seventh was a story unfamiliar to her.

Long, long ago, in the shadow of Mount Fuji, there lived a wealthy and powerful clan. The lord of this clan had five sons, each braver and more handsome than the last.

The youngest, and thus the bravest and most handsome of all, craved adventure, as young men are wont to do. With his father's blessing, he decided to travel to the southernmost tip of Honshū, to help the ordinary people and to seek his fortune.

The first week of his journey went much the way the young man expected. He caught a thief, rescued a child, and was met with praise and admiration everywhere he traveled. But at the end of the first week, he sought hospitality at the home of a wealthy merchant only to be turned away.

The night was cold and wet and though the man did not want to start a fight and he was too proud to beg, he lingered by the door of the manor. There the servant of the lady of the house found him.

"Sir," she said, "I have but my own bed to offer, but if you would join me there, I promise it will be warm and dry."

The man was not eager to share a bed with a servant, and this one not only dressed in rags but her hands and face were dirty. Still, a dry dirty bed was preferable to a muddy one, so he agreed.

That night, as if she cast a spell on him, the young warrior was unable to resist her charms, and he made love to her three times.

The next morning he woke and discovered a red thread tied to his thumb. Puzzled, he lifted his hand and discovered the other end was tied around her littlest finger.

He tried to slip the string off his thumb, but it would not slide over his knuckle, so he tried to cut the string instead. However, though the string was thin as thread, it was as strong as steel and dulled his knife.

The servant girl woke and asked him why he was so upset.

"You think to hinder my journey, by tying this string around me?" he demanded.

"'Twas not I who tied the string," said the young woman.

But the warrior did not believe her. He tried to run away, but still the string would not break, and the young woman was pulled behind him.

Aurelie wanted to roll her eyes at the misogyny of the story, but she couldn't help but find it a little familiar as well. She kept reading, as the man faced challenge after challenge and the servant girl saved him. Slowly, he came to understand that though she was poor and had no background, she would sacrifice everything for him (yeah, the misogyny stayed consistent), and so he agreed to marry her. It seemed like the story should end there, but there was more.

That night, as he slept beside his new wife, the warrior had a terrible dream of monsters made of black smoke that came to eat her.

"Stay away," he begged, for his sword passed through their intangible bodies without hurting them. When his pleas didn't work, he offered, "Take me instead!"

The smoke laughed, a horrid sound that held the cries of the dying.

"You are of no use to us," said the smoke monsters. "Only the babe in her belly has the magic we seek."

And they tore her flesh with their terrible fangs.

He woke pouring sweat and found the cursed thread had disappeared at last.

He turned to his wife, but beside him there was naught but

black ash. The warrior lowered his head and wept.

Aurelie stared at the computer screen in disbelief. "Well."

She shuddered abruptly and shut the browser.

"No wonder it's obscure," she told her empty office. "What a horrid ending!"

10. SUMMONED

オーレリー

A GENTLE knock on Aurelie's open door announced a frowning Mr. Hayashi.

"You won't mind me skipping the mask, since neither of us is at risk."

Aurelie shrugged—she hadn't known they weren't, but she supposed their family probably knew more about the risk of Covid-19 to Unseen than she did.

Mr. Hayashi was as tall as his son, and there was a marked resemblance in their faces. Besides a few fine lines around his eyes, Mr. Hayashi looked only a little older than Kazuki, and Aurelie had the disconcerting realization that she might be closer to his age than to his son's. In fact, she even noted that his well-fitted business attire and tidily arranged hair would have been objectively more appealing to her a month ago. (Now, she was obsessed with how Kazuki's hair fell into his eyes and the way his t-shirts draped his torso, as ridiculous as that was).

All these thoughts bounced frantically through Aurelie's head as she wrung her hands under her desk. And then she stood and bowed, hoping that she wasn't trembling. She would have liked to say the pressure she felt was that of any untenured professor being confronted with a board member of their university, but she admitted (only to herself) that she wanted to impress Kazuki's father.

Her office was not convenient for entertaining—staff were encouraged to bring important guests to the shared sitting room—but Aurelie had been right to get tea ready here. Mr. Hayashi shut the office door after returning her bow.

She collected the tea pot from atop the kerosene heater and poured the bright yellow *sobacha* for both of them. Mr. Hayashi accepted one of the earthenware cups and examined the bamboo leaves painted on one side before holding the tea close to his nose and breathing in the steam.

"If you pour *sobacha* into white porcelain, it's easier to enjoy its color."

He sipped the tea, and Aurelie forced a smile. "Thank you for the advice."

Advice, ha! He was actually saying, "You're a foreigner. You don't know what you're doing." He was establishing dominance, even though they were in her office.

She resented the effort she had put in earlier, reviewing everything Akido had told her about serving guests, as she chose tea and cups.

"Our clan's matriarch would like to invite you to spend New Year's with us at the Forest-Heart Home."

Another order, but since it was phrased with polite indirectness, Aurelie tried sidestepping it. "How kind, but I'd hate to impose, and I think we can probably discuss everything we need to here. Perhaps Kazuki-*san* told you that we had been called?"

Mr. Hayashi nodded.

"Did he also tell you that I am thirty-six years old?"

Mr. Hayashi blinked. He was definitely nonplussed, and, for a moment, Aurelie thought she had found an ally.

"The binding is never wrong," he told her. "*Obā-chama* will help you navigate the difficulties that such a large age-gap may cause."

"I don't think—"

"A foreign Unseen would be welcomed by our family. But a professor who took advantage of my son could not work at our university."

Aurelie's grip tightened so drastically on the cup that she was vaguely surprised it didn't shatter. Still, that seemed better than tapping.

"I see." And though she had a feeling that saying less put her in a better position, she blurted, "My family isn't like yours."

Mr. Hayashi's mouth softened, and he cocked his head, looking more than ever like his son. "I know," he said gently. "In the eighties and nineties, the clan made a big effort to find other families on the Internet. If yours had been anything like ours, there would have been a trace of them. But you don't have to worry—just being what you are will earn you kind treatment."

What I am? thought Aurelie. *Ah, yes, a breeding female.* She didn't express her exasperation. For as much as she hated the implication, she did understand it.

She also didn't want her species to go extinct, on principle.

"We'll meet you at Ōkawara Station tomorrow at 15:13. Kazuki-*kun* will escort you."

Aurelie nodded tightly.

Mr. Hayashi left.

Aurelie allowed her fingers to beat a tattoo on her desk, not sure if she was angry or afraid. She needed an ally, and she could only think of one person who remotely fit that label.

She pulled out her cell and called Emiko.

惠美子

WHEN Aurelie's avatar showed up under the caller ID, Emiko's first thought was that her friend had realized the futility of hiding her existence and had decided to come to New Year's in Nagasaki after all. But then she remembered that Kano had seen Kazuki and his father talking in the courtyard this morning—she closed the door to her bedroom before she answered.

"*Moshi-moshi*, it's Emiko."

"Emi-*chan*, I was, um, invited to the New Year

celebration at the, er, Forest-Heart Home this weekend."

"Is that right? *Invited*, you say?" Emiko was certain that was a questionable word choice.

"Yes, well, you understand perfectly."

"I do." Relief washed over Emiko. At least the truth would be known to everyone, and she could stop covering for the weirdest couple in all of Unseen history. She still couldn't believe their secret had lasted the whole fall! She kept thinking that one of their cousins would see Aurelie—maybe they had but didn't recognize her as Unseen?—or that Kazuki would let something slip, or that she herself would...

"I was hoping that perhaps you could find some time to talk to me today," Aurelie said.

Emiko mulled that over as she stretched out on her bed.

"If you want to know more about the family, you could ask Kazuki-*kun*."

Aurelie sighed. "I truly cannot accept this binding, and I don't want to encourage him."

So they haven't worked it out. Emiko felt suddenly annoyed. "Oh, really? Is that why you've accepted his gifts all term?"

"What else should I do?" protested Aurelie. "He put them in my mailbox—should I return them in class and expose him as my 'secret admirer'?"

"Leave them. Throw them away. You don't have to eat them or read the notes over and over!"

"Over and over! Are you spying on me?"

"Not me," Emiko bit off. "And Kazuki doesn't have

to spy to see what you see. To taste what you taste."

There was a long silence. Appalled, Emiko thought, and she felt a little guilty for scolding Aurelie. Only a little though.

"I see. I will do better. I won't—"

"And why not?" asked Emiko. "You should. You should accept him. He deserves to be happy. Not this sham binding but the real one that has been denied to him. I would give anything to be in your place! Why can't you just appreciate it?"

Again, silence.

"Would you really?" asked the professor softly. "You think the binding is such a good thing? Then you've never seen how it can destroy lives. Destroy a family."

"What do you mean?" asked Emiko, a little shaken by the rawness of Aurelie's voice, the way her words quavered.

"Never mind," Aurelie said. "I hope you can keep your innocence. I'm sorry I bothered you."

And she hung up.

Emiko lowered the phone slowly. That was weird. Should she text Kazuki? It wasn't her business, but...

You know your mate is going to the Forest-Heart Home?

Yeah, thanks.

Emiko felt vaguely offended, even though she had already recognized that it wasn't her business.

But, she suddenly thought, just because what they were doing wasn't her business didn't mean she couldn't join the clan celebration instead of visiting her parents in Nagasaki.

オ ー レ リ ー

ONCE Aurelie resigned herself to meeting the Hayashi matriarch, she wanted to get advice from her mother. Aurelie had forgotten the Unseen clan hierarchy rules if she ever knew them. She wasn't sure how being Japanese affected being Unseen, but Aurelie was sure her mother would have insights for her either way.

Unfortunately, the fourteen-hour time difference to Vermont meant she only had one reasonable time slot for calling, and neither Lisette nor Deborah answered their phones.

Aurelie told herself it didn't matter, but as she sat next to Kazuki on the train (despite the glut of holiday travelers, they hadn't seen anyone they knew), she wished she had managed to get ahold of her family.

She kept trying to focus on the hills and trees as they went by—the autumn foliage was past its prime, but here and there orange and brown still mingled charmingly with the dark green pines.

Kazuki's hand descended on her own, making Aurelie realize that she had been anxiously tapping her fingertips together. She looked at his hand for a moment, with its long fingers that made Aurelie think he should play piano.

Well, maybe he did. She had avoided learning anything about him.

"They'll be more annoyed at me than you," Kazuki

said, his voice a low rumble.

Aurelie pulled her hand out from under his. "Because you didn't tell them about me earlier?"

He nodded.

"It took me a week to tell my family," she said, "And it was easier because they are far away and can't interfere. I wouldn't have told anyone if I were you."

"Well," said Kazuki, returning his hand to his lap. "I did call my sister after our first class."

和希

"YOU told your sister about me?" gaped Aurelie.

Kazuki shrugged one-shoulder. He suddenly felt his admission was tantamount to confessing first—of course, they both knew that he was more invested in the binding than Aurelie was. "I wanted to talk it through with someone."

Kazuki scanned the packed train car so that he didn't have to look at Aurelie. He shouldn't be surprised but it still stung that she so thoroughly wished that their binding never happened.

Kazuki could tell that her efforts to break it were having some effect as well—they were conversing in English, but it wasn't quite as effortless as it had been that first day. He still understood everything, but he was aware that they were using her language, not his. Maybe that was why he was sitting so close to her, why he had stilled the nervous tic of her fingers. He was seeking to strengthen their connection. Preferably before they had to stand before *Obā-chama* in thirty minutes.

"What did she say?" Aurelie asked.

Kazuki blanked for a moment before realizing, "Oh, my sister? She was happy for me. When she learned you had rejected me, she suggested waiting to tell the clan. Guess she wanted to keep the mud off my face."

"Mud? I don't follow?"

Kazuki stretched his arm behind her. He adjusted the blind on the train window, then left his arm lying along the seat back. She turned toward him, hyper-focused.

He leaned closer, and her breath hitched. "If you'd let the binding open between us, you would."

"Would what?" she whispered.

His lips twitched involuntarily. She pretended to be unaffected by him, but she couldn't even follow the conversation when he crowded her.

"You'd follow when I used Japanese idioms. To get mud on one's face means to be shamed or embarrassed."

"Oh." She flushed. "Sure, face is often a metaphor for pride." Her eyes flicked to his arm, and she scooched closer to the window. "You're my student."

Kazuki slid back, leaving two-hands widths between them. The gap felt too large to him.

Maybe if it hadn't been for the other gaps between them—age gap, culture gap, even class gap.

And here he was, stupidly trying to narrow all of these in an hour-long train ride.

Aurelie's fingers started nervously tapping her leg again. Kazuki couldn't help himself from asking, "Do you have any questions before we arrive?"

"I—well, how should I greet your—the matriarch?

She's your grandmother?

"Great-grandmother." Kazuki thought for a moment. "You should address her as *Obā-sama*."

"*Sama*? Not *san*? What's the difference?"

"*Sama* is a little more formal. You've probably been addressed with it at stores and restaurants. *Okyaku-sama*."

"Oh. Yes, I've heard that before. I thought it was one word."

She listened carefully as Kazuki described other protocol, but he didn't take any pleasure in her attentiveness. He knew her well enough to know that she never wanted to look a fool, and if she mastered what he told her, it would make her that much more appealing to his unbound, older cousins.

"What's the difference between *sumimasen* and *gomen nasai* again?" she asked. "I always have trouble with those two."

"They're interchangeable," Kazuki said. Then he reconsidered. "Well, maybe *sumimasen* is better. More polite? You can use that one today."

She repeated the apology twice to herself, and Kazuki closed his eyes.

He imagined the red string that had disappeared. He imagined it thickening, a rope rather than a thread.

What was he doing? Soon he'd be reading his daily astrology chart and buying tarot cards.

But Aurelie suddenly said, "I tried to learn more about the red string of fate." Had she felt his imaginings? "I came across a strange story."

And then she was telling him about a nobleman and

a peasant who had followed him around like a dog.

Kazuki felt himself growing more and more angry as the story went on. When she paused for breath, he said, "So, to you, I'm an unpleasant burden that you can't get rid of?"

Aurelie shifted next to him, but he didn't meet her eyes.

He was tired of being the only one who cared. It was okay at school where there was no one to witness his devotion, but she was going to make him a fool in front of his entire family.

He suddenly regretted coming with her, even confessing his involvement to his father.

No—that would mean giving up on her completely. Admitting defeat to his cousins.

"Kazuki-*san*, I didn't mean—"

He held up a hand. He still wanted her, but he also needed a minute.

"We'll be pulling into Ōkawara Station soon. Let's not fight more."

"But—"

He turned fixedly from her, though the gray-green interior of the train car blurred before his eyes.

11. EXPOSED

IT hadn't occurred to Aurelie that Kazuki would think he was the girl. Yes, Aurelie had found the fairytale analogous to their own situation, but wasn't it obvious that Kazuki was the favored son and she was the peasant? In the US, being Unseen hadn't saved her from the label "white trash." And for Aurelie, it didn't matter how many letters were added after her name: she still felt like that girl who'd grown up with dirt floors and who'd learned basic world history at public libraries while her mother worked odd jobs.

Kazuki turned more sharply from her.

He really was mad.

Aurelie started to speak half a dozen times, but Kazuki kept his shoulders angled away. Aurelie's fingers fluttered in agitation, but was it fair to ask him to listen to her, to grant her understanding, when she was denying his deepest wish?

So she sat in silence beside him, staring out the window while Kazuki stared at the floor of the aisle. He was so unwilling to speak to her that even when the train pulled into Ōkawara and Aurelie pointed out his father, he merely grunted.

He's only twenty-two, she reminded herself. (As of June—she'd checked his birthday in the student records). *This is harder on him than me.* And it felt really hard on her.

This sort of angst, of longing, was meant for teenagers. That's probably why all those forced-romance novels—werewolves and vampires—featured teenagers. Angst looked ugly on a middle-aged woman.

So don't be angsty, she scolded herself and followed him to the exit.

Kazuki went down the metal steps to the platform. Aurelie started to follow and somehow tripped over her own feet. Kazuki turned and caught her effortlessly, and she realized he'd been far more aware of her than he had pretended.

"Thank you," she said. Her hands were resting on his chest, and she wanted to slide them up around his neck.

His brows crawled toward each other, and some of the tension in him eased.

"My pleasure," he told her and swung her to the cement.

Aurelie was confused by his mood change, but she

was so relieved that she didn't step away.

"They suit each other, don't they?" came a male voice.

Aurelie looked toward Mr. Hayashi in surprise. He was talking to another Unseen, a woman. Probably his wife (Kazuki's *mother*).

"I know you were worried about her age, but I think it will be okay. We need to help Kazuki win her. If—"

"She can understand you," said the woman, cutting him off.

Mr. Hayashi stopped talking and looked at Aurelie in surprise. Surprised herself, she looked back at Kazuki.

That's why he had gotten over his bad mood.

The binding had strengthened again.

Because of her own inability to stick to a decision. She had felt him moving away from her, and so she had reached for him through that tie.

So embarrassing.

Kazuki introduced her to his parents with the slightest smirk on his face, and Aurelie secretly liked that smirk. While they all exchanged New Year greetings, Aurelie was grateful for the binding's guidance. As they walked to the car, Kazuki guided her with his hand. It wasn't at all necessary—this was a small enough station that even with the increased holiday traffic, it was hardly overwhelming. Aurelie couldn't bring herself to put distance between them— she valued Kazuki's reassurance more than her own discipline. For someone who had always thought of herself as independent, this was a disturbing realization. As she slid into the back seat of his parents' sedan, she tucked her hands far away from him, though she felt far from resolute. Kazuki tactfully placed their bags between them.

The Hayashis all took off their masks in the car, but Aurelie hesitated. Right now, it felt like armor she couldn't afford to lose.

Of course, wearing it declared her insecurity. Aurelie took off the mask.

Kazuki kept his parents occupied with chatter (surely to spare her their attention). Aurelie studied Mrs. Hayashi and was surprised to realize that she seemed to be of an age with Aurelie's mother.

That wasn't impossible. Aurelie had been born when her mother was sixteen; if Mrs. Hayashi had Kazuki at thirty...

Aurelie tried to imagine her mother talking to Mrs. Hayashi. The image wouldn't come, maybe because she rarely saw her mother visit anyone.

Her mother's work-roughened hands were never still (sometimes Aurelie thought that she was still trying to pay Dan back for marrying her and supporting her two daughters), whereas Mrs. Hayashi had professional nail art and multiple rings bedecking her fingers. Mrs. Hayashi dressed a little like Aurelie herself: high quality fabrics in professional cuts. From her ears dangled gold earrings that Aurelie belatedly recognized as a designer logo. Her clothes were probably brand names, too.

Aurelie didn't think her mother even bought new clothes—last time Aurelie had been to visit, she'd discovered her mother was wearing Aurelie's old clothes from college, patched and repaired.

Aurelie squeezed her hands together so that she wouldn't tap her fingers.

"Here we are," announced Mr. Hayashi, cutting short Kazuki's anecdote about a classmate.

They had reached a tall white wall topped by curved gray tiles, each cap pressed with a trefoil leaf. Directly in front of the sedan were dark wood doors that opened when Mr. Hayashi pressed a button clipped to the car visor. Aurelie of course knew that lots of people had remotes like that for their garages, but she had never seen one for a gate. In fact, she didn't think she'd ever visited a home that was surrounded by a wall.

They pulled through the gate into a forest. Wild pines and bare branches crowded the drive—a shiver of anticipation ran through Aurelie. Even though this place whispered wealth, it reminded her of home. Not home in Vermont, but the wilderness where she had been born.

The trees will hide you. We are the caretakers of the forest, and it is the caretaker of us.

Aurelie pushed that memory away, hating that the words were accompanied by that French bastard's smile.

Suddenly aware she was being watched, Aurelie brought her focus back inside the car. Kazuki and his mother were both watching her, gauging her reaction.

"It's beautiful," Aurelie admitted, begrudging the truth. She didn't suit such a lovely place.

Mrs. Hayashi didn't quite smile, but she was clearly

pleased. Kazuki winked at Aurelie, and she bit her lower lip to keep herself from smiling.

和希

KAZUKI had his fingers interleaved with the red string again. He'd been shocked when it suddenly appeared at the train station. He thought Aurelie's stumble had triggered it, alerting him to her fall and helping him catch her. Like that night when he'd dreamed of her in danger.

It seemed the binding was intended to help them protect each other. Kazuki couldn't understand why Aurelie had such a negative impression of it.

When his father parked the car in the garage, Kazuki leapt out and opened Aurelie's door for her.

She was so surprised that she accepted his hand as she stepped out. Kazuki was vaguely aware of his father's approval and his mother's concern, but mostly he was relishing the clarity with which he could read Aurelie.

She liked the woods and the house, even if she was a little overwhelmed by the clan's wealth.

Kazuki didn't release her hand until she tugged it free, but even then, he could feel her reluctance to let go of him.

From the garage, they followed a short stone path to the main house, and Kazuki expounded on whatever Aurelie focused on.

"The tiles are clay," he told her. "That particular trefoil is the Hayashi family crest. The family was of the samurai class during the shogunate."

"They must be expensive to replace," Aurelie said and blushed.

"Yes," agreed Kazuki, "but the family can afford it. All of our incomes are pooled and invested. One of my cousins is in charge of managing each family member's allowance."

Aurelie's eyebrows shot up. "Who decides how much the allowances are?"

"That cousin, with *Obā-chama*'s approval." He could feel her concerns—it must seem strange to such an independent woman—so Kazuki elaborated. "The allowances are generous though. And you can use them however you want—it's not such a prison as you imagine."

"A prison?" echoed Kazuki's mother. "Of course not! We offer our duty for the family's protection. A good exchange."

Aurelie pressed her lips together, and Kazuki hurried to change the subject.

"The house itself was originally built in the eighteenth century, but it has been expanded several times. You'll notice that most of it is made from pine..."

Aurelie listened attentively, and Kazuki didn't make the mistake of addressing her inner thoughts again.

Inside the *genkan*, Kazuki put Aurelie's overnight bag on a shelf and watched with pleasure as she smoothly left her shoes on the sunken stone floor and stepped into house slippers. She paused to turn her shoes toward the door, carefully lining them up.

It wasn't that Kazuki himself was a stickler for

etiquette, but he knew his mother would be pleased. She had called him last night to express her reservations about a match with a foreign Unseen.

"The family will welcome new blood," she had told him, "but not through you. You must remember, Kazuki, that you are a direct descendant of *Obā-chama*."

"I was called, *Okā-san*. Surely—"

"She's too old. And you are expected to help manage the clan with your wife—a role Emi-*chan* was prepared for."

Kazuki had scoffed. His mother was as aware of his fall in favor as he was. She had paused, and he'd thought she would address it but she'd said, "How could an outsider do that?"

Kazuki had been offended on Aurelie's behalf. Aurelie was smart, sensitive, and strong. Kazuki didn't doubt that she was capable of adapting and managing the clan given time.

Even now, Aurelie was standing still, composed, and at ease while her eyes carefully noted all the details of the *genkan*. They lingered on the trefoil crest carved into the wall before going on to catalogue the house plants.

"Perhaps you'd like to refresh yourself before meeting *Obā-chama*," said Kazuki's mother.

"Yes, thank you."

His parents both went ahead to let *Obā-chama* know they had returned while Kazuki led Aurelie to the washroom.

"Do you...?" she gestured to the door.

"I'll just wash my hands," he told her and indicated

the external sink.

Aurelie nodded and slid the light pine door shut behind her.

Kazuki washed his hands and then his face slowly—he worried that Aurelie would feel self-conscious, so he wanted to keep the water running until she emerged.

She did so sooner than he expected, while water still dripped down his cheeks.

She startled, then smiled in relief. "For a moment, I thought you were crying."

He laughed outright at that, "Crying from happiness maybe."

He regretted the words as her face shifted into discomfort. He grabbed a blue and white *shibori* towel to dry his face and left the sink free for her.

"I know," she said so quietly that he probably would have missed it if it hadn't been for their binding, "that I'm not being fair to you. That I keep flip-flopping. I do like you, Kazuki—beyond finding you attractive, I mean. You are very thoughtful and—well, it doesn't matter. I don't want to be bound to anyone. I'm not what you think."

That last might have been added silently, but Kazuki slipped his hand around her waist, and pulled her back flush with his chest. Her breath hitched.

"I think you're intelligent, independent, and beautiful. Which am I wrong about?"

She blinked rapidly, and Kazuki could feel her desire to put distance between them.

He stepped back.

"I don't know what weighs on you so heavily," he

said, "but I don't think it can be as bad as you think."

"Shall we go? Everyone must be waiting." She took a step forward before Kazuki joined her. They wound their way through the corridors, and Aurelie's curiosity was piqued at the voices they heard.

"There's about thirty people who live here and tomorrow there will be a hundred for the holiday," he explained. "Most nuclear families will celebrate at home. In theory, the entire clan is invited, but practically speaking, there isn't enough room."

"This is nothing like the house where I grew up," Aurelie said, "and yet it's the same too. Are the children homeschooled?"

"No," said Kazuki. "It's hard to do that in Japan." In fact, he wouldn't have understood the word if her meaning hadn't come through their connection. "Were you homeschooled?"

"Until high school."

And then they reached the formal reception room.

"Leave your slippers here," he told her. "This floor is tatami."

オーレリー

KAZUKI slid open a *shoji* door and waved Aurelie into a room that could have been a national treasure. (Maybe it was—she wouldn't be surprised if this entire residence had some special designation from the Japanese government). The walls were painted with a forest: pines and bamboo with little animals— swallows, rabbits, a lizard—hiding everywhere. The style was Japanese, but it was a little different too—the paintings she had seen at the temples had used lots of negative space, but here the subjects were crowded together.

Rather like the wooded yard, it was distinctly Unseen.

Besides the paintings, the room was mostly empty. The only furniture, if that was the right word, was a handful of dark blue *zabuton* cushions. Two were waiting for Aurelie and Kazuki, Kazuki's parents were already arranged on two others, and on the last one was the oldest Unseen that Aurelie had ever encountered.

Obā-chama. Or *sama*, for outsiders like Aurelie.

Fine lines crossed her impassive face and her thin, white hair clung to her skull. Aurelie had heard that Unseen often lived to one hundred and twenty; she guessed that *Obā-chama* was over a hundred.

Obā-chama wore an indigo kimono with white birds diving across the fabric and an orange and white *obi* at her waist. Aurelie suddenly thought Kazuki's use of the past tense when speaking of the family's samurai status had been misleading.

Kazuki bowed, and Aurelie mimicked him, a beat slower than she should have.

He sat cross-legged on the *zabuton,* and Aurelie started to do the same.

Panic (that sounded extreme, but it was panic) flashed from Kazuki.

She got a clear image of a woman kneeling, and she adjusted her legs accordingly, so that she matched Mrs. Hayashi—and *Obā-chama* herself.

"So we meet," said *Obā-chama*, "I am Hayashi Eko.

I hope we'll get along."

Aurelie repeated the Japanese greeting—the same words, yet she was sure hers sounded like a plea rather than the granting of a favor that *Obā-chama* had conveyed.

This woman was a queen, and Aurelie nearly cried when she realized this was how her aunt should have been.

If the French bastard hadn't broken her and claimed her crown.

"Tell me about your family," ordered *Obā-chama*.

Aurelie vaguely summarized the small community in Appalachia, going into more detail to explain that her sister and mother lived in Vermont. (After all, maybe, just maybe Lisette would want to join this clan).

But *Obā-chama* was unimpressed. "Tell me everything."

Aurelie stiffened. It wasn't any of this woman's business, and she opened her mouth defiantly.

But her refusal wouldn't come.

和希

ONE moment Aurelie was speaking normally, saying much the same explanation that she had shared with him about the Unseen community in the United States; the next, she sagged forward, her hands just stopping her face from hitting the tatami. Her short hair fell forward, but it didn't hide her expression from Kazuki's gaze.

Her eyes were unfocused, her cheeks white. Her lips were trembling, and one word escaped them.

"Papa?"

Such an innocuous word, but it might have as well been a scream. Instinctively, Kazuki grabbed the red string, and then he was in her mind. Seeing what she was seeing, though some part of him could still see her prostrate on the tatami mats, tears clinging to her lashes.

オーレリー

Appalachia, West Virginia, US - July 1991

AURELIE was lying on her stomach, looking at the meticulous sketches in her family's botany guide, when an odd sound distracted her. She quickly shut the book—she wasn't supposed to look at it alone, since it was fragile and they only had six books.

The sounds didn't come closer, and Aurelie thought about returning to her book. But she listened a little longer. There were two different sounds: a grunting and a whimpering. Had some of the dogs gotten in the house? Was one of them injured?

Carefully, Aurelie put the book back on the shelf, between *La Peste* and *A Midsummer Night's Dream*. She padded closer to the noises—they were coming from her sister's room. Carefully, she lifted the worn gray curtain a few inches—sometimes the dogs were dangerous when they were hurt.

Her eyes met her sister-cousin's.

Aimee's face was turned toward the door, and she was whimpering.

Their father was lying on top of her, grunting.

He was hurting Aimee, Aurelie was sure of it. Crushing the life out of her—maybe he'd fallen over and couldn't get up.

"Papa?" asked Aurelie.

Aimee shook her head.

"Go away," snarled Papa.

Aurelie ran.

Straight into the bench, which hadn't been pushed under the table, and so hard that her hip throbbed. Instinctively, Aurelie swallowed her cry of pain and kept running. She plowed straight through the vegetable garden heedless of the tomatoes. (Two burst on her skirt; there'd be a scolding for sure).

Through the gate—she did stop to fasten it, only because two of the dogs had chased after her, and she didn't want them to follow. Mom would be down by the river with her aunts. They needed to know that Papa had fallen.

Yes, Papa had fallen, and Aimee was pinned beneath him. That was what she had seen.

Mom and the aunts would know what to do.

She fell once going down the hill, but she was up like a shot, ducking through the brush with the ease of long practice. She practically had every branch memorized.

Aurelie pulled up short at the water's edge, her arms pinwheeling. She almost fell into the water, but Mom caught her.

Mom huffed in exasperation. "Aurelie, you're too big to run into me like this!"

Mom set Aurelie upright and wrapped an arm

around her belly; her big belly, for she was pregnant with Aurelie's baby sister or brother.

"Mom, Papa has fallen, and Aimee is trapped under him! They need help!"

Aurelie hadn't noticed if her aunts were talking before she arrived, but she noticed their silence now.

Mom grabbed Aurelie's upper arm, and her fingers dug in painfully. "What? Say it again, what did you see?"

Aurelie repeated herself. Her tummy felt all bad and knotted. Aimee was scared and hurt, why were they all staring at her like this?

And then Aunt Emily leapt up and ran for the house. Aunt Alice followed, while Mom pulled Aurelie close.

Mom started crying, and Aurelie patted her hair awkwardly.

"It's okay, Mom, I think Aimee isn't too badly hurt... Shh, shh..."

But Aurelie had been wrong. Nothing was okay.

Because Aimee's belly started to grow, just like Mom's. The aunts were always whispering and arguing, and Aurelie kept out of their way.

On the day that Aimee's labor started, Aurelie and her other sister-cousins were sent out into the yard to shell beans. The beans did need to be shelled, but even at six, Aurelie knew they were being gotten out of the way.

Inside the house, the aunts were whispering again. But the whispers rose in volume until they were shouting. Aurelie wasn't the only one who forgot to shell the beans, turning toward the window to hear the argument better.

"If only Emily had never gone to France," moaned Aunt Susan.

Aunt Alice snapped, "It's already done. Besides, there aren't any boys. We need to survive."

"What's the point of surviving if we have to live like this?" That was Mom, and the crack of a hand across a cheek followed. Aurelie jumped up and looked through the window.

Her mother's pale cheek was red with blood. Her mother sat unmoving—it wasn't like Mom not to defend herself, but Lisette was in Mom's arms, and Mom's blouse was open. *She's nursing. Aunt Alice hit her while she was nursing.*

Aurelie took off, running away from the house, running as madly as that day when the aunts started warring with each other.

She heard a token protest from behind her, from her next oldest sister-cousin after Aimee, but Aurelie ignored it, and no one came after her. She focused on the way the mud squished between her toes.

She ran as fast as she could, and when she reached her favorite hemlock, she climbed it. The sweet and spicy smell of the bark soothed her, and she sat three feet from the top until the sun set.

It was dark when she got back to the house, and Aurelie figured there wouldn't be any food left, but a bowl of bean stew was waiting on the table. When Aurelie crawled into bed, Mom was crying. Aurelie kissed Lisette's head and whispered, "I'm sorry Aunt Alice slapped you, Mommy."

The crying halted.

"So that's why you took off. Next time, don't stay out so late. Anyway, I don't even care about that." She took a deep breath. "Aimee and the babe didn't make it." She was quiet for a moment before adding, "It was a boy."

Didn't make it. "Aimee died?"

Mom huffed. "Yes. Now go to sleep."

But the worst was yet to come, for two days later, Aunt Emily, Aimee's mom, hung herself from the tree outside the house. The one that was right in front of Papa's bedroom.

The aunts tried to usher all their daughters inside, but Aurelie saw it anyway.

Aunt Alice took charge in the months that followed. She was far stricter than Aunt Emily ever had been, meeting any angry word with an even angrier slap.

Aurelie volunteered to collect brush and go fishing and harvest mushrooms whenever she could. She made sure to be least in sight when anyone was needed for sweeping or cooking, though she didn't mind peeling potatoes or shucking beans, since they did those in the yard, out of reach of Aunt Alice's wood spoon.

And that was the new normal. Nightmares of Aunt Emily's purple face, everyone tense and angry with each other, and babies. There were always babies, but they were all girls, and sometimes Aurelie thought of her mother's whisper.

It was a boy.

But mostly Aurelie stayed away from the house.

And then, when Aurelie was ten, Papa ruffled her hair and said, "I can't believe how tall you are getting!

You're the truest Unseen among us, spending so much time in the woods. The magic must run deep in you."

Aurelie beamed with happiness, but when she looked at the table, she saw Mom didn't look happy at all.

That night, Mom woke her up. It was quiet and dark, the room painted silver by moonlight.

Mom pressed a finger against Aurelie's lips and gave her a bag.

The bag was heavy, but not as heavy as sleeping Lisette, whom Mom carried.

When they had gone further from the house than even Aurelie dared wander on her own and the sun edged the leaves overhead with gold, Aurelie's tummy growled unhappily. She asked Mom, "What will Papa say?"

"Don't call that French bastard that!" hissed Mom. "And I don't care what he—or Alice or any of them— say. He raped me, but he's not gonna rape my girls."

和希

Forest-Heart Home, Kyoto Prefecture, Japan - November 2021

IT was the red string.

Kazuki had never realized it before, but he now saw a string running from *Obā-chama* to him. His to Aurelie was also visible; through that connection, *Obā-chama* was forcing Aurelie to expose her memories to them, even though Aurelie had literally collapsed from the pain.

This is why they call it a binding, not a bond. Bound, not bonded.

In the present, Aurelie wept softly; in the past, she sat on a street corner, pinning her little sister to her side, while her mother negotiated with a stranger for food.

Obā-chama was torturing her, humiliating her, through the binding.

At last he understood why Aurelie didn't want any part of it.

So he cut it.

THWARTED

NOOOOOO!

SO CLOSE.

WHY?

NOT FAIR.　Not fair.

So hungry.　SO HUNGRY.

What now?

QUIET. I'M THINKING
WE INTERVENE. WE HELP.

Help prey?　HA!

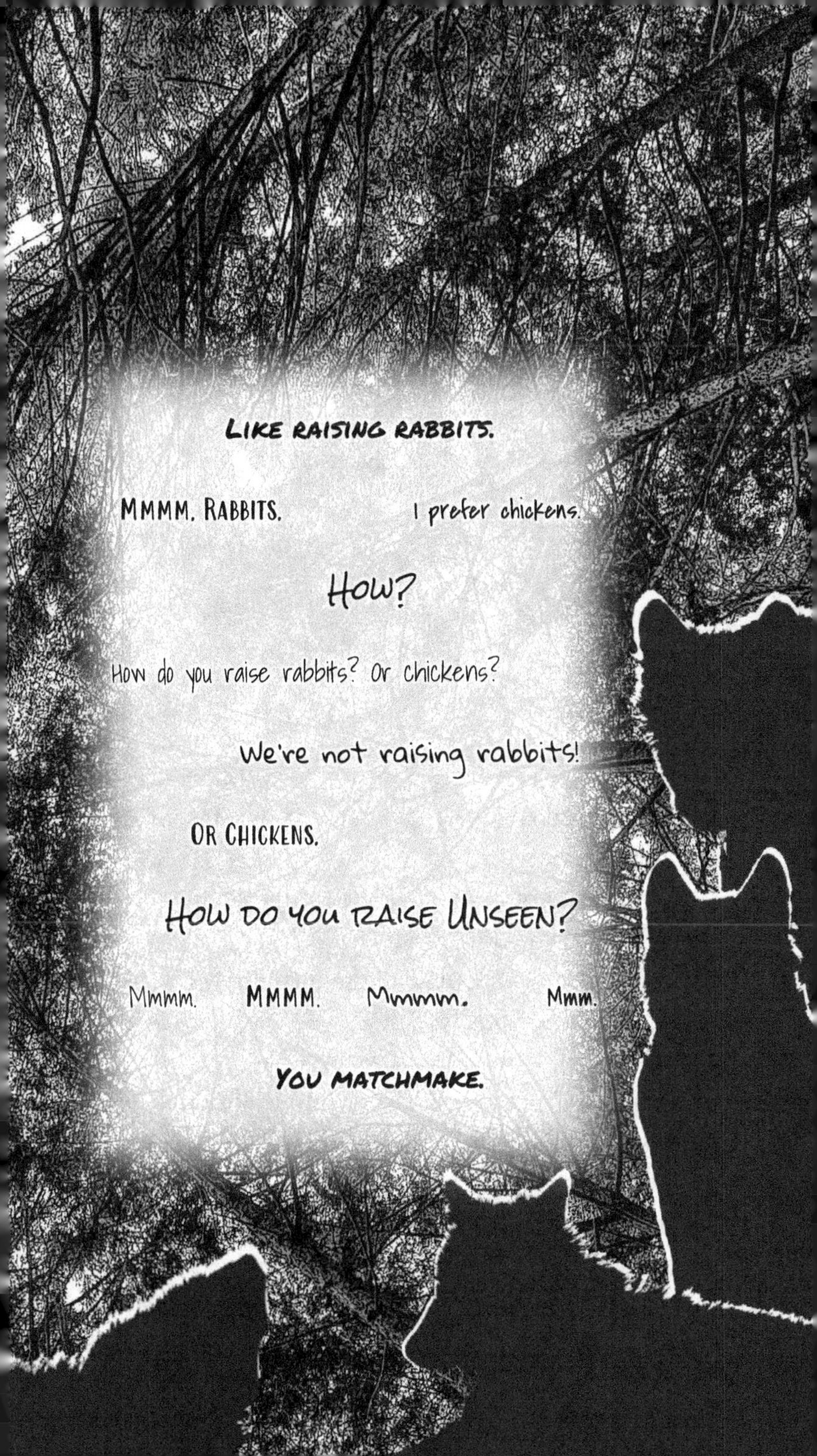

LIKE RAISING RABBITS.

MMMM. RABBITS.

I prefer chickens.

HOW?

How do you raise rabbits? Or chickens?

We're not raising rabbits!

OR CHICKENS.

HOW DO YOU RAISE UNSEEN?

Mmmm.   MMMM.   Mmmm.   Mmm.

YOU MATCHMAKE.

12. BEREFT

和希

AURELIE jerked upright when the string snapped, and then collapsed.

Kazuki caught her before she hit the floor.

"What did you do?" cried *Obā-chama*.

"What were *you* doing?" Kazuki countered.

"Kazuki-*kun*!" cried his mother. "Apologize to *Obā-chama*."

Kazuki was practically shaking. Aurelie had trusted him to protect her from his family, and he hadn't.

He still hadn't fully processed what he had seen in her mind—like Aurelie herself, he didn't want to believe that there was a father alive who'd rape his daughters. He wasn't totally naïve; he knew there was messed up shit in the world, but it had never been an intimate reality for him. And, even if her memories hadn't been so traumatic, how dared *Obā-chama* force them out like that?

What he wanted to do was sweep Aurelie up in his arms and walk out of the room. If she weren't quite so tall and heavy, he would have. Awkwardly, he pulled her arm over his shoulder and stood; her head lolled against his neck.

Kazuki began to half-drag her from the room when his father stood and collected Aurelie's feet.

Kazuki's mother stood, and her hands fluttered with indecision. Kazuki ignored her, and his father said only, "We can lay her down in the Maple Room."

Kazuki's great-aunt saw them in the hallway. She gaped briefly, then led the way to the Maple Room, opening doors for them. They had to stop to change their grips on the stairs, but they managed.

"Is this the American?" she asked. "What happened?"

Kazuki grunted at the first question, but he ignored the second. To his surprise, his father said, "You'd know better than us. *Obā-chama* was using Kazuki's binding, wasn't she?"

"Yes," said Kazuki, "she was walking through Aurelie's memories."

"Memories?" echoed his great-aunt. "That's wonderful—your binding must be very strong. But why did she faint?"

"The memory," Kazuki answered. How could Aurelie not have collapsed under that burden?

"Is that so?" His great-aunt sounded surprised, but

she left it there, to Kazuki's relief.

Most of the bedrooms in the Forest-Heart Home featured traditional *tatami* and *futon*, but the Maple Room had a Western bed—probably why his father had chosen it. Well, that, and it was reserved for guests. In fact, someone had already brought up Aurelie's overnight bag.

His father and he arranged Aurelie on the bed, and Kazuki tugged the duvet over her.

He turned to find his great-aunt observing, a frown between her brows.

"*Oba-san*," he said, "I need to ask you about magic."

オーレリー

AURELIE awoke with tears on her face. She couldn't remember the last time she felt so alone.

Wait, yes, she could. It had been in Nara Park.

Why couldn't she feel Kazuki?

She sat up slowly and immediately sagged against an unfamiliar headboard.

In an unfamiliar room.

The first thing that caught her eye was a beautiful *bonsai*, a Japanese maple that was only a foot tall. The floor was hardwood (more maple, if she knew her trees, which she did).

She was still at the Hayashi estate, she was sure.

She tried to remember what had happened.

She remembered entering the room with *Obā-chama* and the old woman's invasive questions. She hadn't wanted to answer, but then something had happened. She had been eight again, on that day when she saw that French bastard raping her cousin.

To her surprise, the memory wasn't as overwhelming as it usually was. It was almost as if it was someone else's. Or—it was like Kazuki had been with her, holding her hand. He knew, he understood, that she couldn't have saved Aimee. She'd been too young, too helpless. It was as if he had covered her eyes when Aunt Emily hung herself. As if he had walked through the woods when they fled home, telling her she could do it.

How absurd! He wasn't even born back then.

Aurelie kept thinking, trying to remember what came next, but it hurt too much. Like someone had ripped her heart out.

Aurelie pressed a hand to her chest. It still felt hollow and aching.

What the hell had happened?

和希

KAZUKI sat with his great-aunt, her husband, and his grandparents. Before them was a steaming pot of tea and five cups that Kazuki had filled, though they had all been forgotten.

"The binding is the magic of the Unseen," said his grandmother—his father's mother, and *Obā-chama's* daughter-in-law. Her fingers were moving absently, as if twisting a bit of thread, and Kazuki was sure that she was playing with her own red string, even though he couldn't see it.

Kazuki's grandfather bobbed his head at his wife's words, but he didn't interject.

"All Unseen are born with magic potential, but it's the binding that releases it. In its weakest form, the binding allows a couple to feel each other's emotions and physical needs. But stronger bindings bring the double senses—you can see, feel, hear, and smell whatever your mate is experiencing—and sometimes you can share thoughts. And then even past that, is the ability to rifle through each other's memories."

Kazuki hunched his shoulders. "That's horrible."

"Oh, no," protested his great-aunt, "the binding is wonderful. It protects us and makes us stronger. Yuri-*chan* said, 'rifle,' but that's not the right word. None of us have bindings that strong, you see, but I remember my grandmother's description. You travel through their memories with them. It's a gift, letting you share your lives more fully. To achieve a deeper understanding."

Unless they aren't memories they want to share, Kazuki thought sadly. His great-aunt's grandmother (his great-great-grandmother) had led a life of luxury, a beloved child of the Hayashi clan. She wouldn't have had memories like Aurelie's.

He supposed that did soften his anger at *Obā-chama* though—even though Aurelie had been resistant, it probably hadn't occurred to her that she might find anything like that. She probably thought, like great-aunt, that it was a gift.

"Why could *Obā-chama* use the binding though?"

"Ah, that is clan magic, and the reason my mother leads the clan," said his great-aunt, "You see, my parents had the strongest binding of their generation.

The strongest threads."

Kazuki didn't fully follow, but he was starting to understand. "You mean she has more magic. And she is connected to each member of the family, like the mate bindings?"

"Yes," said his grandmother. "You have unusually strong magic, too."

So that was why *Obā-chama* had wanted him to the lead the clan. Not because he was a good student or because he was a natural leader, but because she thought he would have a strong binding, one that would let him control the family. And that was why she had pushed him down a different path when that binding didn't appear. His mother was completely wrong—Kazuki and Emiko would never lead the clan. "I was supposed to have a strong binding because of that. But I didn't."

"But now you do!" said his great-aunt enthusiastically. Then, more tentatively, "Did you—did you see the red strings?"

So that's a known phenomenon. Kazuki nodded, "I did, but..." he hesitated. "The binding is broken now."

"Broken?" echoed his grandfather. "What happened?"

Kazuki shrugged, not sure how to explain what he had done. He had seen the red string and snapped it.

"Kazuki."

Kazuki whipped his head around and found *Obā-chama* standing in the doorway.

"Let's talk."

In perfect synchronization, his four elders rose to

their feet and left the room. *Obā-chama* approached slowly—there was the slightest shuffle to her step. She was, after all, over a hundred.

Kazuki rose to help her sit, but she waved him off.

"Kazuki," she asked, "what did you do?"

"What do you mean?"

"Earlier, I saw the binding between you and Aurelie-*san* was loose. I tried to anchor it for you. But suddenly—"

Kazuki flushed. "She doesn't want to be bound. So I cut the thread."

Obā-chama sagged forward and went so far as to support herself with the table.

"You impulsive child," she said, her voice sad rather than angry. "How could you do that to her?"

"I was protecting her!" Kazuki growled.

Obā-chama looked at him keenly. "Is that so?" She shook her head. "You're in for a rough time."

Kazuki crossed his arms. "What's that supposed to mean?"

"That child's potential for magic is even deeper than your own. If you give her up, one of your cousins will bind with her. And then I will take them as my successor, not you."

Kazuki frowned. "You mean to say you want Aurelie—and whomever she marries—to be the head of the family?"

"The boy can learn." *Obā-chama* folded her hands over each other.

Kazuki shook his head. "She won't be bound to anyone." But he wondered—if it were Kento or Shigeru, would Aurelie still be reluctant?

Surely she would. He had seen in her mind, in her heart. It hadn't been him she had rejected so utterly but the binding itself.

"She's her own person, *Obā-chama*," Kazuki said. "I won't let you force her."

"I won't have to," said *Obā-chama*. "She will choose this on her own. It's our nature to bind ourselves to our community. The bindings make us strong. And there's nothing she craves more than strength."

Kazuki still felt lost, but he couldn't argue with that last.

オーレリー

DESPITE her aching chest, Aurelie got out of the bed, but she felt too nervous to leave the room.

To say she was in enemy territory would be obvious hyperbole, yet there was a grain of truth to the thought. Instead of going to the door, she stepped closer to the window. It was a second story room (who had carried her here?), and it afforded her a view of the compound.

Her initial impression of a wilderness was quite right, despite the high wall that encircled it. Dark green pines, crimson maples, pale yellow gingkoes, and many bare branches. As she watched, birds burst from the trees (she didn't recognize them from this distance, but they were a variety of songbird, driving off a poacher, she thought). She suddenly wanted to see this place in every season—blanketed in snow, blooming with new buds, erupting with every shade of green.

If she accepted her binding with Kazuki, she would.

He's too young for you.

That was an excuse. She knew how badly he wanted her; she felt the same burning desire. It wasn't like they were human after all, with thousands—millions—of potential mates their own age.

You're an outsider.

Sure, she was an American. She didn't understand all the elements of their culture. But between the binding and Aurelie's own willingness to adapt, that was hardly insurmountable.

It's not safe.

Aurelie frowned. She'd believed that for so long—her mother had explained it over and over, how Aunt Emily's binding had destroyed their family.

Except... Kazuki wasn't like that French bastard. He was mindful of her wishes, and he was respectful of her. Even today, he'd answered her questions on the train so thoughtfully and he had guided her without crowding her. And look at his parents—neither was controlling the other. They were partners. The whole clan felt like a safety net; maybe the problem wasn't the binding, maybe it was the French bastard.

That French bastard is your "Papa."

Aurelie flinched.

Unseen had migrated to Japan over a thousand years ago, and they had thrived. They had stayed hidden, but they held power and wealth and they lived like civilized people.

They hadn't hidden in the mountains, avoiding the government and raping their daughters under the pretense of preserving the species.

She was suddenly glad that Kazuki *hadn't* really been with her for all those difficult days.

Maybe that was the real reason she'd been so afraid of the binding—she had so desperately wanted to pretend to be the woman he saw. *Smart, independent, and beautiful.*

She ran from the binding because it would expose her family's secrets. If he knew—how could she face him?

Never mind binding and marriage, how could she stand in front of him as a teacher without collapsing from shame?

The door slid open with a soft shush.

Aurelie turned and met Kazuki's eyes. They were wide with surprise.

"You awake?" He spoke in English, and Aurelie noticed his accent for the first time. He was understandable, but their binding was not helping. He stepped into the room and shut the door. "Are you okay?"

No, she felt like she might never smile again.

"I'm fine. What happened? The last thing I remember, *Obā-chama* was asking me about Unseen in the US."

He bowed to her. She knew that bowing was more common here, but that made her uncomfortable.

"I'm sorry, Dubois-*sensei*. *Obā-chama* evoked your memories. We saw your childhood. I severed our bond."

Oh. Oh, oh, oh.

He had *seen*. He *knew*.

And like she'd expected, that knowledge had knocked her off the pedestal. He no longer wanted to be bound to her. He was disgusted by the reality.

She squeezed her hands into fists.

This is what she had wanted. (Lies, she had never *wanted* this). She would have preferred it if she could have remained an ideal (how could she be so pathetic), but this was what she had been asking for.

She spoke Japanese because it let her distance herself from her words. "I see. Thank you." She returned his bow.

"*Anō, Obā-chama* wants to talk to you. If you wish—"

"I'll talk to her," she decided. She certainly didn't want to wait until tomorrow when a hundred strangers would be visiting. Maybe she could even settle this and leave tonight.

He pressed his lips into a thin line. He opened his mouth twice, but he said only, "Okay, okay. Come with me."

13. RELIEVED

恵美子

EMIKO associated her clan's Forest-Heart Home with peace and tranquility, but tension swamped her as soon as she entered the door.

It was hard to say why she felt that way—it was quiet, as usual, and no one was in sight. But the air felt oppressive and the walls too close.

Maybe it was the manifestation of her own guilt for stalking Kazuki and Aurelie.

But something *was* off. By the time Emiko switched her outdoor shoes for house slippers, Haruko stood waiting, her face even more solemn than usual and her hands tightly clasped.

Haruko was the infamous cousin who had taken a

human lover; she was now the housekeeper of the Forest-Heart Home and rarely left.

"Emi-*chan*, we weren't expecting you." Haruko sighed. "Though I suppose if I were in your place, I might very well have shown up, too. Have you met the American?"

Emiko nodded. "She's my professor."

"A professor?" echoed Haruko. "Not a student? How old is she?"

Emiko shrugged. "I suppose around your age."

Haruko looked horrified. "But I changed Kazuki-*kun*'s diapers! Perhaps we should be grateful the binding broke."

Emiko, who had been stepping into the house proper, stumbled, and Haruko had to catch her.

"The binding broke? Bindings can break?"

"It seems so. No one knows what's going on. But that's what Kazuki-*san* told Mariko-*oba*-san. That the binding was broken."

"Poor Kazuki-*kun*. Where is he now?"

"I think he went to check on the American. She fainted."

Emiko hesitated. "Do you think I could see *Obā-chama*?"

Haruko hesitated. "I was about to bring her some tea. Why don't you carry it for me?"

オ ー レ リ ー

AS soon as Aurelie saw Emiko, she remembered the girl's declaration that Kazuki deserved better than Aurelie.

Well, she thought unhappily, *it seems* Obā-chama *agrees. Now that Kazuki has realized it as well, they must be planning to reinstate Emiko as his partner.*

But if that were the plan, it didn't seem Kazuki was aware of it. "What are you doing here?" he asked Emiko.

"Visiting *Obā-chama*," said Emiko. She blushed though, and Aurelie knew that wasn't the whole truth.

Obā-chama said something to Kazuki in Japanese. He replied—arguing, Aurelie thought—but *Obā-chama* repeated herself. Kazuki sort-of bowed and strode angrily from the room. Aurelie suddenly felt totally alone.

Obā-chama then turned to Aurelie and invited her to sit. Aurelie went to one of the *zabuton* and remembered just in time to fold her knees rather than sit cross-legged.

Obā-chama then said something rather long and fast, but before Aurelie could panic, Emiko translated.

"*Obā-chama* wanted to speak to you alone, but her English isn't very good, and she thought it might be easier if I translated. Is this acceptable to you?"

"Yes," said Aurelie, but she couldn't help but ask, "Why doesn't Kazuki translate?"

Emiko repeated her question (which Aurelie followed easily enough), but she had no idea what *Obā-chama* replied.

Emiko looked a little lost herself, but she said, "*Obā-chama* is mad at Kazuki and thinks he needs to be punished."

Aurelie found her fingers starting to tap, so she

twisted her hands together. "Why is she mad at Kazuki?"

The answer shocked her. "Because he cut the binding. Are you okay?"

Aurelie nodded and then touched her chest self-consciously. "Actually... it hurts here."

Obā-chama nodded, as if she understood the words even without the translation.

Then there was a long burst of Japanese that led Emiko to ask several questions before saying, in English, "*Obā-chama* has only read about broken bindings a handful of times, but she believes the pain you are feeling, the emptiness, is because of that. The sole way to heal is to build other connections, other bindings. She says—" here Emiko cleared her throat, "well, she says that you and I have a thin binding already."

Aurelie was shocked—it must have shown on her face because Emiko blushed.

"I was surprised, too. *Obā-chama* says that all members of the clan are bound to each other, but in recent years we hardly notice because the threads have grown thin and weak. It's a testimony to the strength of your magic that she can see a binding between us."

Aurelie studied *Obā-chama*. The old woman's eyes were clear and sharp, hardly given to flights of fancy.

"She also wanted to talk about her walk in your memories?"

Aurelie whipped her attention back to Emiko, who looked vaguely confused.

But Aurelie understood. *Obā-chama*, the regal

queen, had witnessed the transgressions of her family as well as Kazuki. Appalled, Aurelie slowly looked back at *Obā-chama.*

She expected condemnation. Scorn.

Instead, she found practical compassion. No shock, some sorrow, but mostly strength.

"She felt you had more to share."

A distant voice—it sounded like her mother—told Aurelie to be careful. Not to share herself; to be angry that *Obā-chama* had already brought so much out.

But Aurelie felt nothing but relief, relief so strong that the room blurred before her eyes.

For the first time in her life, she analyzed the trauma of her family as she would a historic conflict. She was punishing herself for her father's transgressions.

Yes, her father, who had controlled her family with fear. A fear that was undoubtedly real for him, though that in no way excused the violence he had inflicted.

Emiko wrapped an arm around Aurelie's shoulder, and her hand squeezed one of Aurelie's reassuringly. Aurelie realized the room was blurry because her eyes were full of tears. Emiko looked strange, and for a moment, Aurelie saw a flash of red. Aurelie blinked away the tears, and the hint of red disappeared, too.

She squeezed Emiko's hand in reassurance and turned toward *Obā-chama.* "I do. I do have more to share."

Through Emiko, *Obā-chama* asked, "So you are not angry at me for walking through your memories?"

"Angry?" echoed Aurelie. "No—it hurt, in the

moment, but...I feel relieved. It was cathartic." (Emiko asked what cathartic meant).

"Kazuki is angry," admitted *Obā-chama*.

He must be frustrated that he was called to me, thought Aurelie. "Ah," she said aloud. "I'm so sorry about that. But it's my past. My truth. It's painful, but now—sharing has made it less so."

Obā-chama nodded.

"The binding brings relief and healing," Emiko translated.

Obā-chama asked a question, and Aurelie jerked in surprise when the English words, "that French bastard," were a part of it. Emiko asked how he came to Aurelie's family.

Aurelie thought about it for a moment. "I need to back up—you have to understand, a lot of this happened before I was born. So I can only relate what I was told."

Aurelie shifted uncomfortably on her knees, and Emiko said, "Why don't we sit cross-legged? I also don't have the endurance for this."

After they rearranged themselves (*Obā-chama* remained kneeling), Aurelie said, "There was an epidemic in the fifties. Something like a flu or pneumonia, and it devastated the community. All the men in my aunt's generation died.

"My aunt was expected to take over managing the community, and she decided that survival necessitated finding more Unseen. This was in early sixties—my mom knows the exact year, but I forget."

Faces, long pushed from her thoughts, swam before

Aurelie's eyes.

"The community didn't keep great records, but we all knew we'd come from England in the late 16th century. I've wondered if they were the lost Roanoke colony. However, my aunt didn't believe there was any purpose to going to England. Our own stories said that fleeing England was out of desperation, and we should never return there. However, she also believed the family had originally come from France, during the Norman conquest."

She was rambling—Emiko struggled to translate, and did *Obā-chama* even know of Roanoke or the Normans?

"So my aunt went to Normandy. In France," she added for Emiko's benefit. "And she was called. To—" Aurelie hesitated, "to the French bastard. My father. He was happy to come join them in US, for he was completely alone." Aurelie couldn't resist tapping her fingers. "They probably couldn't have managed that today. My mother had a huge amount of trouble getting social security numbers for my sister and I when we left the community, but back then... I guess it was easier to convince people there'd been paperwork errors before every agency had databases."

"He was alone in France?" asked *Obā-chama*.

"Yes. Well. Actually..."

オーレリー

Normandy, France – May 2012

AURELIE stood on the cliffs of Etrétat, the channel

lashing their base and the deep blue sky brushed with wispy white clouds.

They were just as her father had described them.

She understood—and supported—her mother's decision to take her and Lisette away from him, but he had always told wonderful stories, his dark eyes glinting with humor and his face transforming as he acted out different characters. His hands had swept up and out like puppets danced on the ends, and when he laughed, the deep, rich sound had rolled through her.

When he had spoken of these cliffs, his eyes had gone soft and faraway, his voice wistful and sad. He had painted such wonder and beauty, that Aurelie scanned the sparkling waves for a glimpse of a mermaid tail or selkie face.

If they'd been human, maybe she would have visited France with him. Maybe he would be showing his home to her, and they'd walk along the pale sandy beaches talking about history together.

Of course, if they'd been human, she wouldn't exist because her mother would never have borne the child of her rapist. And Aunt Emily would never have even found him in the first place—

Aurelie turned away from the beautiful view as if it were lying to her.

Her father had often spoken of his home, and Aurelie had memorized its address as a child. But it had been empty for nearly fifty years. Would there still be anything there?

These roads weren't meant for pedestrians, but there wasn't that much traffic, so it was easy enough to step off into a field when a car did pass by. And the day was nice and warm—maybe it was good she had postponed this trip for so long, for late spring was surely a better season for it than the fall or winter would have been.

An hour later, she reached a heavily wooded area— it wasn't a forest by Aurelie's standards, though the French would probably beg to differ—and a dirt drive that clearly hadn't seen much traffic in the past thirty years.

At the end of it, she found the Dubois ancestral home. In horrible disrepair, a shack more than a house, and covered with ivy. She circled it warily, looking for signs of ownership. The door was locked, but the windows were easy enough to go through since the ivy already had.

It was quite dim inside, so she activated her phone screen and turned the brightness all the way up. (If it was really so "smart," then why didn't it have a flashlight?)

The ghostly white light made the inside of the shack feel even creepier than the dimness, but it also revealed furniture.

Aurelie started opening drawers, a vague cloud of guilt hanging over her.

This was my family's home, she reminded herself.

There wasn't much in the drawers but dust. Her fingers found detailed carvings in the wood, but the phone barely illuminated them. She supposed her father had taken everything personal with him—or burned it. Unseen knew better than to leave traces behind, though she hoped there would be something. She searched two more cupboards, and she was rewarded at last with a folio filled with paper. Maybe the paper was useless, for it to have been left, but she'd examine it anyway. It was old (probably over a hundred years), so she wrapped it in her flannel shirt before placing it in her backpack.

"Hey! What are you doing?"

Aurelie jumped at the abrupt yell and bumped her thigh on the corner of the cupboard.

She turned toward the voice and saw a dark-haired man at the shack's window.

She wasn't sure if she should try to run or not, but after a moment, she walked to the window.

The man stepped back as she reached the light. He was wearing a fleece jacket despite the heat—maybe it was thinner than it looked.

"*Zut!* Those genes run strong. You a Dubois?" the man asked.

"I'm Robert's daughter," Aurelie admitted, hoping her accent was good enough to let her pass for French.

"Well, I'll be." The man sort of—well, smacked his lips, and Aurelie instinctively crossed her arms over her chest. "You better climb out of there—the structure's not the sturdiest."

Aurelie obliged, aware of the man's staring. (What were the chances she'd run into a sociopath?) When her feet were on solid ground again, he said, "The two of them always kept to themselves so much—I'm shocked Robert had a daughter."

"The two of them?" she echoed.

"Robert and his sister. Elise."

"I didn't know he had a sister," she blurted before she could think better of it.

The man's expression darkened. "Yes. Well. Not surprised that he wouldn't talk about her. Practically kept her closed up in this house till she died. Forgive me saying so, but the two of them were a bit unnatural."

He looked at the house behind her. "You claiming the house? Far as I know, it's still in Robert's name, but lots of people have talked about ripping it down. Shouldn't let a house rot like this."

Aurelie flushed. "I'm sorry, I'm not. I just wanted to see if it were still here."

"Where's Robert anyway?"

Aurelie hesitated. She didn't like chatting with strangers, and this man was making her uncomfortable, but she craved whatever crumbs he could offer about her father.

"He's passed," she lied. "Leaving a lot of unanswered questions. I was hoping..." She looked at the house sadly, and she heard that moist, lip-smacking sound again.

"Perhaps I can buy you a coffee?" She'd passed something like a café twenty minutes ago.

He giggled, a surprisingly high sound for such a big man. "Not much of one for coffee. But I can tell you about Robert and Elise."

He leaned forward, and Aurelie had to resist the urge to lean back. "The two of them rarely went out, only *he* ever talked to anyone outside the house, but then she was pregnant."

He raised his brows and waggled them.

Aurelie hated him in that moment, but not as much as she hated her father.

"She had gotten pretty big—I saw her sometimes, living next door, and people in town wondered if something ought to be done about it. For being so unnatural. And then..." He sliced at his wrist with his fingers. "Killed herself. From shame, I should think."

オーレリー

Kyoto Prefecture, Japan – December 30, 2021

"IT'S not really relevant, but the neighbor said he raped his sister. She killed herself in late pregnancy. I always wondered—did my aunt know that, and bring him back to us anyway? Or did he hide it from her?" Aurelie's hands fisted.

Obā-chama's arms wrapped around her, and Emiko squeezed her fingers again. (How long had they been holding hands?)

Aurelie waited for one of them to say, "Your aunt wanted the family to survive," or "At least you are here now."

Instead, *Obā-chama* stroked Aurelie's hair softly, and offered a phrase that needed no translation: "I'm sorry."

Aurelie wrapped her arms around the old woman, laid her head on that frail breast and cried her eyes out.

14. WELCOMED

和希

KAZUKI slid the shoji shut behind him and stared a few beats at the golden *noren* that hung in front of it. He was annoyed that Emiko had been allowed to stay, while he had been pushed out.

Ever since meeting Aurelie, he had fancied himself in a blockbuster—a movie that parents showed their kids twenty years later. East meeting west, the discovery of other Unseen, a fate that stretched around the world. Up until now, he had felt like the lead of the script.

But he had been wrong. Aurelie was the lead, and he wasn't even the love interest. At best, he was the second lead, whose purpose was to show how desirable the heroine was by having a handsome, devoted man chasing her even though his wooing went unacknowledged.

He was tempted to linger, to listen to whatever *Obā-chama*, Emiko, and Aurelie discussed, but he definitely didn't want anyone to walk by and catch him eavesdropping.

Besides, didn't he know what they were going to talk about anyway? *Obā-chama* was going to try to convince Aurelie that she wanted to have little Hayashi babies. Kazuki didn't like abandoning Aurelie to that pressure, but she was an adult.

And had been one fourteen years longer than he.

He turned away from the door and started down the hall, checking the time on his phone. Dinner would be soon; he should go to the kitchen and see what he could do to help.

He could hear chatter as he approached, but everyone fell silent when he stepped through the door.

His great-aunt and uncle gave him sympathetic looks, and Kazuki hunched his shoulders awkwardly. He hated how coming home could make his poise and confidence in the wider world disappear.

Haruko, his fifth-cousin twice removed or something like that, stepped forward and directed him to stacks of dishes sitting on the kitchen table. Haruko had been held up as a warning to uncalled Unseen like Kazuki. Ever since her indiscretion with a human, she had been responsible for managing the estate, where no humans were allowed.

"Help me set the table," she said briskly.

"Placemats?" asked Kazuki.

"Already out," said Haruko. She picked up a stack of small brown plates, each painted with a cream-colored rabbit and the moon, and Kazuki took the blue bowls with pale dots that sat next to them.

"What is she like?" Haruko asked as she set her first plate down on the low dining table.

No need to ask who she was: Aurelie.

Gorgeous. Brilliant, independent, and insecure. Kazuki placed a bowl in the upper left corner of a placemat.

"Palest hair I've ever seen. Like moonlight." *Kuso.* Like moonlight? He'd been trying to sound nonchalant. He cleared his throat, hoping Haruko would forget he said that. "She speaks conversational Japanese pretty well. Don't talk to her in English unless you want to realize how not proficient you are—she's a history professor, and she uses big words."

Haruko chuckled. "Too bad she doesn't speak French. I'm better at that than English."

Kazuki looked at Haruko in surprise. "She does speak French. I didn't know you did."

"Most of my branch does."

Haruko's branch intersected with the main six or maybe seven generations back, but no one had ever tried to make Kazuki learn French. "Why?"

Haruko was setting one of the rabbit plates in the middle of a placemat, and she seemed more interested in the rabbit's orientation than Kazuki's question. He thought she was going to ignore him, but when she spoke, he realized that she had been deliberating.

"We've been told not to discuss it, but I guess your foreigner changes things. About four-hundred years ago, a foreigner married into our family. My eleven-times great-grandfather."

"What?" exclaimed Kazuki. He dropped the blue bowl he was holding, but the high-quality clay was resilient. He set the bowl upright and checked the table. No scratch, thankfully.

Haruko ignored Kazuki's fumble and continued to arrange her plates. "He was the lone survivor of his clan, and the family was afraid that revealing his existence would lure the family's youth abroad, into danger."

"Okay," said Kazuki slowly, even as he quickly placed the rest of his bowls. "Four hundred years ago—wouldn't that be during *sakoku*?" Japan had isolated itself from the rest of the world in the early seventeenth century. "Didn't we help implement that policy?"

"Because of my ancestor," explained Haruko. "Yours, too. His son had an unusual amount of magic and married into the main line. It was fear that whatever had killed his clan would come here and kill ours."

Kazuki shivered at Haruko's words. Whatever had killed the other Unseen? What could that be except humans?

"So he entered Japan before *sakoku* and then helped enact it?"

Haruko chuckled. "He didn't, but our clan did. He kept a low profile, I believe, given that he was an undocumented immigrant at the time. If you want, you can read the records later. Come, let's get more dishes."

オーレリー

AURELIE felt safe, seen, and connected. Not so intensely as she had been with Kazuki, but *Obā-chama*'s calm acceptance of that which upset her the most had bound them together. She could tell that *Obā-chama* was starting to feel hungry (it was dinnertime), and Aurelie found she could understand *Obā-chama*'s speech. At her side, Aurelie knew how Emiko was sitting without even looking at her. Could feel her concern, her care. *Obā*-chama was right that they had a binding too, strengthened now by the fact Aurelie and Emiko were both connected to *Obā-chama* as well.

These gentle bindings—less invasive than what she had shared with Kazuki—made Aurelie understand why Aunt Emily had gone to France.

Why she might have married that French bastard even knowing what he'd done.

To be surrounded by understanding, resilience, and acceptance—it was heady. Addictive.

It was how family should be.

If this is what her family had before that French bastard came, Aunt Emily couldn't have comprehended the risk of trusting others.

Oh, if Aunt Emily had known what he had done to his sister, she shouldn't have brought him home, bound or not. But...

The Hayashis were a clan that Aurelie wanted to know more about. To connect with—maybe not a mate binding, but *this* was okay.

(And that hole in her heart where Kazuki had been—she'd get used to it?)

Or maybe she could fill it.

"*Obā-chama,*" murmured Aurelie. She could use the insider's name now.

"This is the magic of the Unseen," said *Obā-chama.* "That we can connect to each other; protect each other. And your magic is strong, stronger than ours has been for some time."

Aurelie didn't believe in magic, of course, but other words occurred to her. Genetic diversity. Hive mind.

"I'm so glad you came to us," murmured *Obā-chama.*

"Me, too," said Emiko. "I'm glad you're not alone anymore."

An hour ago, those words would have made Aurelie bristle, but now—tears welled, and she took Emiko's hand. "Thank you."

Then her insecurities chimed in.

"But—what if I don't breed?" Aurelie asked. "The binding with Kazuki is broken..."

Obā-chama smiled faintly. "I *do* hope that you'll bind anew and bring more children to our family. But I welcome you into our family either way."

She was telling the truth—the soft binding made that clear. Aurelie's value to *Obā-chama* wasn't contingent on her binding and reproducing.

This was on par with receiving her offer from Yale's history department for grad school.

Aurelie shook her head in denial, even though she believed it. She just wanted to hear it said again.

Obā-chama wrapped her hands around Aurelie's

face, which should have made her feel like a child, but made her feel special. Loved.

How could a stranger make her feel more loved than her family ever had?

But that was the magic of the binding. Aurelie winced at her own word choice. *Wonder* of the binding, then. The world was full of wonder, even if there was no magic.

"You impress me. Not because of your magic, which isn't something you had any say in, but the fact you came here. That you went looking for answers, and you faced that which frightened you. I now have hope there are other Unseen in the world and that you could find them."

Emiko made a small noise, and both Aurelie and *Obā-chama* looked at her.

"Ah, yes," said *Obā-chama*, "you are interested in such an endeavor, aren't you, Emi-*chan*?"

Emiko nodded, and Aurelie could almost see it. Traveling with Emiko, exploring the world, and seeking traces of the Unseen. Except she thought Kazuki and his fearlessness would make a good companion, too, which broke the daydream.

Aurelie said carefully, "I would be open to such an undertaking. Looking for answers about the Unseen is what brought me to Japan in the first place."

Obā-chama tilted her head. "Oh? Why Japan?"

"Letters," answered Aurelie. "In France, there were letters in a portfolio. In Japanese."

She blushed, remembering how she had mistaken the characters for an Unseen language before realizing they were far more common. Probably that French bastard hadn't been able to read them, which is why he had left them in the house.

The letters hadn't said much—her many-times-great-uncles had been obsessed with Japan for they believed its isolationist tendencies would make it an ideal home for Unseen. One of them had gone to Holland (for only the Dutch traded with Japan during those centuries) and then Nagasaki to pursue this wild theory. The letters had stopped abruptly, and Aurelie had assumed that he had died.

Aurelie had thought going to Japan would be dangerous, but she'd been willing to take the risk to learn why the Unseen had been so determined to hide.

Obā-chama's face remained serene and pensive, but her feelings grew increasingly tense as Aurelie spoke.

"I know who you are speaking of," she admitted. "The clan found him and adopted him."

Emiko gaped. "What! There have been other foreign Unseen?"

"Just the one," said *Obā-chama*, "and his family sent word that he must not come home for they were being hunted. That was their last missive."

"Hunted?" echoed Aurelie. "By whom?"

Obā-chama shook her head. "We have only guesses. But if our legends are right, the right question is 'by *what*?'"

"By what?" asked Aurelie.

"Wolves," said *Obā-chama*.

"EMI-*CHAN* said your foreigner is a professor," said Haruko. "Around my age?"

Kazuki could hear the disapproval in her tone. "She's younger than you." He was pretty sure. "She's a young professor." Kazuki set down two drinking glasses.

"Is she thirty?" asked Haruko.

"Thirty-six," mumbled Kazuki, "But I'm an adult!"

"Barely," muttered Haruko.

Kazuki went to the kitchen to fetch more cups.

オーレリー

"LITERAL wolves?" Aurelie couldn't believe it. "That's why we are so compelled to hide?"

"That's what our stories say."

Aurelie shook her head. "Most wolves are near extinction now—are there even any in Japan?"

"Not wild ones," said *Obā-chama*, "Not anymore, though there used to be."

"It must be a metaphor. *Human* wolves," Aurelie argued, then blushed at her gall.

Obā-chama cocked her head, her wispy white hair adding piquancy to the movement. "I have wondered if humans would help or eliminate us."

"They don't have the best track record," acknowledged Aurelie, "Besides the hundreds of species that have been driven into extinction, I have often thought that they would prefer to place us in camps or reservations, as is often done with 'other' humans."

"If you believe humanity is what threatens us

though, why did you come to Japan looking for answers?"

Aurelie bit her lip. "I believe that here," she tapped her temple, "but not here." She pressed her fist against her chest. "I've been trying to convince myself the threat to our species is humans. After all, they now have dozens of organizations that prevent the extinction of other species. If it's humans that threaten us, it's time to come forward. To use their resources to unite us across the globe."

Obā-chama nodded seriously. "I have thought this, too, but I also feel certain that we must hide to survive."

"If I could read the stories that you spoke of..."

Obā-chama laughed. "Yes. All in good time. But there is something more pressing for now. I want to arrange one-on-one meetings for you with the eligible men of the clan."

"Blind dates?" Aurelie wasn't much of one for TV, but she suddenly imagined handing out long-stemmed red roses to Unseen bachelors. *Does Kazuki like roses?*

Obā-chama laughed. "They are *omiai*. Will you do it?"

Aurelie looked at Emiko for guidance.

Emiko shrugged. "It's up to you. I've done them; no binding for me, just many stilted conversations."

Aurelie wasn't exactly comfortable with binding, but she *liked* this less invasive binding she had with *Obā-chama*. (If she were honest, she already missed her binding with Kazuki).

Plus, there's no way what happened back home would happen here. The Hayashi clan was large and rule-following. Aurelie didn't have to trust her mate because the clan would ensure that he didn't do things like rape her sisters and daughters. She saw now that her fears were born of paranoia, a natural reaction to a traumatic experience, but totally unfounded in reality. But understanding her feelings didn't make them go away.

"After New Year's?" Aurelie asked. "I need a little time to adjust. And some weekends won't work, unless they came to Nara..."

She shifted uncomfortably, and *Obā-chama* set a hand on Aurelie's. "You won't meet them alone. We will do it here."

Aurelie breathed a little deeper. *Obā-chama* understood her fears like a therapist (not that Aurelie had ever gone to one).

"Okay," Aurelie agreed. "I'll go on your *omiai*."

和希

KAZUKI was relieved when *Obā-chama*, Aurelie, and Emiko entered the dining room because Haruko was too polite to keep drilling him about their age-gap in front of Aurelie.

They all sat down on the *zabuton* tucked around table. There was a flurry of activity as rice, fish, vegetables, and drinks were distributed. Kazuki knew it must be overwhelming to Aurelie, and he wished he could help her through the binding.

Although.

She didn't seem as lost as he expected. Some of the greats used words that should have been unfamiliar to her, but Aurelie seemed to be following the conversation fine. What was going on?

When the plates were filled, *Obā-chama* cleared her throat.

Everyone turned to her expectantly.

"Au-*chan* has agreed to meet some potential mates. The *omiai* will be held here on weekends over the next few months."

"What?" demanded Kazuki. "*Omiai*? Why?"

"I thought Kazuki-*kun* and she were bound," said his mother.

"Kazuki-*kun* snapped the binding," said *Obā-chama*, calmly. "Au-*chan* has agreed that it is still desirable to marry into the family," *What! This must be a joke,* thought Kazuki, "and we must hope that she will be called again. So we will have *omiai*."

Obā-chama popped a slice of salmon into her mouth and started chewing.

Kazuki had a lot to chew over as well, if only he could swallow his pride first.

15. BEFRIENDED

ON New Year's morning, Aurelie took her time showering and drying off. Without *Obā-chama* right by her side, she was regretting her decision to stay for the celebrations. At least she had appropriate armor: fine wool trousers and a lilac silk blouse. She fluffed her hair and stepped into the hall—directly into the path of an Unseen woman about her age.

Aurelie remembered her face from dinner last night, but not her name. (This spoke to her state of stress, for normally Aurelie was excellent with names).

The woman had an unusually prominent jaw, which was emphasized by her hair being held away from her face with a flower-print headband. The stranger glared at Aurelie, her mouth pinching and her brows snapping together.

Aurelie felt her cheeks heat, and she mumbled an apology. In fact, she even felt tears prick at her eyes before the woman's hostility, and she blinked rapidly to hold them at bay. She must not have wholly succeeded, for the other woman's face abruptly softened. When she spoke, her voice was as soothing as hot cocoa.

"I'm Morimoto Haruko. The house will be hectic with arrivals soon. I'm on my way out to run some errands for the holiday. Would you like to come with me?"

Aurelie was shocked by the offer. It wasn't very appealing either; Haruko didn't seem wholly welcoming. And yet...

Aurelie refused to turn molehills into mountains.

"Please," she said.

Haruko grunted in approval. "Let's get you breakfast, quickly then. Is there anything else you need?"

Aurelie shook her head, and, perhaps fifteen minutes later, some yogurt and fruit were in her belly, and she was in the smallest minivan she'd ever seen.

She was musing that Haruko was rather pushy (almost American, versus the Japanese indirectness to which she was quickly becoming accustomed), but she supposed that if she were in charge of getting this house ready for seventy guests, she'd be in a rush as well. Plus, she was kindly (hopefully) helping Aurelie escape the chaos of the house, so Aurelie wouldn't hold it against her.

Haruko's foot seemed to be a bit heavier than Kazuki's father's, which made the steep roads seem even narrower than Aurelie remembered.

They rode in silence for a bit, giving Aurelie time to take in the rear of the van, filled with empty crates. The silence wasn't unwelcome, but Aurelie's curiosity was growing. "Are those for groceries?"

She received an "mmm" that she chose to interpret as affirmative. Then Haruko sighed and said, "I'm sorry, I don't mean to be rude. Actually, I am in charge of running the Forest-Heart Home, and I have a lot to do."

Aurelie understood that, but *Haruko* had invited *her*. She said as much before she thought better of it, and Haruko laughed sheepishly. "You're right, of course. It was on impulse. When I saw you come out of the washroom... I realized this might be my only opportunity to talk to you alone. But why did you accept the invitation?"

Now it was Aurelie's turn to be embarrassed. "I was also being impulsive. The Forest-Heart Home is intimidating to me, and I haven't been around so many Unseen in a long time. I don't think I've ever been around a hundred."

This admission drew more questions from Haruko, and Aurelie soon realized she was making another Unseen friend. Emiko being her first. Like Emiko, Haruko was full of curiosity and eager to learn. Unlike Emiko, she was four years older than Aurelie, and the two of them understood the resignation to loneliness, for it turned out that Haruko was also unbound.

Even after that revelation though, it caught Aurelie off guard when Haruko said, "It seems we aren't going to bind with each other."

Aurelie wondered if she had misunderstood, but she asked, "Was this an *omiai*?"

Haruko smiled, but it was more bitter than happy. "*Obā-chama* wouldn't organize an *omiai* for the two of us. But in the clan records, there are bindings between Unseen of the same-sex. Not common, but they are there."

"I didn't know that," admitted Aurelie, "my mother taught me the binding was all about propagation." Aurelie could sense there was some pain, some secret behind Haruko's revelation, but she also thought it wasn't her business. And Haruko seemed reluctant to say more, even though she had introduced the subject. So Aurelie changed it. "I don't know much about the binding at all. I didn't even realize there were bindings between non-mates."

"Oh, yes," said Haruko, "we're all bound to the clan, to our parents, and to our children. But the binding between two partners is usually the strongest."

"You, Kazuki, and Emiko are all unbound. Is that common?"

"No, not at all. There are currently five unbound Unseen in the clan—you'll meet Kento-*san* tonight, and *Obā-chama* will certainly arrange an *omiai* with Shigeru-*san*. That means we have five unbound out of a thousand, when historically the rate has been one in ten-thousand."

Aurelie made a sound, somewhere between surprise

and interest, and Haruko added, "I've entered all the clan data into a spreadsheet."

Aurelie grinned. "That's wonderful. There's nothing quite like data-driven analysis, is there?"

Haruko looked over at her, as if afraid that Aurelie was poking fun, but a moment later, she grinned as well. "There really isn't."

Aurelie started talking about her studies, her efforts to understand Unseen history, and somehow that naturally led to airing her family's dirty laundry *again*, after years of ignoring the stench. But now she understood that others' acceptance was the only true detergent.

As the little green van parked in front of a brown warehouse labelled "co-op," Aurelie silenced her confessions. Haruko reached over and squeezed Aurelie's hand.

"I see now why you thought the binding was only about the physical survival of our species," Haruko said, "but in my experience, it's about happiness, too. Maybe to be happy *is* to survive. We need joy, motivation, to live and raise the next generation. As for your family... I have no explanation for you. Perhaps the circumstances were so desperate that the magic was left with no other choice."

Magic, thought Aurelie. *There's that word again.* It sounded different in Haruko's voice, though. Instead of the mystique that *Obā-chama* had offered, Haruko said it as if it were simply the most appropriate word to describe the phenomenon.

They put on masks and got out of the car. A wiry,

elderly man wearing a knit skull cap greeted them. He looked visibly puzzled by Aurelie, so Haruko explained that she was a foreign professor from Hayashi University. This in no way abated the man's curiosity, and Aurelie realized that a visitor to the insular Hayashis must be big news in the area. She distracted the man by asking about his business and was rewarded by deep eye crinkles and a strawberry candy when they finished loading the food into the car. (Aurelie couldn't help but anticipate the evening meal, as she surveyed the yams, pears, unfamiliar root vegetables, and Styrofoam coolers that the man said were full of fresh fish).

They stopped twice more, to collect a shocking (to Aurelie) amount of *sake* as well as *shimekazari*, a kind of wreath made of rice straw and beautifully folded accents.

"Let's stop at Koishidani Shrine," said Haruko. "You'll like it."

Aurelie did like it very much, though she thought guiltily of the fish in the car. The shrine was small though—they could cover its ground in five minutes. Haruko taught her how to pray properly at the small vermillion structure: throw a coin in the box, bow twice, clap twice, and bow again when the prayer is finished.

Aurelie didn't know who or what to pray to, so she thought, *If the random entropy of the universe would be favorable to me, I'd be grateful.* (Did that mean she had prayed or not?)

Then the tiny van was zipping back up the hills to

the Forest-Heart Home. When they reached the gate at noon, a white sports car was opening the gate ahead of them.

Haruko frowned, and Aurelie asked, "What's wrong? Are we late?"

Haruko shook her head and flushed. "That's Kento-*san*. One of the unbound clan members."

和希

THE plaintive notes of a *biwa* echoed throughout the large kitchen while Kazuki and Emiko turned little doughballs into flat rounds with smooth pine rolling pins. Along with several others, they had been roped into dumpling making, and, despite their youth, they worked at one-fifth the pace of Kazuki's great-aunt. She was in charge of the efforts and was also responsible for choosing the old record of even older music.

The kitchen door slid open, and a familiar voice said, "*The Tale of the Heike*? Really? How about some Yoasobi instead?"

Kazuki looked up to find his sister; behind her stood her husband, smiling apologetically for her brashness.

"My kitchen, my music," said his great-aunt, placing her fiftieth (or so) dumpling wrapper in a stack.

Yuriko sighed with great exaggeration. "Only for you, Auntie." She and her husband washed their hands and joined the dumpling making.

She was far better at the task than Kazuki and Emiko, and her husband was equally skilled, but before Kazuki could be grateful for their contribution, Yuriko asked, "So did *Obā-chama* approve of your binding? Are you going to have a wedding for a graduation celebration?"

That's what Yuriko had done.

"Um," said Kazuki.

"He snapped the binding," said his great-aunt, "and *Obā-chama* is arranging *omiai* for the foreigner."

"Whoa. What?"

Kazuki was forced to reiterate the whole awkward story, not that it brought clarity to the matter.

"So back to grad school instead of marriage, huh?"

Kazuki accidentally tore his dumpling wrapper. Yuriko frowned. "What's with that reaction?"

Kazuki shrugged.

She elbowed him—why had Emiko moved over to allow Yuriko to sit next to him?

"I—I just realized that I have to submit some documents for that."

"For grad school? What documents? When do they need to be submitted?"

"Um. Maybe last week. A reference from... my English immersion professor."

"You mean Aurelie-*sensei*'s recommendation?" Emiko asked, leaning around Yuriko.

Kazuki willed the blood to stop filling his cheeks; it didn't work. Everyone continued to stare at him. "I'll figure it out, okay?"

"Figure what out?" Three more people had entered the kitchen—Aurelie, Haruko, and, *kuso*, Kento. They were each carrying a large crate full of food. Kazuki felt absurdly jealous that Kento was helping while he hadn't even realized that Aurelie had left the house—he had assumed she was hiding in her room.

He pushed away from the table so roughly that his chair tumbled backward onto the floor. "Nothing! I don't need help," which was blatantly untrue, since he at least needed Aurelie's letter of recommendation. Thankfully, no one contradicted him. Too embarrassed to stay there, he strode from the room.

Kazuki wanted to be alone in his room, but he knew that state couldn't last long. Several men were sharing it for New Year's—his brother-in-law or, even worse, Kento could join him at any moment. He headed for the entry instead.

賢人

A KNOT of tension formed in Kento's shoulders as a black Honda Street followed him into the Forest-Heart Home. He recognized it as Haruko's, even though he couldn't see the driver. Kento always felt unfairly guilty and awkward around Haruko because *Ōba-chama* had once proposed marriage between the two of them. Kento had agreed, but Haruko had run off with a human woman in protest. When the clan reprimanded her, Kento couldn't shake the feeling that it was his fault.

The twenty-year-old Honda didn't help. Haruko didn't have her own salary, but the clan could easily support her needs, including a new car. But Haruko always refused to buy one; she also usually refused her allowance for clothing and miscellany. When they parked, Kento was unsurprised to see Haruko's winter jacket had patches on the right shoulder and left elbow. He couldn't help but self-consciously adjust his cashmere scarf that he'd bought yesterday. Then a second car door shut, and he glanced over in surprise. He'd been so focused on Haruko that he hadn't realized that she even had a passenger with her. And a stranger at that.

Kento briefly panicked—had Haruko brought home a human lover *again*?

"Kento-*san*, hello," said Haruko. "This is Dubois-*sensei*. She's a professor at Hayashi University who will be celebrating the New Year with us."

Kento looked at Haruko in shock. An outsider was celebrating with the family?

Well, it wasn't as if they practiced ritual sacrifice or celebrated the new year any differently than humans (he didn't think, anyway), but *still*.

Haruko's expression was odd. Her eyes, narrow and assessing, darted back and forth between him and the stranger.

"Hello, nice to meet you," mumbled the professor, sounding as happy as a *sumo* wrestler in a train restroom. "Are we bringing the food to the kitchen or..."

Kento was vaguely confused, but Haruko popped the rear door and grunted confirmation. (Haruko was quite the grunter; she could say yes, no, and maybe with only her throat).

Realizing they were returning with groceries, Kento took a crate as well. In fact, he took the heaviest one, which contained nine bottles of expensive sake, despite Haruko's doubtful expression; he might like to dress nicely but that didn't mean he was weak.

As he fell in behind the stranger, he realized he hadn't returned her greeting, so nonplussed had he been. Surely it was too late now?

In the kitchen, about ten clan members were busy assembling dumplings. That was typical, but bizarrely, as soon as they entered, his cousin Kazuki practically ran from the room.

Kento didn't know Kazuki particularly well—they were about twenty years apart in age—but usually Kazuki was smiling (maybe smirking) and projecting confidence. Kento didn't think fleeing was Kazuki's usual style. Wait, wasn't Kazuki a student at Hayashi University? Did he know this professor?

Kento suddenly suspected the surprise guest was tied to Kazuki. Was the golden boy failing her class, and the family trying to butter her up? Maybe Kazuki had invited her home by accident and didn't know how to handle it.

Impulsively (which was not *his* usual style), Kento announced, "I'm going to go greet Kazuki," and he also escaped the room.

He caught up to his young cousin in the *genkan*, where Kazuki was donning his shoes. Kento put on his as well, though Kazuki paused to glare at him.

Kento was socially awkward at the best of times, so he pretended to be oblivious and asked Kazuki where he was headed.

"Out," said Kazuki shortly.

Kento treated that as an invitation. When they had put a little distance between themselves and the house (relatively rapidly, even though Kazuki wasn't *quite* running), Kento asked, "Why's that professor here? Did you mess up?"

He had realized that Kazuki was unusually volatile, of course, but he was still shocked when the younger man grabbed the collar of his jacket and half raised his hand, as if he might hit Kento.

A moment later, the hand dropped, and Kazuki released the jacket. "Yeah, I screwed up, lucky for you."

"Lucky for me?" echoed Kento. "What do you mean?"

"The *omiai*?"

"*Omiai*? I don't know what you are talking about."

Kazuki's face scrunched up, and his eyes scanned Kento's face several times. Abruptly, he sighed, exhaling most of his anger. "Sorry. You met Aurelie Dubois just now, didn't you?"

"Yes. I thought humans weren't allowed here. That's why I thought you must have done something—she's your professor? Or..."

Kazuki started laughing, so hard that he doubled over and grabbed Kento's arm for balance.

Kento repeatedly asked what Kazuki was laughing about before the younger man finally managed, "She's Unseen!"

"Who?"

"Aurelie! My professor! She's Unseen." Kazuki straightened. "We were called, but I snapped the binding, and now *Obā-chama* wants to arrange *omiai* with you and Shigeru-*san* to see if you'll be called."

Kento tried to process that, but he couldn't. Yet

again, he asked, "What?"

They ended up walking and talking for an hour or two, Kazuki's frustration and confusion resulting in long rambling tangents about second leads and only being around to show how desirable the main lead is. Missing his chance to confess and serving as a pitiful witness to someone else's happy ending.

When Kazuki subsided into silence, Kento struggled to find the right words. He failed at that, so he settled for the ones he had.

"I know you're a film studies major, but you're confusing dramas with reality. There's no such thing as a 'second lead'—we're all the main characters in our lives."

Kazuki's jaw dropped, but he snapped it shut, waiting for Kento to continue. So he did.

"There's no 'getting to confess.' No writer making a convenient moment or snatching away your chance. If you like the professor, tell her. Chase her. Do something about it."

"Why are you giving me this advice?" demanded Kazuki. "Don't you want to chase her yourself?"

Kento hesitated. "Yes and no. I'm forty-two, and I guess I gave up the hope of a calling a decade ago, and I haven't yet wrapped my mind around the possibility. What's more, I mistook her for a human. Somehow I don't think there will be a calling. If I was to court her, it'd be with the knowledge we were both settling."

Kazuki rubbed his eyes. "She seems willing to settle, so long as it's not with me."

He sounded unattractively bitter, but Kento didn't

blame him. "Why do you say that?"

"Since I met her, she has been unwavering in her resistance to the binding. But as soon as it broke, she happily connected with *Obā-chama*. It made me realize that she's already closer to Emiko-*san* than she is to me, and didn't you see the way she connected to Haruko-*san*? They only met last night!"

"Maybe you are overthinking," Kento suggested. "From all you've told me, the professor does care about you. She obviously thinks about you a lot. And her growing closer to the family means growing closer to you too. Creating relationships with them will give the two of you more in common."

Kazuki blinked. "That makes a shocking amount of sense. Wow, when you say it that way, I really like her becoming friends with everyone. Us sharing a family..."

His lips twisted several times, leading Kento to prompt, "But?"

"Even supposing you're right—that she's not totally opposed to a relationship with me—that maybe she's still meant to be with me rather than you or Shigeru— what do I do? *Obā-chama* isn't organizing *omiai* for me. She's made it clear that I don't deserve this binding."

Kento knocked Kazuki gently on the head. "Now you are talking like one of those second-leads you so despise. Why would you need someone else to arrange an *omiai*? Make your own dates."

"My own dates?" Kazuki looked like a kitten who'd fallen into a pond. He needed a little more help before he could swim.

"Like humans do," Kento said.

"Yes," said Kazuki, his brow knitting, "but I am only familiar with fictional dating."

"Same," admitted Kento, "but I know how to find real advice." He pulled out his phone, typed "date ideas" into Google, and showed the results to Kazuki.

Kazuki snorted but rubbed his chin thoughtfully. "Hiking and *karaoke*? You think that could work?"

Kento shrugged. "Wouldn't hurt to try, would it?"

Kazuki smiled. "Thank you, Kento-*san*. I—I'm sorry I was so rude earlier."

"That's alright. Be happy, so I don't regret this later, yeah?"

Kazuki's smile faded, and he looked at Kento earnestly. "That's a big ask, but I'll do my best."

Kazuki was ready to return to the house, but Kento decided to walk longer. He honestly believed that he had little chance of forming a partnership with Aurelie Dubois. But he couldn't help but think of the other Unseen in America, Aurelie's relatives.

Maybe, just maybe, there was a partner there for him, too.

デボラ

DEBORAH hissed at the computer screen, even though it wasn't to blame for the information on it.

Obtaining a US passport had been a little confusing to a woman who hadn't had a social security number until she was twenty-nine, but she had managed it. She was even grateful for the challenge because it distracted her from Dan's health.

She supposed she should consider herself lucky that

she could worry—she couldn't help but think she wouldn't have that privilege much longer. He had come home before Thanksgiving, against the doctor's advice but on his own insistence. He was a terrible patient—he said that the meds made him feel foggy, and he'd throw them away if Deborah didn't watch him swallow. Moreover, he kept trying to do his daily routine even though his presence of mind was insufficient. He ruined a Teflon pan trying to cook eggs over easy and boiled the tea kettle dry twice (both times Deborah had already made him a full pot of his favorite Red Zinger).

When she first met Dan, he had seemed like a father figure to her. He was more than twenty years older, and he known the world. Now, she felt like she was the parent, and it was tough.

Representing Dan to his doctors was the hardest part. He adamantly disagreed with most of their advice (such as remaining at the hospital until the seizures were sorted out). Deborah would have preferred to follow their recommendations to the letter, but she also felt Dan had a right to autonomy over his body. And yet—where was the line? Did he fully understand what was told to him? Sometimes Deborah thought yes, that despite his forgetfulness and slow processing, he retained his ability to make decisions. Other times, she felt she was being reckless with an old man who couldn't make decisions for himself.

But mostly she thought he knew he was risking his health for his happiness, and, since it didn't put anyone else at risk, she didn't have the heart to deny him his home or his wits.

Dan had wanted to stay up late to celebrate the New Year, but he had nodded off while reading a book. Luckily, he had already been in the living room bed that they'd set up when he came home (the stairs were tough for him).

Deborah should have gone to sleep when Dan did, but instead she had wandered over to their computer and started looking over travel options to Japan.

Unfortunately, the mandatory two-week quarantine there meant everything was nigh impossible for her. She'd have to go for at least three weeks, and how could she leave Dan for that long?

She couldn't. That was the answer. Dan and she might not have the usual husband-wife relationship, but they were family.

Deborah hadn't really felt the pandemic. Yes, she wore a mask when she went to the store, but she mostly spent all her time at the farm anyway. Dan's card night had been cancelled last March, but cases had never spiked in Vermont the way they had in the rest of the country, and even that had resumed quickly. Deborah had been very worried when Dan had his stroke and had been hospitalized for a week in October, and there were still some extra hoops to jump through for visiting, but Deborah and Lisette had recklessly taken the human vaccine (hadn't it been tested on other animals anyway?) and that hadn't been too bad. Since Deborah didn't read much news, she hadn't fully realized the difficulty of travel.

Deborah rubbed her temples, trying to decide

whether she was wasting time even looking at going to Japan. At any rate, it felt like a terrible way to spend the last hours of 2021. Maybe everything would make sense in the morning and in the new year. She shut off the laptop and went to check on Dan once more.

He was stretched out on a twin bed, a massive lump in the darkness. They needed to buy a hospital bed because Dan was too heavy for Deborah to lift alone. She and Lisette managed together, but Lisette was often gone for work. Even though he seemed fine, Deborah adjusted his blanket.

"Thank you for saving us," she whispered.

His hand suddenly latched onto her arm—it was a rough and awkward grip, for the stroke had impaired his hand.

"Deborah," he said, a little slow and sloppy. "You know you saved me, too? Gave me a purpose. Pulled me out of my mourning." He sighed. "I can't take care of anyone anymore though. The girls are grown but... You'll take care of yourself, won't you?"

Deborah placed her hand over his. She could feel his swollen veins.

She blinked back tears. "Over the past years—if you hadn't married me, you might have found someone else. Someone you could love..."

He laughed a little. "Still worrying about that, after all these years?" She couldn't see his expression, but she saw him shake his head. "I wasn't looking for another wife, it just made it easier to take care of you." His grip tightened suddenly. "My fair folk. I was happy to share my home with you."

Deborah swallowed. She never quite knew what to say to that—it was both ridiculous and yet too close to the truth for comfort. She patted his hand.

"Good night," she told him.

"G'night," he replied, and took his hand back.

The new year came reluctantly. Deborah woke late because the day was overcast and drizzling. She would have welcomed snow, but the not quite freezing rain was miserable. She stalled getting up for a few more minutes before going downstairs. She set the tea kettle on the stove and called Happy New Year to Dan.

He didn't reply. Surprised, for he usually rose early even though he couldn't do his farm chores anymore, Deborah went to the living room.

The bed was empty. Deborah searched the house, the barn, and the yard. The green Toyota Corolla, which Dan was definitely not cleared to drive, was gone. Lisette had the day off and was still abed, but as soon as Deborah told her what happened, she jumped up. Still in her PJs, she took her pickup to look for Dan. Deborah hesitated, for they didn't want legal trouble, but after a few minutes she decided to call the state police.

The trooper was concerned that an elderly man prone to seizures was driving, and he lectured Deborah quite stringently not to leave the keys out where Dan could take them.

Deborah couldn't bring herself to tell him the suspicion that had been growing ever since she first saw the empty bed.

Dan was a tough, sometimes lonely New England

farmer who didn't believe in a higher power. Over the past few years, every time one of his acquaintances entered a community home, he'd grouse that he'd never let things go that far. "I'll take care of things before I let someone change my diapers," he'd say and laugh.

Deborah had never quite known how to respond. She also hated the idea of being infirm, though mostly because it sparked her paranoia of discovery—if she were in a home, would her species be revealed? It had made her uneasy, to hear him speak of such things, and yet she wasn't sure if he was serious anyway (there'd been that laugh after all).

When Lisette returned though, Deborah felt compelled to share her fears. "Would Dan have left a note," Deborah asked, "if that was his intention?"

Lisette pulled off her baseball cap, fluffed her hair, and put the cap back on. "Remember when he tried to fill out that form at the hospital?"

Dan's hand had shaken, and his letters had come out a spidery mess. A note would have been beyond his abilities.

Deborah felt shaky. She pressed the back of her hand to her eyes.

"Mom, don't cry!" She could feel Lisette fluttering near her before awkwardly patting her back.

"I'm not," Deborah said. "I just keep remembering his words last night. He was saying goodbye, but I didn't realize." She closed her eyes. "I hope he hasn't injured himself. He'd be miserable."

Lisette's hand stilled on her back. "Yes," she agreed

softly, "he would be devastated." A long pause, and then she added, "I'll keep driving around…"

Deborah nodded.

After Lisette left, Deborah debated texting Aurelie. Aurelie had said she was off until the fifth, and they were supposed to do a few extra video calls, though Aurelie had cancelled the one last night without explanation.

But even if she told Aurelie that Dan was missing, that Deborah feared he had given up on life…

What could Aurelie do? She was an ocean and a continent away.

If Deborah told Aurelie, it would just be a burden on her. Aurelie had obviously been guilty she couldn't help with Dan's treatment plans. (Not that Deborah needed her. It was tiring to always drive to Burlington for the hospital appointments, but she had the time).

In the end, Deborah decided not to text Aurelie, for there was nothing her daughter could do.

But never had Deborah felt so alone, not even when she had been with her two young daughters at the homeless shelter.

16. ADRIFT

SCHOOL resumed Wednesday after New Year's, which ought to have been plenty of time to process the revelations of the weekend but hadn't been. Maybe it was the fact Aurelie hadn't been able to get ahold of her mother or sister since canceling their Zoom call on New Year's morning (she hadn't known what to say). At any rate, she pulled her mail out of the box without processing what it was. But as she stared at the bold white letters, "Pocky," emblazoned on red, her heart started jumping between her throat and her gut like a hyper chihuahua.

Kazuki?

There was no note, but she pressed the box tight against her chest.

Who would give her chocolate besides Kazuki? But he had broken their binding. Why would he continue to court her?

Confused, she dropped the treat into her purse and headed upstairs.

Akido's door was open, so Aurelie stuck her head in to say good morning. Akido wasn't there though—instead a tiny Japanese woman was packing up Akido's desk. She stroked her hands nervously when she saw Aurelie, making Aurelie feel like she was bullying her with her mere presence.

Aurelie greeted her and asked after her missing colleague.

"My husband in car accident. Not okay. Hospital. A few months."

This nearly incoherent answer had been given in English, even though Aurelie had spoken Japanese.

"I'm so sorry," she had said, again in the woman's native tongue. "Please let me know if I can do anything. Akido-*sensei* has helped me so much—"

"Yes, yes," his wife said, returning to English, which she clearly wasn't confident in, and bowing as well.

Realizing that the woman wasn't comfortable with her and wanted her to leave, Aurelie gave a bow of her own.

She felt mortified as she walked away, and even though a quick glance up and down the hall revealed no witnesses, Aurelie couldn't quite shake the feeling that someone was watching her.

She sent a short text message to Akido, expressing

her regrets over his accident and extending the same offer of help that she had made to his wife.

Aurelie rubbed her face, trying to push all the weirdness and tension out with her fingers. (It didn't work).

She dropped her purse on her desk and was distracted by a rattling sound.

Oh, the candy from Kazuki.

It was a bit early for sugar, but she needed a mood boost. She opened the box and pulled out one slim chocolate-coated stick. She took a bite with relish, for she had learned that Kazuki always chose the tastiest snacks, only to spit into a tissue.

That had tasted like...bread.

She checked the ingredients, and her eyes locked on the *kanji* for wheat flour. (She had memorized them even before arriving in Japan).

She closed the box and set it on her desk. The next minute she stood up and threw it in the garbage. (She ought to offer them to someone else, but Akido was out, and she was too upset to go further afield).

Why would Kazuki give her wheat? Was he so mad that he wanted her to get sick?

Even if he were mad, Aurelie hadn't thought he was malicious like that.

She paced back and forth, debating whether she should text him. If he had done it to be mean, she didn't want him to know how upset she was.

She sat down to work, but she couldn't focus.

Finally she pulled out her phone. After agonizing over the words for too long, she wrote,

What's up with the Pocky?

It felt like forever before he replied.

You shouldn't eat Pocky, it will make you sick. If you want to try matcha flavor, there's other chocolate.

I don't want to try it. It was in my mailbox.

0.0

Sorry, I don't know about that.

Aurelie believed him. She ought to be relieved that he hadn't tried to poison her, but she felt overwhelmingly disappointed. She had thought the gift meant that he still cared about her.

But really, now that their binding was broken, why would he bother with an old, foreign professor?

和希

EVEN after he replied to Aurelie, Kazuki kept looking at the text thread.

"What's wrong?" asked Emiko. Quietly, for they were in the library and a handful of cousins were with them.

Kazuki flushed and immediately flipped his phone screen to the table.

Emiko rolled her eyes, and Kazuki realized she knew exactly who he'd been texting.

"Someone left Pocky in her mailbox. She thought it was me."

Emiko frowned. "Did she eat them?"

"No."

"That's weird. A coworker? Or maybe it was a

mistake."

"Yeah. Maybe."

But Kazuki felt uneasy. A little like he had that night when he had dreamed of the big dog. If Aurelie was in danger again, would he feel anything?

Not that wheat was that dangerous—it would cause stomach pain. Not death.

"You're not giving up, are you?"

Kazuki was confused by the question and fully met Emiko's eyes.

"I wouldn't, if it were me. I would tell everyone."

"Tell everyone what?" asked Kano, Emiko's best friend when she wasn't busy with her boyfriend.

Kazuki flushed. He had been cowardly not to tell his other cousins, but how much worse would it be to tell them now?

Of course, it would be all over the family soon enough. So he might as well try to control the narrative.

"There's a foreign Unseen on campus," Kazuki said. "She went to the Forest-Heart Home for New Year's, and *Obā-chama* is trying to find her a mate."

"What!" exclaimed Kano and then all of their cousins were peppering Emiko and him with questions.

"I can't believe the two of you didn't tell us you had an Unseen professor!" said Ryōta. "I'm a little offended, honestly."

Kazuki was about to apologize when Kano broke in snidely, "But don't you see? Kazuki-*kun* must have thought he could bind with her."

She was angry on Emiko's behalf.

"Eww. Isn't she old?" said Ryōta.

Kazuki's cheeks were hot. He couldn't think of a response. But Emiko saved him.

"Age doesn't matter with a binding," said Emiko, "and you can't understand how it feels to be uncalled. I think Kazuki-*kun* should go for it."

Kano looked shocked. "But he's your fiancé!"

Emiko smiled dryly. "It's not the same for us as it is for you. If it were a male Unseen who'd appeared out of nowhere, I'd be pursuing him."

And Kazuki found his voice. "I'm going to pursue. I mean, yes, it's a lot more likely that she'll end up with Kento-*san* or Shigeru-*san*, but like Emiko-*san* says, it's worth a try."

"I think you would have felt it already," said Kano irritably, "if you were going to be called."

Kazuki nodded but said nothing.

オーレリー

ON Thursday (or "Tree-day" in Japanese, which Aurelie rather preferred), Aurelie met the woman who would be covering Akido's classes.

Ōkami was a dark-haired woman so thin that she made Aurelie look like a buxom farm girl.

Ōkami surprised Aurelie by offering a handshake (goodness, was she nothing but skin and bone?). Ōkami smacked her lips twice while still holding Aurelie's hand in a grip that was surprisingly fierce for such a slight woman and even more surprising for a Japanese—shaking hands was not as common here.

The handshake and the lip-smacking were unsettling, but what really bothered Aurelie was the fetid breath that accompanied her new colleague's greeting.

Aurelie fought to conceal her gag and wondered if the woman had an eating disorder. Aurelie immediately scolded herself for judging (plenty of well-meaning and some annoying people had accused Aurelie of anorexia) and then thought it might be a medical condition. *Or maybe she's just thin and forgot to brush her teeth. Be grateful that humans like Ōkami-sensei make your own appearance less notable.*

Aurelie felt so guilty over her less-than-complimentary reaction that she put extra effort into making herself amenable to Ōkami. She wanted to pay forward Akido's kindness. Ōkami might be Japanese, but she was still starting a new job.

"Are you headed to your office?" asked Aurelie. "Shall we walk together?"

Ōkami's eyes curved in a smile, and they fell in step with each other.

"Where were you teaching before this?" asked Aurelie.

"Ah, well, when my daughter was born..." Ōkami launched into a long and complicated story about her struggle to balance family and career that Aurelie found far more interesting than she would have a few months ago.

If she was bound again, if she had a baby, would she stay home to raise the child? Would she even be a good mother? Did the Hayashi clan have expectations?

What was best for a child? For her?

By the time she and Ōkami parted between their

offices, Aurelie was thinking they'd get along. Ōkami was a little awkward, but she was kind and humble. Aurelie was so glad to have another friendly colleague (poor Akido hadn't replied to any of her texts).

Impulsively, she asked if Ōkami would like to have lunch together.

Ōkami smacked her lips and nodded. "I would enjoy that."

和希

KAZUKI had an excellent, if embarrassing, reason to see Aurelie on Thursday: the reference for grad school.

Luckily for him, the forms were due tomorrow, not last week as he had thought. (Emiko had snorted over this, saying everything always worked out for Kazuki. He decided to take her words as a blessing).

In fact, he had realized everything was uncertain until it wasn't. Look at today—the air was damp and heavy, but even the radar wasn't sure if it would rain. On days like today, Kazuki felt potential building up— it kept him alert and engaged.

Instead of mourning the binding, he needed to embrace the tension between Aurelie and himself. He had watched her closely over the weekend, and had been surprised to realize he could often decipher her thoughts, even without the binding. The challenge excited him.

Will they, won't they? Films embraced such agony; Kazuki could as well.

Aurelie opened her office door just as Kazuki raised his fist to knock, meaning she was briefly less than a foot from him. He felt hot—or maybe that was the heat from her office escaping into the chill hallway.

Aurelie flushed and stepped back. "Can I help you?"

"I have a form I need you to complete," Kazuki said.

"Oh. Sure. Uh—" her flush deepened. "I was on my way to the restroom." She bit her lower lip, then in a rush, "You can wait in my office if you'd like. It's cold in the hall." She shyly moved aside to let Kazuki in, then left with an awkward bob of her head.

Kazuki felt like something important had happened, but it took him a moment to pin down what: she trusted him.

Not a big deal in one way—he had always had good relationships with his professors, and his grades were high enough that he didn't need to cheat. But Aurelie's trust was special.

Only... Maybe she shouldn't have trusted him. As a student, yes, he could be respectful, but as a lover, he had an overwhelming desire to learn her secrets. Kazuki hesitated, then moved to her desk. He opened one drawer, and then another. Her erasers and pencils were practical and simple—none of the common *kawaii* branding. Everything was quite orderly, if a little bare—he wondered if that was her taste or if she just hadn't been here long enough to acquire more.

And then he found a drawer filled with his notes. And one note he didn't recognize—he couldn't see the writing, but it was on plain dotted paper, and he had always used pretty stationary.

He pulled it out and unfolded it. There were only two words and a few letters on the page, and it took him a moment to see his own name.

Kind

Audacious

Z

U

K

I

She had tried to write him a poem, like the one he'd written her. Had she been stumped by Z? It wasn't a common letter in English.

Quickly, he refolded the letter and dropped it back in the drawer.

He took a seat in her armchair and wondered what it meant.

Literally. What the heck did "audacious" mean?

After a moment, he pulled out his phone and typed it in—luckily the autosuggest took over after the fourth letter.

The second definition immediately caught his attention: *lacking respect*?

She thought he didn't respect her?

He thought of the first word—*kind*. Kind and lack of respect didn't make sense. He considered the first definition again—*taking bold risks*. Maybe she thought he was bold. Bold could be good—like brave, right? He could take kind and brave.

"What's so funny?" asked Aurelie.

Kazuki jumped out of the chair; he hadn't heard her return.

"Sorry?"

"You were smiling—never mind, it's not my

business."

"Oh, oh, just a text. My sister sent a funny meme." He cleared his throat.

"Oh—that's nice. Okay, so a form? What's it for?" Aurelie asked.

Her question had been directed toward the ceiling, but her avoidance of his gaze didn't trouble him for it showed how aware of him she was.

"Grad school. I need an evaluation from my English immersion professor."

"Grad school?" she echoed in surprise. "For film studies? I didn't know that's what you wanted to do. You intend on entering academia?"

"Maybe." Kazuki hesitated, reluctant to reveal his own insecurities. But maybe that would be a good thing—after all, she must feel so awkward that he knew about...

"When I was little, it was expected that I would take over managing the family. Then, when I wasn't called, that changed. But *Obā-chama* never said what I'd do instead. Usually our future is settled by the family, but, every time I've consulted her, she has been vague. So I don't know what I want to do, and grad school is a respectable way to waste time."

Aurelie stopped and glared at him. He was glad to have her attention, though that wasn't the reaction he'd been seeking.

"What?" he asked.

"Grad school is expensive and a lot of work," she said stiffly.

He turned that over for a moment. For her, grad

school had been her dream, a point of pride. Her career proved something.

And here he was doing the same thing, just because. His privilege must grate on her—mock her even.

"I didn't mean to denigrate it," he said, "or you. I admire everything you've accomplished."

Kazuki would have liked to kiss her, but he knew the timing wasn't right. Instead, he settled for enjoying her autumn rose scent as he showed her the form online.

"Wait! This is due tomorrow?" Aurelie exclaimed as she looked it over.

It was Kazuki's turn to flush. "Sorry."

"When did you find out about it?" Her eyes narrowed in accusation.

He cleared his throat. "Um, last semester."

"So why are you only asking me now? Have you asked your other professors?"

"There's just one. Yes, I asked him last semester because I've had him before. I didn't ask you because..."

Aurelie was still frowning at him.

"I was thinking I might not go after all, this fall."

"What? Why?"

"Well." He pulled back and looked at his shoes. They were canvas slip-ons, a light tan color. "If, if, *ēto*, I got married after graduation and had a child..." The shoes *had been* light tan. Now they were a sort of dusty brown. Maybe he should wash them? "...grad school wouldn't be convenient."

He should definitely wash the shoes.

Why wasn't Aurelie saying anything? He dared a

peek at her face.

She looked even paler than usual, and her eyes were wide. She looked like she might cry.

She abruptly swiped at her eyes.

"Sorry," she said, and her voice cracked. "It's dry in here. Because of the kerosene heater."

Kazuki glanced at the small heater by the window. There was a small kettle on it, providing a steady output of steam.

"I'll do this now, don't worry," she went on.

"Would you like help with the Japanese?" he asked. She wouldn't welcome a hug, would she? She had been grateful that he'd broken the binding...

"There's an English option," she pointed out.

"Ah, so there is." Kazuki blushed.

"I'm sorry," she said suddenly, and she reached halfway toward him before jerking her hand back.

Sorry? About what?

Impulsively, he asked, "Au-*chan*," the name he wished to call her, "will you get lunch with me?"

She went stiff, and her fingers drummed the desk. "Don't call me that. And I'm busy for lunch."

There was a knock on the door.

The door that Aurelie had left ajar.

Good thing Aurelie had reprimanded him, for the woman at the door had definitely heard his invitation.

She was studying Kazuki curiously, and he studied her back. Even though Aurelie wasn't his lover, she was in a foreign country—someone had to keep track of the people around her.

This woman was gaunt. By her age, she was

probably a professor, though Kazuki didn't recognize her. She was dressed professionally, in a gray suit, but her short black hair was shaggy, like a rocker. Or—maybe it wasn't. When he looked closer, it was evenly cut and neatly brushed, but somehow, something seemed rough and unkempt about her.

"Am I interrupting?" she asked, smacking her lips.

"Not at all," said Aurelie. "I've finished helping Hayashi-*san*, and I'm ready to go to lunch. Ah, Hayashi-*san* is one of my senior students. And this is Ōkami-*sensei*. She's filling in for Akido-*sensei*."

"Akido-*sensei*?" asked Kazuki, looking back at Aurelie. "Did something happen to him?" Akido had taught the general history course that Kazuki took as a freshman. He was popular because he was both cheerful and an easy grader.

"Car accident," said Aurelie. "Over New Year's."

"Oh, no, I'm sorry." Then, realizing he was being rude to Ōkami, he bowed and welcomed her.

When he straightened, he was unsettled by the look in her eyes. Not disapproval, but appraisal of a challenge. Or of a meal.

It was weird. He didn't want to leave Aurelie alone with her, even though she looked too sickly to offer any physical threat.

He excused himself, but in the hall, he stopped at Akido's old office to check the *kanji*. Unfortunately, the name plate hadn't been updated. It was probably "big" something or other, even though his mind had leapt to the very unlikely "wolf."

オーレリー

"HE has a crush on you." Ōkami was still looking at the door by which Kazuki had just left.

Unnerved, Aurelie hid in truth. "That kid is twenty-two!"

"How old are you?" asked Ōkami, not visibly perturbed by Aurelie's reaction.

"Almost thirty-seven."

"Fourteen years. That's a big age gap, but no one blinks when twenty-four-year-old women date thirty-eight-year-old men. Don't let the patriarchy ruin your love life!" Ōkami grinned, and Aurelie couldn't tell if she was joking or in earnest.

Maybe both.

"He's my student!" sputtered Aurelie.

"Ah. Yes, that would be unethical," sighed Ōkami. "I'm afraid pop culture has romanticized student-teacher relationships." Then her eyebrows waggled. "But didn't you say he's a senior? You could wait a few months, couldn't you?"

"Ōkami-*sensei*," gasped Aurelie. Had she really invited this woman to lunch?

17. SIDELINED

STARING through the hospital window, Dan hooked up to a ventilator, Deborah asked herself yet again if she shouldn't have called the police.

They found Dan before Lisette. He had been driving home—he had gone to visit the hill where he'd scattered his wife and son's ashes—and when the sirens turned on, he had panicked. He had driven the Corolla into a ditch, and then been taken by ambulance to the hospital in Burlington.

The accident wasn't good, but it hadn't been too serious. Which left her to wonder...

If Deborah hadn't called the police—if they hadn't tried to pull Dan over—if Dan hadn't gotten concussed—if the hospital hadn't insisted on keeping him for observation—would he still have gotten Covid?

恵美子

SATURDAY before the full moon saw Emiko on the Local Kameyama train, fulfilling her duty as the biggest (and only?) Kazulie shipper. As such, she was helping Kazuki figure out his dating plan because, wow, did he need it, and, hey, it was kind of fun. A lot more fun than moping over the fact that she hadn't been called, anyway.

Today was Aurelie's first *omiai*, with cousin Shigeru, a thirty-year-old entrepreneur.

Their first mission in Operation Get the Girl was to stakeout the Forest-Heart Home so that Aurelie went home with Kazuki rather than Shigeru.

Emiko's plotting was rudely interrupted when Kazuki grabbed her wrist and squeezed.

"Ow!" she said. "What's wrong now?"

Despite agreeing with Emiko's plan, Kazuki kept freaking out.

"What if they kiss?"

Emiko smirked. "You punch Shigeru-*san*."

Kazuki nodded, and Emiko lost the smirk. "Kazuki-*kun*! I'm kidding. Don't punch Shigeru-*san*." She thought about it more seriously.

"If they kiss—you have to be calm about it. In fact, I think you should even act like it's no big deal. Aurelie-*sensei* obviously likes you, but she views you as kid. So act mature and become her friend. I think you need to sneak up on her."

"That's not a bad plan," Kazuki agreed. "I want to ask you something."

She nodded, but he sucked his cheeks in and out rather than continuing. Finally, "I appreciate your support. But I keep wondering—is it because you think I'm doomed to fail? You're helping me get it out of my system?"

Emiko was surprised. She thought about being offended, but then she realized this was about Kazuki, and she laughed instead. "I never realized you were so insecure before," she said.

He at last released her arm and crossed his own over his chest. Not looking at all mature.

"I think you're going to succeed. I've seen the way she looks at you—honestly, I even heard some of the women in our class gossiping that they saw her checking you out."

"Really?" He perked up and stopped sulking.

Emiko leaned back and studied Kazuki closely. It was strangely comfortable because now they were friends and she knew that was all they'd ever be. She could see his flaws and his strengths; she could care about them, but there was also a distance. What he did, what he was, only mattered as much as she chose to let it. The weight, the obligation she had felt when they were supposed to be partners was gone.

Among Kazuki's strengths were loyalty, and among his flaws was sentimentality. Both of which contradicted recent events. "Kazuki-*kun*, I know you want to be with Aurelie-*sensei*. So why did you break the binding?"

Kazuki's eyes snapped to hers. "*Obā-chama* was making her remember something traumatic. I wanted to protect her."

That fit Kazuki, but it didn't match what she had seen between Aurelie and *Obā-chama* when she was translating.

"I don't think Aurelie-*sensei* was upset about remembering. She shared more memories with *Obā-chama*. Maybe you misunderstood."

Kazuki stared at his hands, then shook his head so hard that his rocker-hair danced.

"You wouldn't say that if you had seen her. She looked...broken. Every other time I've seen her, she's been so confident. So in control."

"Nobody is like that all the time," Emiko mused. "Everyone has broken parts. And those parts need to be shared, too."

"Maybe," said Kazuki, but Emiko could tell he didn't agree.

Stubbornness was another of his weaknesses. Thank goodness she didn't have to deal with that one anymore.

オーレリー

"...ALL to say, if you know a good vet please point them my way," Shigeru laughed heartily.

The two of them were having a private dinner at the Forest-Heart Home. There was fried chicken, an array of local vegetables, and ample beer—especially considering Aurelie wasn't drinking any of it. (Shigeru seemed to have trouble grasping the fact she didn't drink—he had explained three times that Kirin *Nodogoshi* was made with soy protein rather than wheat, as if he thought she was afraid of gluten-poisoning).

Shigeru was easily compensating for Aurelie's abstention. She had never seen someone drink so much, though he didn't seem drunk. Maybe his size helped? With an almost chubby face and shoulders that strained his suit jacket, Aurelie was wondering if the slim build she associated with Unseen in fact reflected the scarcity of food in Appalachia.

"I do know a good vet," Aurelie replied to Shigeru's comment, offering a social smile, "but she's in the US."

Shigeru's nose wrinkled. "Oh, no, thank you. No foreigners!"

Aurelie was taken aback, and it must have shown on her face for Shigeru quickly added, "Present company excluded! You're great. Most foreigners come to Japan not even knowing the language. They expect *us* to adapt to *them*. But you're different. You're fluent."

Aurelie tried another polite smile, but it twisted as it came out. Her Japanese was improving rapidly, but outside of the Forest-Heart Home, she was far from fluent. Should she admit how bindings helped?

She settled for, "I think travelers should make an effort to learn the language and culture of the country they are visiting."

"Yes, exactly," agreed Shigeru. He grinned broadly at her and shocked her by stretching his hand toward her face.

Aurelie jerked back out of reach.

He blinked and laughed awkwardly. "You've got something here." He waved at the left side of the face, and Aurelie wiped her cheek with a napkin.

"Is that better?"

"Yeah, you got it. Guess you don't feel comfortable with me, huh?" Shigeru grimaced and took a big gulp of his beer.

"Oh, no, I mean, it's always awkward the first time you meet someone." *Unless it's Kazuki.*

And suddenly, she was so sad that she had never had a date with Kazuki.

It would be as inappropriate as it would have been last month of course, but, now that her chance was gone, she really, really wanted it.

Kazuki wouldn't stick his foot in his mouth, insulting her for being a foreigner. He had always been keenly aware of Aurelie's needs and feelings, even though he was so young.

Of course he was! He had the binding to help—and he's good at English. Shigeru probably isn't...

Just then there was an odd buzzing. Aurelie was confused until Shigeru pulled out his phone—it was vibrating.

"Oh, I need to take this," he told Aurelie and pressed the phone to his ear.

"Hi, Jeff, I thought we were speaking tomorrow?"

Aurelie blinked—Shigeru was speaking English. Perfectly.

"Oh, I see. Give me a sec." He covered the phone's speaker with his hand and told Aurelie he needed to settle something.

Aurelie stared at the three empty gold cans. She couldn't decide if the creature in the logo was a horse or a dragon or a deer. She felt too embarrassed to ask Shigeru, even though she would've asked Kazuki. Would he know? Did he even drink beer? Well, he was a college student, so he probably did.

Maybe she should have one—Lisette would say she needed to loosen up.

But Aurelie hated being loose, hated being sloppy or wild. She sipped at the oolong tea Shigeru had poured for her when she passed on the beer. She liked the taste okay, but it was definitely caffeinated. She'd probably be up all night at this rate.

A moment later, Shigeru sat back down.

"Sorry," he said, returning to his native tongue, "our American partner had an unexpected issue."

"No problem," said Aurelie. "When did you learn English?"

"Oh, in school. It's not hard."

"Some people do find learning a foreign language hard though," she pointed out.

He shrugged. "So, what do you like to do for fun?"

和希

SINCE Kazuki didn't want to call for a ride, he and Emiko took a local bus to the golf course near the Forest-Heart Home and then walked the rest of the way. The first person they encountered was Haruko, folding linens on the long dining table.

Her eyes widened. "Isn't it still January? I didn't know it was legal for twenty-somethings to visit the elderly more than once a month."

Emiko laughed, but Kazuki felt guilty. He didn't mean to neglect his parents and grandparents—as a freshman he had visited regularly. But somehow, after realizing that he wasn't going to lead the clan after all, he stopped coming home.

It was different for Emiko—her family lived a few hours south by bullet train. To her, this was just the clan estate.

Haruko seemed to realize that she had touched a nerve, and she smiled kindly at Kazuki.

"I think your parents went out to watch a movie. Your grandparents are playing cards. Shigeru-*san* and Dubois-*sensei* are in the Green Room. I can't let you go in there."

"I wouldn't interrupt someone else's *omiai*," he said, possibly lying. "I'm going to go play cards. Do you want to come, Emiko-*san*?"

She shook her head. "I want to visit with Haruko-*san*." She was already donning a light pink apron with the brown bear Rilakkuma on the front.

Kazuki was glad for the moment alone. He was grateful that Emiko had come with him of course—it was such a relief that they were purely friends now, and he appreciated her suggestions. But he also felt the need to regroup. Despite having gotten back on track with grad school, he didn't know what he was going to do with his life. He still would prefer a wedding that derailed his plans. He stopped to look at a carved deer that hid in a recess of the hallway. Thin cables held it in place in case of an earthquake.

Kazuki had expected to be those cables for the family. To hold everyone steady whenever external forces shook them. His feeling of being pushed aside, of being sidelined, hadn't just started since the binding broke. It started three years ago, when his unbound state started rumors.

Obā-chama had always favored Kazuki; it hadn't been a secret that she expected him and his mate to lead the clan. He had been happy about that—he liked listening to stories of their past, socializing with the elders, keeping track of his cousins and their children. He supposed that he might enjoy working as a manager at a large company, but managing the family was so much more meaningful to him. It hadn't mattered what he majored in; *Obā-chama*'s focus was that he be active in clubs and intramural sports while at Hayashi University, practicing his networking and building close friendships with his cousins.

But at the end of his freshman year, he had been called home.

Obā-chama had sat in her receiving room and he had poured her tea. She hadn't bothered to drink before saying, "Maybe you should switch majors, Kazuki-*kun*. How about finance? Or computers?"

"Why?" he'd asked.

"Well, what will you do with film studies?"

He had laughed. "What will I do with finance? Or computers?"

But she hadn't laughed with him.

"Those things won't help me lead the family," he pointed out.

"The leader of this family must be called and bound to a mate." She had at last reached for the tea, using it as an excuse to avoid Kazuki's eyes.

He had felt like crying and had blinked rapidly.

He blinked now as well—how awkward to visit his grandparents with tears in his eyes!

He turned abruptly from the deer and continued down the hallway.

He soon found his elders sitting in the living room, brilliant pendant lights illuminating playing cards arrayed on a folding table.

"Good evening," he told them, the cheer in his voice ringing false to his own ears.

Apparently, it did to his grandparents as well—or maybe he should pay more attention to the lesser bindings he had with them. Maybe their uncanny understanding of him was due to those.

At any rate, his grandmother folded her hand and beckoned him closer.

She rose and enveloped him in a hug. She was a slight woman, if a tall one, but Kazuki felt her strength and was comforted.

"Regretting snapping that binding?" drawled his grandfather.

"Oh, hush," said his great-aunt. "He regretted that immediately, don't rub it in."

Kazuki rolled his eyes and pulled up an extra folding stool.

"I don't suppose you have any suggestions about getting called a second time? Legends about impulsive lovers who got another chance?"

"Hmmm," said his great-aunt, as she discarded, "that's a tricky one. I'd suggest the full moon. Probably why *Obā-chama* picked this weekend when the professor said she couldn't do Tuesday."

Obā-chama had wanted Aurelie to travel two hours each way on a weeknight? Kazuki would have been more shocked if Aurelie had agreed. Refraining from comment, he asked, "The full moon?"

Kazuki knew his family loved *tsukimi*, full moon viewing parties in autumn that dated back to the Heian period, but he had assigned their passion to a yearning for a past age. He hadn't realized it was, well, magic. "What does the full moon do?"

His grandmother tsked. "You've heard legends about red string. Who ties it in the first place?"

"The old man in the moon?" said Kazuki. "You mean he's real?"

All four elders burst into laughter, their faces folding into mirth.

"Of course not!" said his grandfather. "The moon is an airless rock in space. But there's a root of truth. Our power, our bindings strengthen during a full moon."

Kazuki wondered how Aurelie would dismiss this legend—probably something to do with werewolves.

"Okay, so I should seduce her under a full moon?"

His grandmother swatted his arm.

"What?" he protested. "I'm old enough to know where bindings come from!"

All the elders laughed again.

"I've heard worse ideas," said his grandfather with a wink. Then he grew somber, "But, Kazuki-*kun*, I've never heard of anyone repairing a ripped binding."

"Have you even heard of a ripped binding before?" Kazuki asked.

"I have," said his great-uncle seriously, "I have heard of two cases."

"Who?" demanded his great-aunt.

His great-uncle snorted. "It's not as if you knew them! These were stories, even when I was a boy. Haruko-*san* could probably find you the texts, for she's always going through the old tales, but I do remember that in one of them, the woman snapped her binding when her family brought shame to the clan. Her whole branch was asked to commit *seppuku*, and she hoped her fiancé would be forgiven if ties were broken." His great-uncle gathered the cards and started shuffling, the shush of his bridge testifying to his many years of play.

He started dealing out new hands, adding Kazuki in without asking. "But her fiancé refused to be separated from her. He saved her life after she cut herself and their binding was restored."

"Isn't *seppuku*..." Kazuki drew his hand across his belly, miming disembowelment.

His great-uncle nodded.

"I don't see how anyone could survive that," Kazuki argued.

"The red string," said his grandmother, "lets us protect each other. There are many miracles if you believe old stories."

If Kazuki sliced open his gut, he was pretty sure that Aurelie would stay far away from him for the rest of her life.

"What about the other case?" he asked his grandfather.

"Almost the same story. Except the binding didn't take a second time, and the wife killed herself after failing to save her husband."

"Oh," said Kazuki. "Great."

18. SUNG

オーレリー

DINNER was finished; Shigeru was nursing his beer, and Aurelie was politely sipping her oolong.

This being her first date (besides one awkward encounter in grad school that she hadn't realized *was* a date until after), she didn't know how to end it. Should she say thank you? Give him a hug? Make an excuse about being tired?

"Should we have sex now?" Shigeru asked.

Aurelie choked on the tea, and Shigeru came around the table to pound her back (far more enthusiastically than was necessary).

"No," said Aurelie, when she could speak again, "we

should shake hands and part as friends."

Shigeru's shoulders slumped, and his mouth pouted a bit. "Are you sure? I know we haven't been called yet, but maybe sex would trigger it. Your body is nice."

Aurelie rolled her eyes. She wasn't offended exactly—Shigeru was probably a thirty-year-old virgin. He had to be as curious about sex as she used to be. She briefly considered humoring him, since this might be his only chance to experience it—no bound Unseen in his clan would be willing.

But she wasn't a martyr. She had no interest in sex with him, and pity wasn't enough of a reason to force herself.

"No, I'm sorry, but that's not how the calling works, and I don't want to."

Shigeru nodded once. He was unhappy, but he was also being respectful. Aurelie wondered if she should mention her sister to him—but no, she should tell Lisette first.

"I'm going to head home now—are you also leaving?"

Shigeru shook his head. "They prepared a room for us, just in case, and it's three hours to my house. I'll stay overnight."

Aurelie nodded awkwardly and left without even offering the hug.

She made her way to the door hoping not to run into anyone, but a familiar voice caught her attention, and after a brief hesitation, she turned down a side hall. Through a slightly ajar *shoji* door, she saw Kazuki. He was playing cards (some kind of poker, maybe) with four older Unseen. Laughter filled the air, as warm and welcoming as the sizzle of onions in butter. She stepped closer, not intending to go in, but wanting to enjoy it a moment longer.

Kazuki's eyes snapped to her, as if the binding still tied them together.

His laughing mouth pressed into a flat line, and the humor in his eyes faded; Aurelie's belly did a somersault. Aurelie couldn't decide if she should enter and greet the elders or flee before anyone else noticed her.

Kazuki didn't suffer such self-doubt.

With the fierce energy that disappeared with one's twenties, he surged up and opened the door fully, exposing Aurelie to his grandparents.

"It looks like the *omiai* wasn't successful," said one elderly woman. Aurelie wasn't sure if she was Kazuki's grandmother or his great-aunt.

Aurelie blushed. "Shigeru-*san* was friendly, but we weren't called."

"It's late," said Kazuki, "Do you need help finding your room for the night?"

"I'm not staying," declared Aurelie. "I'll sleep better at home."

Kazuki nodded and said, "Then I'll catch the train with you."

"Oh, no, I didn't mean to interrupt your game—"

"It's not a problem," Kazuki said, "Travelling alone late at night can be dangerous."

"In Japan?" snorted Aurelie. "I dropped my wallet full of cash in the road, and it was returned to me without a *yen* missing."

Kazuki nodded, though his face remained solemn. "Japan prides itself on being a safe country, but women are regularly harassed on trains. That's why in Tokyo there are women-only cars at rush hour."

"I don't think—"

"Let him escort you," interrupted Kazuki's great-aunt. "Just this morning I read an editorial about how perverts target foreign women. That lovely blond hair attracts too much attention."

"Dubois-*sensei*," Kazuki interjected, "I would do the same for any of my cousins. We are family now that *Obā-chama* approved of you."

Aurelie was surprised. Family. A word that had brought terrible memories; a word that now brought hope; not a word she wanted on Kazuki's lips. (Her own lips would be better there).

She nodded stiffly and thanked him.

和希

KAZUKI didn't feel the least guilty for misleading Aurelie about the purity of his intentions. He didn't think it was good for her to take a train alone after 21:00—and it wasn't as if he was going to hit on her. He would follow Emiko's advice to sneak up on Aurelie.

Friendship first, romance second. The opposite of every Unseen binding ever, but hey, he understood the friends-to-lovers trope. Shouldn't be that hard to mimic.

"Can you think of anything as awkward as an *omiai*?" Kazuki asked Aurelie with a laugh once they were ensconced in two gray and green train seats.

"No—but how would you know?" Her eyes were wary, her mouth tight. She suspected his sneaking already!

"Are you kidding? Do you know how many *Obā-chama* arranged for me when I didn't bind by eighteen? And for the past year, they have all been with sixteen-year-olds."

"You're kidding!" said Aurelie. "That's terrible. Poor girls."

"Poor girls!" Kazuki scoffed and clutched his chest. "What about me? Do you know how many middle-aged ladies sniffed at me when I was just doing what my family told me to?"

Aurelie snorted and then burst into laughter. She even wiped a tear from her crinkled eyes before adjusting her mask!

"Are you laughing at me?" he asked, making sure his own eyes were conveying amusement.

"With you, with you," she insisted. "I'm sorry, I'm a bit keyed up. It's not that funny. I had too much caffeine, and I was so on edge!"

"You need to relax," said Kazuki. Of course, the best place to release stress was... "How about we go to *karaoke*?"

"*Karaoke*?" she echoed. "What, sing in a bar in front of strangers? No, thank you."

It was Kazuki's turn to snort. "I know what you're talking about—I've seen it in American movies—but that's not what *karaoke* is like in Japan. You get a private room, there's a big screen with the lyrics and music, some mics and tambourines."

Aurelie's brows raised. "Tambourines? Really?"

"You would be missing out on a quintessentially Japanese experience if you don't go."

Still she hesitated. "Maybe it's not appropriate to go with a student."

He shrugged. "If you don't feel comfortable with me—"

"Oh, no, it's not that." Her hand came close to his arm, but it swerved for her pocket at the last moment. "You said it was late—but not too late for *karaoke*?"

"No—it's most popular at night. But you must be tired?"

"Yes, but I'm not going to sleep for hours. I think I drank ten cups of oolong tea!"

"Then you have no excuse."

He didn't expect her to agree, but she shrugged.

"All right. Let's do it."

Kazuki pulled out his phone and was relieved that his hand wasn't shaking. Nonchalant was the vibe he needed, not desperate. He searched for a *karaoke* spot—he wasn't that worried about running into classmates, but also didn't see the need to be stupidly careless.

"Okay," he said, "this should be good. *Raburī Karaoke.* We'll get off one stop early." He winked at Aurelie. "This will be fun."

オーレリー

AURELIE stood in the parlor of a small *karaoke* joint, hanging back as Kazuki completed a transaction with the clerk. *It's not too late to turn around—you could walk out the door.*

He glanced at her over his shoulder, his brows quirked in challenge, as if he knew what she was thinking. Aurelie was glad her mask hid her blush. She squared her shoulders and returned his gaze; she wasn't a coward.

A moment later, Kazuki directed her into a short hall, its walls plastered with music posters; Aurelie stepped past him and wondered if he really thought of her as family.

An aunt? An older sister? He definitely didn't feel like a little brother to her—he didn't feel like a student either though, and that was what he was. Despite his careless attitude, Aurelie knew a professor and college student hanging out at 10 pm was sketchy.

Aurelie had spent her life being careful, rule-abiding, and rational. Where was her restraint tonight?

In one of Shigeru's empty beer bottles, probably. Strangely, it had been her inhibitions that he'd drunk away instead of his own.

Kazuki opened the door to a tiny room—smaller than a college dorm single—all done in beige and green. There was a square table with an L-shaped padded booth. On the opposite wall was a TV and speaker system, looking oddly expensive against the cheap furnishings.

Aurelie removed her mask and sat, folding her limbs close to her torso, as she had in his parents' car. The booth was surprisingly comfortable, and the room smelled clean. Completely at ease, Kazuki collected two wireless mics and a tablet from the far wall.

He showed her how to select both refreshments and songs using the tablet. He paused. "Would you like a beer?" he asked.

"No—but I'd take a ginger ale."

He tapped the soda twice and clicked submit.

"Oh, you should get a beer, if you want," she told him.

He shrugged. "I wouldn't have ordered one even if you had."

And Aurelie relaxed. Goddammit, but Lisette was right. She was into him.

She had always been into him, but when he had wanted her, she had kept him at an arm's length. But now—well, now she knew nothing was going to happen, and so she didn't have to guard against it. It was a crush: her first.

Pathetic, but that was why she was here. She had a crush, a secret crush, and she wanted to enjoy it. That was her freedom now that he was no longer interested...

Since New Year's, there'd been nothing. No notes in her mailbox, and he'd kept his distance in class. Oh, he'd invited her to lunch when he'd asked about the form, but now she was realizing that he had just wanted to clear the air.

It was terrible and wonderful at the same time. Her crush was safe because he had regulated her to young aunt or much older sister.

Now that she had realized it, she should insist on leaving. She shouldn't indulge herself this way.

But!

But she had spent two months denying her reckless, selfish desires. Two months running from the binding.

There was no binding now, and she could let herself feel everything precisely because he didn't know what she was feeling.

"Want to sing first?" he asked her.

"No!" she giggled. (Giggled!) "Definitely not!"

He laughed, a low rich sound that danced on her arms. "Then I will." His fingers tapped quickly on the tablet, and then he stood up.

The TV opposite them started playing an anime video, and Kazuki swayed with the music.

When the first words appeared on the screen, Kazuki was perfectly in sync with them, and Aurelie knew she was going to look like an idiot in three minutes—he sounded like a real singer! He even danced a bit, and Aurelie found herself clapping along and laughing from sheer pleasure.

"That was wonderful!" she exclaimed when he finished. "I can't go after that!"

His lips quirked. "You absolutely can. And moreover, you must!"

He passed Aurelie the tablet, and she realized she should have been brainstorming her song while he was singing. Under pressure, she searched the first band she thought of—Eve6, which had dominated her high school music scene.

As the lyrics to *Here's to the Night* ran across the bottom of the screen, Aurelie realized in horror that she was singing about a one-night stand. (How had she not known that? She had sung along to it so many times). Kazuki had chosen a song about friendship and being there for each other—would he read into the meaning of this one?

And—why had she chosen a song by a man? She couldn't hit these notes! It was different from singing along, when her out-of-tune crooning was covered by the artist's voice.

She was relieved when the song ended, and Kazuki immediately started a new song.

"Listen to this one," he told her with a grin, "so you remember the right number next time."

Named *Call 1-1-9*, the chorus repeated the emergency number she had forgotten a few weeks ago over and over. She laughed and vowed to pick her next song more carefully.

But every one she thought of was a love song, and she knew that she'd feel like she was singing to Kazuki. It was unfortunate Kazuki was so skilled in English— she'd love to do a song that he couldn't understand at all.

French! She'd gotten into French singers during her post-grad research.

Unfortunately, this *karaoke* selection didn't have the first two artists that she searched. But—Edith Piaf! She was so famous...

And there was the *La Vie en Rose.* She felt rather pretentious, and she was no chanteuse, but at least it was in the right range.

She made the mistake of looking at Kazuki while she sang, and his eyes held hers.

The song ended, and he stood up and walked close.

Aurelie tilted her head back to maintain eye contact.

He turned toward the TV and started singing about butter in English. Aurelie was surprised and impressed—she vaguely recognized that uber-famous Korean boy band.

"You like Korean music?" she asked him.

"Some," he grinned, "I like K-dramas."

"You like dramas?" She wrinkled her nose. "Like soap operas?"

"Not really," he said, "American soap operas tend to go on forever hinging on improbable twists. K-dramas love coincidences—fate—but especially modern ones are tightly plotted. Like sixteen-hour movies. I enjoy the occasional K-drama. What do you like to watch?"

"Oh..." Aurelie had to think about it because honestly she didn't watch much. "I used to be obsessed with rom-coms when I was in high school. *She's All That* was my favorite."

"I don't know it. Can you sing any songs from it?"

"It's not a musical," she demurred, but she totally could. And while Kazuki continued to smile at her, she cued up Sixpence None the Richer's *Kiss Me*.

A moment later she wanted to sink into the floor. If *Here's to the Night* had made her self-conscious, this made her blush so badly that her cheeks felt sunburnt.

But as soon as she finished, Kazuki launched into the same song. In Japanese!

He seemed to have no trouble transposing the notes so that it suited his rich tenor.

It was a good thing she already knew her crush was

hopeless—he was way out of her league. (Of course, given the scarcity of Unseen, it didn't make sense to have multiple leagues. But if they did, then he would be).

"I thought you didn't know the movie!" she protested when he finished.

He laughed, wholly unrepentant. "I don't," he said, "but my sister loves that song."

和希

KAZUKI had suggested *karaoke* on impulse, but he couldn't have come up with anything better if he had planned it.

At first, Aurelie was adorably awkward, blushing fiercely every time she realized she was lyrically propositioning Kazuki. Though it was hard—no need to say what "it" was—he pretended to be oblivious to the provocation. Each song set her a little more at ease, soon they were laughing and chatting in a way they never had before. Emiko's strategy was working, and Kazuki thought if they could do this a few more times, she'd see things his way.

Of course, tonight he'd gotten lucky. She clearly hadn't hit it off with Shigeru and had needed to unwind after. That reminded him that technically she still had an *omiai* with Kento. Kento had denied any interest, but would he change his mind if Aurelie found him to her taste? Shigeru was fun and cheerful, but he was also loud and brash. Kento was serious and intense, rather like Aurelie herself. He was definitely more controlled than Kazuki.

But that would be all wrong for Aurelie—she needed someone to balance her, not encourage her in her tendencies. Kazuki could be that counterpoint; he could be the person who brought her to *karaoke* when she was too keyed up to sleep. Who teased her when she took life too seriously, who reminded her that she wasn't alone when she needed someone to confide in.

The next song she chose was one Kazuki had heard before. Oh, he didn't know the words, but the melody was familiar, and most importantly, it was a duet. Aurelie didn't seem to know that—she startled when he took the man's lines.

Just Give Me a Reason was perhaps too on point, but in her up-too-late state, Aurelie didn't object to his singing with her. In fact, she even swayed against him, and impulsively, Kazuki wrapped an arm around her shoulder—he was careful to keep it casual, friendly— and together they sang about learning to love again.

There was a question in Aurelie's eyes that Kazuki wanted to answer, but he knew that, even though she was asking, she wasn't quite ready for a reply.

So he kept his own expression innocent and smiled back.

19. CONFUSED

和希

SHORTLY after declaring herself *Just a Girl*, Aurelie started crashing. Kazuki called a taxi for them—she said she could return to her apartment alone, but he insisted on escorting her.

He was glad he did when she dozed off as the car started moving, her head sliding against his shoulder. He looked down at her face and marveled at how her lashes and eyebrows practically glowed, like the white lace that covered the taxi seats. They were almost invisible in daylight, but in the dark they seemed like moonlight adorning her face.

That made him wonder what she would look like under true moonlight.

When their chances of restoring the binding would be strongest.

He suddenly imagined seducing her in a field, where the moon would paint her silver.

A romantic notion, but probably much less comfortable than his bed.

And he was now uncomfortable at the thought of it. He shifted in his seat, wishing he was wearing looser jeans, and thought of the other things his grandparents said.

Would it really take one of their lives being in danger to restore the binding?

He couldn't risk that—if their odds were fifty-fifty of restoring the binding or dying, he'd rather remain unbound.

He felt so stupid for having snapped the binding in the first place—and yet…

It was only now that Aurelie was opening to him. It went against all conventional wisdom of course, but to her the binding had been a thing of danger and regret.

If he had known someone who had abused a binding the way her father—*that French bastard*—had, well, he would be leery of it too. He needed to prove to her that he was safe. That she could trust him with or without the binding.

Very gently, lest he wake her, he settled his hand atop hers.

Less than ten minutes later, they pulled in front of her apartment, and he used that same hand to shake her awake.

He didn't escort her in, for he was afraid that he'd

try to stay the night if he did and that would not be sneaky.

恵美子

AT breakfast, Emiko was scanning the table for Kazuki when Haruko said, "I dropped Kazuki-*kun* and Dubois-*sensei* at the train station last night."

Emiko was caught off-guard by the hurt that filled her. It wasn't that she was hurt by his actions—that had in fact been their strategy—but he hadn't even texted her.

"Oh, good," she said, with false cheer.

"You're more generous than me," said Shigeru as he pulled out the chair next to her.

Emiko met Shigeru's eyes and recognized the jealousy and loneliness there.

It's not fair, she suddenly thought. *Shigeru would be a perfectly acceptable mate. Why haven't we been called to each other?*

In the past, she had never seriously considered Shigeru for he was eight years older than her—if twenty-two and thirty felt like a large gap, it had been unthinkable at sixteen and twenty-four.

But he was handsome enough, with a wide mouth that was given to smiling and an unusually broad chest.

Why had she never had an *omiai* with him? Tried to induce the calling?

The rest of the family continued to chat and enjoy their breakfast, but Emiko couldn't join them. Oh, she kept eating, but she barely tasted the food. She was debating how to ask Shigeru out.

When he rose, she did as well, and followed him to the kitchen. She thanked him prettily when he offered to wash her dishes, but she lingered.

He darted her a curious look.

She blurted, "Dubois-*sensei* and Kazuki-*kun* have more years between them than you and I."

He had been drying his hands on a dish towel—now they stilled, the lightly woven cloth bunched in them. "That's true."

"Do you want to—go for a walk? Before you leave? I always find the woods here good for my state of mind."

He kept staring at her, his dark eyes unreadable. And then, he hung the dishtowel in its ring and gestured toward the door.

"Let's go."

Emiko nodded. They both took a few minutes in the entry to don coats, gloves, and their shoes.

And then they were in the unseasonably warm air, which held the delicate spice of pine trees.

They walked slowly, silently, until they were out of sight of the house. Emiko wasn't sure if she stopped or if he did, but he reached for her. His hands on her shoulders, he gently turned her to face him.

She was a little nervous because she had no idea what she would do if this failed. He leaned in; she screwed her eyes closed and puckered her lips.

His landed on hers softly.

They stood there, frozen, and Emiko began to count in her head. How long to wait before it was appropriate to step back? When did desire begin?

It occurred to her that in *manga*, the girl always

wrapped her arms around the boy's neck.

Emiko did and brought her body flush with Shigeru's. She was surprised by how large and hard he was—she supposed hugging a tree must feel like this.

They ground their lips into each other's. Then there was some slobber, wet and sloppy, and Emiko couldn't take it anymore.

She and Shigeru stepped back simultaneously, the only moment they'd been in sync during the kiss.

He shrugged and attempted to smile.

Emiko sighed. "Well, it was worth a try."

He nodded. "I can't even be annoyed at the American anymore," he admitted. "It would have been useless. Why do you think our sexuality is a switch like that? If we were like humans, wouldn't it be easier to breed?"

He was probably asking flippantly, but Emiko thought about it.

"If you go by sheer percentages, there's probably more humans who end up alone," she pointed out. "In our family, there's what, five of us? Five in a thousand is very low."

He snorted. "True. But being one of the five, I'd take being attracted to everyone instead of this fated stuff any day."

Emiko smiled tightly and started back to the house. She didn't want to be as selfish as Shigeru, but she felt the same way.

オーレリー

A PROLONGED buzzing woke Aurelie.

"Hello," she said, pressing the phone to her ear without even checking the caller.

"Hello, Dubois-*sensei*, it's Ōkami. Today I will go to the National Museum, and I thought you might like to accompany me."

Aurelie pulled her phone far enough away to check the time. It was a little after ten, and she forced herself to sit up. Getting so off schedule had been fine through grad school, but she'd be regretting this all week.

Except then you would have missed last night.

Okay, so no regrets.

"Oh, um, yes, I'd like that," she said. (She'd been meaning to go, even though it sounded as appealing as walking in boots filled with snow right now). "What time were you thinking?"

"How about two?"

Aurelie double-checked the time, "Great, that's perfect."

"Then I'll see you out front."

Aurelie showered, wishing for the hundredth time that her showerhead was mounted a little higher on the wall, and tried not to think about last night.

Except—why not? Why shouldn't she savor the memories? Who would it hurt?

And she sang *Just Give Me a Reason*, Kazuki accompanying her in her imagination.

She was still humming it by the time she was standing in front of the Nara National Museum and a hand settled on her shoulder.

Aurelie jumped a little (if only because someone touching her was a rare occurrence) and found Ōkami standing behind her, her thin lips stretched into a wide, closed-mouth smile.

The museum was full of old and beautiful objects. They all were worthy of attention, though their mostly Buddhist roots didn't impress her. (Aurelie didn't much care for religion; even pacifism hadn't stopped the wars in the name of Buddhism).

At the moment she was studying a black lacquer feretory that resembled a large lantern. It had two doors that were opened to reveal the paintings on their interiors (four Buddhist deities who were dressed in gold armor and resembled *samurai* to Aurelie's admittedly untrained eye). Inside was a repository of sutras, small scrolls that undoubtedly preached peace and mindfulness in the pursuit of enlightenment. (She didn't mean to mock—what she had read of the Tripitaka had made her reflective, but looking at the art flanking the scrolls, she was reminded that many early Buddhist monks in Japan were warriors and of the controversial contributions that Japanese Buddhist temples made in World War II to suppress China).

"So how was your weekend?"

Aurelie startled again—Ōkami moved with uncanny silence. "Um—" It took Aurelie a moment to drag her thoughts from history, and, feeling the awkwardness of the delay, she blurted, "I had a date."

"A date? It's been so many years since my husband courted me! How was it?"

"Uh... Not great. We didn't vibe."

Ōkami nodded. "Chemistry is important. And I don't just mean physical chemistry. Being able to hold a conversation with your partner—wanting to talk to them—makes communication easier and life better."

"Right," Aurelie was agreeing out of politeness, but she remembered again how easy it had been to talk to Kazuki last night. Going to *karaoke* should have been terribly awkward, but it hadn't been.

Honestly, she wished he was here now. He'd be talking about the objects in front of her instead of gossiping.

But it seemed that Ōkami sensed Aurelie's annoyance, for she started talking about the feretory that Aurelie was studying. Aurelie wasn't terribly impressed with her observations (she seemed to be reading the labels aloud) but still, they passed an enjoyable two hours meandering through the exhibits. When they parted, Aurelie mused that once you had one friend, the next came a lot easier.

和希

ON MONDAY, Kazuki was sitting in Aurelie's lecture and taking notes on courtly love, wondering if any of these rules could benefit him in his own pursuit of Aurelie, when one of his classmates raised her hand.

"Yes, Suzuki-*san*?" said Aurelie.

"So were such big age gaps typical in marriage?"

Kazuki smiled behind his mask when Aurelie's eyes darted to him before sweeping the whole classroom.

"Marriages among the nobility, where land right and family alliances were the priority, often had large age gaps, but it doesn't seem like that was typical among the lower classes, where marriages were often based on mutual interest. Of course, we don't have many detailed records of such marriages, so there's some speculation involved."

"I see. I can't imagine marrying an old man. It's so creepy!"

"I don't think it's such a big deal," said Emiko, and Kazuki knew she was speaking for him. "There's more important things than age in a relationship."

"Like common interests," retorted Suzuki, "but people of a similar age are more likely to have those! They grew up with the same music, the same shows..."

"Well, since there was no TV in the middle ages," interrupted Aurelie dryly, "and much less variety in music, that probably wasn't an obstacle."

Several students laughed—Kazuki remembered again how shocked Aurelie was when he mentioned watching dramas. Well, that wasn't just age-gap but culture-gap too.

Good thing he had long, strong legs. He would jump those gaps eventually.

"But I do feel badly for those young women who were married to men two or three times their age," Aurelie continued. "Many of these brides were children by modern standards, and it's hard to imagine them having babies at that age. Some scholars think that this was understood, and in fact they were not expected to have intimate relations with their husbands until they were older. But given how many adult men take advantage of girls today, I think that is a naïve take in most cases." Then she said, and Kazuki sat a little straighter, "Someone recently told me that even teacher-student romances are popular in Japan. Is that true?"

Who had told her that? Kazuki had been careful not to mention it, for most of those were obviously fetish-fiction. Not exactly what he was going for.

"Yes," said Nakamura, a male junior, "there's *Sensei!* and *Meet Me After School. Why Are You Here, Sensei?!* and *Lucky Guy.*"

"Isn't that Korean?" snorted Suzuki, who'd asked the original question, "and just because it's your kink doesn't mean it's 'popular,'" she told Nakamura.

"Age-gap romance in general is popular," argued Emiko, "though usually older man, younger woman."

Kazuki flushed under his mask. He knew Emiko was trying to be supportive, but it was too obvious that she was thinking about him and Aurelie rather than the middle ages. At least to him—and it would be to Aurelie as well.

"Ah, well," said Aurelie, "that was the usual in the middle ages as well. I'm sorry to have introduced this tangent, we had better get back on track. You only have one more lecture before finals."

Soon, thought Kazuki. *Soon, I won't be her student anymore.*

20. COMFORTED

和希

KAZUKI expected Aurelie to have a second *omiai* the weekend before finals began, but he heard through the grapevine that both she and Kento had claimed to be too busy.

Kazuki had decided to visit the Forest-Heart Home anyway—he wanted to explore the archives on the estate. It was a good excuse to speak to Aurelie, as he could ask if there was anything she wanted him to set aside for her. Early Friday afternoon he dropped by her office.

But when he reached the door, she wasn't alone. The substitute professor, Not-Wolf, was inside. The door was ajar, and their English conversation carried into the hall.

"But you should go out on your birthday to celebrate!"

It was Aurelie's birthday? Today?

Aurelie's low laugh reached the hallway. "I'm celebrating with my family!"

Ōkami's reply was skeptical. "So what, you're going to sit at home all Saturday on a video call?"

Not today then—tomorrow.

"Pretty much," said Aurelie. "You're close to your family. Wouldn't you do that if you hadn't seen them in four months?"

Aurelie's birthday—how to celebrate birthdays sneakily?

"Sure, but all day? You'll develop claustrophobia. You aren't going to go on another date this weekend?"

Aurelie snorted, "With who? I told you the last was a bust. Besides birthdays should be spent with those who already care about you rather than someone you have to impress."

Ōkami laughed low, and the sound raised the hairs on the back of Kazuki's neck. "What if it was with that senior? I bet you'd go on a date then."

"Ōkami-*sensei*! Please don't joke about such things."

Aurelie sounded half-strangled, and Kazuki couldn't blame her. Not that he saw a problem with them dating, but a human professor encouraging it?

Maybe Ōkami shared Nakamura's kink.

Kazuki lingered a few moments, hoping to get more information about Aurelie's plans, before backing away slowly. Fetish or no, if Ōkami suspected a romance between Aurelie and himself, he needed to be more circumspect.

And yet when he realized that the door to Ōkami's office was ajar, he opened it fully.

It would be unwise to poke around, given that Ōkami would have left it open with the intention of returning shortly. She was only about fifteen feet away.

And a quick glance told Kazuki there was nothing to see there anyway.

Literally nothing. The shelves were still full of Akido's books, but the desk was completely bare. No laptop, not even an empty coffee mug.

He heard Aurelie's door swing, and he stepped back out. He walked down the hall as quickly as possible and was relieved when no one called him back.

デボラ

DEBORAH felt guilty for avoiding Aurelie's calls, but she couldn't do so any longer. Dan had died. (Deborah had foolishly argued that Dan had been vaccinated when the doctor informed her; the doctor had said that his age and pre-existing conditions had been a factor).

Deborah tried to tell herself that it was better for Dan's sake that it had been fast, but it didn't feel better for her. She still couldn't quite believe it had happened. But it had. So, the second to last weekend of January, she screwed her courage to the sticking place and scheduled a video call with Aurelie.

"I have something to tell you," Deborah said as soon as the call started. Lisette sat next to her, eyes averted.

Aurelie smiled encouragingly, oddly expectant, as if she was expecting good news or congratulations.

"Dan died," Deborah continued.

Aurelie's face blanked and shuttered. Aurelie's hand went to the side of her face, and her index finger tapped her temple, the only evidence that video hadn't frozen.

Deborah babbled out the details, but even when she subsided into silence, Aurelie didn't speak.

Lisette in contrast had been waiting impatiently. Now she burst out with, "So? Are you coming home for the funeral?"

Aurelie flinched. "Well—there's finals, and the entrance exams, then graduation..."

"Don't you get bereavement leave or something?"

Aurelie shook her head. "I don't know; I don't remember. Travel right now—I don't think I can do it."

"Are you sure?" asked Deborah. "Maybe you should leave Japan."

Aurelie's eyes fell almost closed, and her delicate mouth thinned to invisibility. "If the funeral could wait until March—"

"We aren't going to do that," scowled Lisette. "It's absurd of you to ask!"

Deborah winced; she hoped they wouldn't fight. Aurelie and Lisette were usually cordial, but only because they didn't push at each other, not because they understood each other. They were quite different. Lisette had an earthiness, a willingness to get messy that suited a farm vet perfectly. Aurelie was a thinker. Even as a little girl in Appalachia, she would shirk her chores to hide in the house with one of the six books that the family owned. Yes, Aurelie was practical, and

Lisette had done well in school, but they didn't get each other.

"You care more about this job than us." Lisette continued bitterly. "You haven't been home since you went to France. Are we too boring for you?"

This must be a push day, brought on by the loss of Dan.

"You refused to let us visit North Carolina and then you just flew out of DC," continued Lisette. "It's like you don't even like us really," Lisette laughed bitterly, and the insecurity hurt Deborah's heart. Partially because it was echoed there, and she too wanted to hear Aurelie's response. Lisette didn't remember that French bastard or her cousins, but Aurelie did. Deborah hadn't said anything when Aurelie did her post-doc in France, but she knew it was because Aurelie still hadn't let go of him. Deborah took a sip of her Raspberry Zinger tea.

"I didn't come home first because he showed up at my house," Aurelie said, and Deborah sloshed some of the dark red tea onto her jeans. Her mind had jumped to the French bastard when Aurelie spoke, but surely—

"Who?" demanded Lisette.

"That French bastard," Aurelie said and went to sip her own tea. She paused though, looked down at the cup, and set it down again. Was it empty? Deborah wished she could reach through the screen to refill it.

Deborah asked, "Why didn't you tell me?"

"Why didn't you tell me about Dan?" Aurelie's question shoved a splinter under Deborah's fingernail.

"There wasn't anything you could do," said

Deborah.

"Exactly," said Aurelie, still cold and calm. That was Aurelie though—as smooth and refined as the gold she was named after. "Since there was nothing you could do, I didn't want to risk him learning where you and Lisette were."

"You *talked* to him?" asked Deborah, her heart beating fast, even though this must have happened at least ten months ago—that was when Aurelie began applying to jobs abroad.

Aurelie fiddled with something out of sight and nodded while looking at it.

"Shit," said Deborah and Lisette at the same time.

"Why are you bothering to tell us now?" Lisette's query was sharp with anger. Deborah patted her hand soothingly, but Lisette jerked it away. "Why not keep it a secret forever?"

Aurelie looked up. "I was planning to, but I realized I was wrong."

Deborah winced at the implication—she'd been wrong to keep Dan's disappearance and illness secret.

Aurelie pressed a hand to her heart. "I thought I was protecting you, but I realized sharing makes us stronger. Growing up with the aunties, I was so afraid of those ties. Of the weight of family. But here..."

"See," sneered Lisette, "I told you that it would do you good to fuck."

"Lisette!" snapped Deborah.

Lisette stood up and walked away from the table.

Deborah looked back at Aurelie. Deborah wondered if there were other secrets she was hiding. She had always known that Aurelie didn't feel the need to speak, to unburden herself, as Lisette did, but never had Deborah thought she would keep mum about meeting that French bastard.

"Aurelie," she said, "I have a passport. Before I couldn't leave Dan. But now..." She couldn't finish the sentence. "Maybe I could visit after the funeral."

Aurelie's brow knit. "You're that worried about the Hayashis?"

"Yes," said Deborah.

Aurelie stopped tapping her fingers and scrubbed her face. "You are scared of the bindings. Because that—because my father abused them. He used them to hurt you and your sisters and my cousins. But it's not like that here. The family, the clan is strong and healthy, Mom. There's a *thousand* of them, for goodness' sake. They—family is healthy for them. It provides protection and—"

Aurelie swung her face away from the camera abruptly.

"I'm sorry, baby," Deborah got out. "I know it was hard on you to leave the family—"

"No! No, Mom, it wasn't. I'm, I'm so grateful that you had the courage to get Lisette and me out of there. It's just, I'm realizing that there are other options. I thought I had to choose either family and abuse or being alone but safe, but now..." Aurelie looked back at the camera.

"Mom, you *should* come to Japan. You should meet *Obā-chama* and the rest of the Hayashi clan. You—it won't be like with your sisters, but you won't be alone anymore."

Deborah suddenly found it hard to breathe. She couldn't process everything that Aurelie was saying, but she managed, "I'm not alone now. I have Lisette and..."

That was it. She had only Lisette and these weekly calls with Aurelie.

"Mom, don't cry," Aurelie begged.

The tears from earlier had become uncontrollable sobs.

Lisette ran into the room. "Mom!" she exclaimed and flung her arms around Deborah, squeezing her too tightly. "Nice, Aurelie, real nice. Thanks for the comfort!"

"It's not Aurelie's fault," Deborah protested, but Aurelie sighed.

"I'm sorry, Mom, Lis. Look, let's talk again tomorrow, okay? Take care."

"You too, baby," said Deborah, but she wasn't sure if Aurelie heard before the call disconnected.

"What did she say?" demanded Lisette. Now it was Deborah's turn to sigh.

"Nothing. I just remembered old hurts that haven't gone away—Aurelie didn't cause them or bring them up. You shouldn't be so hard on your sister, Lisette."

Lisette slipped her arms around Deborah and lay her head on her breast. "I'm sorry, Mom. I didn't mean to fight. It's just—I can't believe she's not coming home."

Deborah rubbed Lisette's back. "It's hard on her too, sweetie."

和希

KAZUKI carefully rolled a painted scroll, mindful that his fingers touched only the backing paper, and returned it to its shelf.

"I told you there wasn't much to find," said Haruko. She was watching him with interest, her hip propped against the table in the middle of the environment-controlled archive room.

Kazuki nodded and removed the next scroll.

"Why are you so interested in wolves anyway?" asked Haruko.

"Just a feeling," Kazuki admitted.

He could feel Haruko hesitating. "What is it?" he prompted.

"There isn't much in the old materials, but I've been trying to record the oral traditions. There're stories there, especially from our secret French ancestor."

Kazuki turned. "Why didn't you open with that?"

Haruko smiled. "If it was useful, I would have. They are all vague, folktale-esque."

Kazuki shrugged. "I'd still like to see them."

Haruko nodded. She pointed at the black desktop tower that Kazuki had trouble believing still worked—it was probably older than he was. "*Obā-chama* has decided they can't go online, despite having nothing particularly Unseen about them. They're all local to that machine."

"Password?" asked Kazuki.

"There isn't one," said Haruko.

There were about two dozen stories, but most of

them were variations of "Little Red Riding Hood." What intrigued Kazuki was the wolves in these stories weren't all big-eyed, big-eared, and big-toothed. Some of them had dark hair or long nails or smelled like smoke. Of course, Kazuki realized that all of this might well be nonsense, but he filed away the descriptions anyway.

There were also two verses, written in both French and Japanese. In Japanese, at least, they were a singsong pattern that a child could easily remember.

'Ware the dark, the moon that's full,
'Ware the smile, the skin that's dull,
'Ware the teeth, the lips that smack,
'Ware the wolves, gathered in a pack.

In the shadows, on the wind,
Clear to see, hard to find.
Smoke and teeth, beast or shadow,
Protect the babe of the morrow.

Both rhymes were clearly a warning. Of course, they were also nonsense. "Babe of the morrow?" Just an awkward way to describe the future so that the syllables were right?

Kazuki had planned on staying the night at the Forest-Heart Home, but something about the verses teased at the edge of his mind, and he wanted to see Aurelie.

Haruko was making dinner in the kitchen when Kazuki made his way out.

"You aren't staying?" she asked in surprise, and Kazuki felt a pang of guilt.

Most of the house's residents were many years her senior; he thought of her gentle teasing that he and Emiko didn't visit often enough.

"I'm sorry," he said, "I—I want to check on Aurelie."

Haruko frowned, turning toward Kazuki more fully. "What alarmed you?"

Now he felt paranoid. "There was a verse..."

Haruko recited something in French, and then in Japanese.

"Yes, that one," admitted Kazuki.

"There aren't any wolves left in Japan," she reminded him gently.

"I know, but it probably doesn't mean literal wolves."

"There's no danger here at all," Haruko added. "That's why we have thrived for so long."

Kazuki hesitated, then said, "What if something followed Aurelie?"

When Haruko's face folded into skepticism, Kazuki said, "There's a reason we're all so afraid. A reason those poems have been passed down through so many generations. A reason most Unseen have died out."

"Yes..." said Haruko, though she still looked doubtful.

オーレリー

AFTER two weeks of her mother and sister missing her calls (deliberately, she now realized), Aurelie thought their Zoom request was because of her birthday. But Deborah and Lisette had forgotten about it—not that she blamed them. The stress they must have been under, caring for Dan and then his death. Her turning thirty-seven was a blip under that behemoth. Her mom sobbing...

As soon as the video cut, Aurelie let herself cry, too. She had resented Dan so much that she hadn't acknowledged how much she cared about him. He had been a deeply kind man. That was even why he had met her family—he'd volunteered at a homeless shelter to serve Thanksgiving dinner. Aurelie could still remember the deep brackets of his smile when he offered her whipped cream on an apple in lieu of pie (stupid gluten). There had been something so genuinely kind in his blue eyes that Aurelie had felt reassured. And then, when he saw four-year-old Lisette, he had offered them his son's winter clothes.

Deborah had been suspicious at first (hypervigilance, Aurelie now realized), but Dan's continued kindness had won her over, and eventually she had agreed to live with him and then, a few years later, they had married.

Did she have to miss Dan's funeral? She wanted to say goodbye. But she had three finals to give and grade—how could she cancel her office hours this week? And then, between finals and graduation, she had committed to grading the English portion of the university entrance exam. She couldn't just up and go for two to three weeks, plus the travel would be expensive.

It wasn't like it would bring Dan back.

But maybe it would comfort Mom.

Aurelie had rarely hugged her family, but she yearned to now. She wished they were closer—physically, but emotionally too. There was too much unsaid between them—which was partially her fault.

She had been wrong to keep secrets. And she hadn't even told them what she had discovered in France.

She had intended to take that tragedy to her grave, but she had told *Obā-chama*, and it had felt so right. Hiding it in darkness had granted the secret a far more sinister cast than daylight ever could. Acknowledging her painful family trauma had also eased the burden in her heart.

And that made her realize that she owed Kazuki an apology.

She heard a ringing sound, and it took her a moment to realize it was her doorbell. Aurelie blinked in surprise. It had only rang one other time since she moved in, when a package came.

The doorbell rang again, and Aurelie shut her laptop before hurrying to the door. She felt vaguely uneasy—ever since North Carolina, she dreaded unexpected visitors at the door. She was in Japan though, so there was no way it was her father. (She was pretty sure he was technically an illegal alien in the US). Most likely it was a Christian group come to win converts (her neighbor had warned her that they came by regularly, even though they weren't supposed to solicit inside the building).

The sound of the bolt retracting made her flinch. Annoyed with herself, Aurelie hurriedly pulled it open only to remember she should have grabbed a mask. But that worry faded as she recognized Kazuki. He was wearing her old leather jacket and holding a white plastic bag with condensation on the inside.

He tugged his mask down to his chin and grinned at her. "Have you tried *oden* yet?"

Aurelie stood frozen in the door a moment. She was tempted to check her own pulse because her heart felt like it was going to beat right out of her throat.

What was going on? Why was he here? Once again worried about his not-sister, not-aunt?

She moved away from the door so he could enter, and said faintly, "No, what's *oden*?"

Kazuki's smile had faded, and his eyes flicked anxiously over her face. Was it obvious that she'd been crying? His smile returned, slightly forced. "It's a stew. Popular in the winter, though it's available year-round at the *conbini*. Shall we eat together?"

His mouth quirked in a lopsided smile, and Aurelie marveled at his composure.

Then again, he was just offering some soup—not all the things she wanted.

"That would be nice. Thanks for thinking of me." She let him in.

To her apartment. Not her heart.

和希

STRETCHED out on the *zabuton* in Aurelie's common room, discussing seasonal dishes, Kazuki gathered his courage. Something had obviously gone wrong today. Besides her red-rimmed eyes, he'd seen some fancy *mochi* sitting unopened on the kitchen counter, and he had the feeling they were meant as birthday cake. Why hadn't she eaten them with her family earlier?

Finally, Kazuki asked, "What upset you earlier? Before I came?"

Aurelie's smile turned brittle. It broke, and she sighed. "I mentioned my stepfather to you before, haven't I? His health suffered shortly after I came here. I just found out he died."

Kazuki blurted, "On your *birthday*? I'm so sorry!"

"Well, he didn't die on my birthday, but yes, I found out today—wait. How did you know...?"

Kazuki felt his cheeks heat. "I dropped by your office yesterday and overheard you and Ōkami-*sensei* speaking."

Aurelie gaped at him, then started crying. Without thinking, he moved to her side and wrapped his arms around her. She pressed her face against his neck, and he could feel her tears on his skin.

It was the most intimate thing he'd ever experienced. Gently, he stroked her head and back; she was practically limp against him.

Once she had cried herself empty, Aurelie started asking him questions about leave. He didn't know all the answers, but he helped her find them in the staff portal. Unfortunately, it became obvious that a three-week bereavement leave wasn't an option, and that was more than her paid leave as well.

"I can't go; it just doesn't make sense," she declared.

"I could ask my father—"

She shook her head but squeezed his hand gratefully. "I'll go home after graduation, when there's a break anyway. Then I can stay longer."

Her gaze drifted to their linked fingers, and slowly her expression closed. She dropped his hand.

"I'm sorry—I, I was overwhelmed..."

Kazuki wanted to linger. To stay as late as she let him and even overnight. Not for seduction—just to be there.

But the *oden* containers were empty on the table, and he could see her recalling broken bindings and student-teacher etiquette.

It was time for a strategic retreat.

Kazuki slowly straightened, and Aurelie's eyes snapped to him. He didn't miss the way they traced his face and shoulders before Aurelie blushed and looked away again.

"I'm sorry about your stepfather," Kazuki said, "If you think of anything I can help with, please let me know." He checked the time on his phone. "The next bus is in ten minutes—or I could stay another hour if you..."

"No, you should go home." Aurelie leapt to her feet, and for a brief moment her hand settled on his arm. She jerked back as if scalded. "Thank you so much for the *oden* and for—well. I felt like I had a friend."

Kazuki could tell that she hadn't meant to be so honest, for she paled and her fingers started fluttering. If there'd been anything within tapping distance, they'd be beating a tattoo.

Although it might have been a little too bold, Kazuki caught those fingers and stilled them.

"I am your friend," he told her.

Her eyes widened and filled with worry.

"Now that you've been honored by *Obā-chama*, I daresay everyone in the clan will be your friend if you let them." He winked, and she relaxed. He released her hand. He reached for the white Styrofoam bowls that had been filled with *oden.*

"I'll get them!" Again Aurelie's hands brushed his. She quickly deposited the bowls in the bag that Kazuki had brought them in. "You don't want to miss your bus!" she reminded him.

Kazuki didn't—he boarded the bus and got off near his home on autopilot, hashing over the evening and his next move.

In fact, he was so distracted that he bumped into a man wearing a thick fleecy jacket—he noticed the fleece because he steadied the other fellow and was startled at how deep his fingers sank into the faux-fur.

Recognizing him, Kazuki flashed a quick smile. A minute later though, Kazuki remembered *where* he had seen the guy before—outside *Aurelie's* apartment, throwing away trash.

What were the chances that a guy who lived in Aurelie's complex happened to be outside Kazuki's at 23:00?

Kazuki turned back, to talk to him, maybe even to challenge him.

But the man wasn't there. Kazuki ran back to the spot and looked up and down the street. But besides a little steam drifting up from a street drain, everything was absolutely still.

Kazuki walked slowly back up his stairs.

Maybe he had imagined it. He rubbed his fingers together, getting rid of the impression of fleece that lingered on them.

21. MISSED

リ ッ セ ッ ト

THE funeral parlor limited in-person guests to ten, so they set up a Zoom broadcast. Lisette sent a Zoom link to Aurelie. Lisette had realized that the funeral was set for two in the morning in Japan, which was definitely past Aurelie's bedtime, so she didn't expect her sister to attend, but she started the call and prepared to feel bitter.

But Aurelie *did* show up, and Lisette felt terribly guilty instead.

When all was said and done, there wasn't that much to the service. Dan and Deborah had discussed things ahead of time, and he hadn't wanted anything religious, so it was just the funeral director saying a bunch of empty words. His bridge partner of thirty years spoke as well, and Lisette cried. Deborah suggested Lisette say something as well, but Lisette couldn't. She knew that Aurelie never truly thought of Dan as family, but Lisette had.

Who cared if they were different species? He'd been her dad.

Deborah held her hand then, and they collected the box of his ashes together.

"Are you going to scatter them with Ellen's?" Aurelie asked—Lisette jumped at the question.

"Yes, and Tyler's," said Deborah.

"It's sleeting there, isn't it?" asked Aurelie.

"What, I suppose you want us to wait until you get home to scatter the ashes," snarled Lisette. She was frustrated that she did, but she couldn't help it. She wanted Aurelie to break down, to show that she felt the way Lisette did.

Aurelie said, too mildly, "Not if you don't want to. I'll visit the hill when I get home."

"I think we—" started Deborah, but Lisette cut her off. Like a petulant teenager.

"No, we're not going to make Dan wait any longer to join them."

Aurelie got a weird expression. It was probably supposed to be a smile, but it looked like she was constipated.

"Of course," said Aurelie. "I'll let you both go then. Please be careful; don't slip."

Lisette felt even worse when she saw the disappointment in Deborah's eyes.

オ ー レ リ ー

A WEEK after Dan's funeral, Aurelie found herself wishing that she could answer the questions in her life as well as her students had answered those on her finals.

Was she wrong not to have taken unpaid leave for the funeral? She had attended via Zoom—the funeral home had set up a link, since attendance was limited due to the pandemic anyway. But she knew it wasn't the same. Had she been wrong to prioritize her life here over her family's feelings?

But Vermont felt like the past; Japan was starting to feel like the present and future. It was such a relief that Kazuki didn't condemn her for that. Instead, he had been there for her over the past two weeks, which came with its own set of questions...

If her family's dirty secret had so repulsed Kazuki that he'd broken the binding, why did he want to be friends? Why was he being so nice to her?

Was she just enjoying a one-sided crush, or was she setting herself up for heartbreak? Did she care that Kazuki was her much younger student, or was that an arbitrary rule that didn't apply? Maybe, now that finals were done, he wasn't her student? But no, she couldn't think like that. Once he graduated...

Oh, Aurelie, for shame!

At first she had been afraid of the binding, but she was the one who was too old. Anyone looking at their relationship would look at her in askance—not Dubois-*sensei*, but dubious *sensei*. And yet—could a relationship with Kazuki be wrong when it felt so natural, so comfortable?

Aurelie did what everyone should do when they were confused: she hit the pavement.

It was in the forties (or single digits, since she was trying to think in Celsius), so she wore some thick joggers and an even thicker sweatshirt. She ran far and fast, south of her apartment on the narrow roads between small dark houses and flooded rice paddies. Aurelie wondered idly if they ever froze—the rice stalks that still pierced the water here and there would make the surface rough, but they were big enough to skate on, if they did. She hadn't gone skating since undergrad in Vermont. Not that she would go on a stranger's rice paddy. And they probably didn't freeze anyway, since it only seemed to get cold enough overnight.

She bent her head into the wind that was attacking her nose and let her feet fly.

Only to collide with someone.

They both nearly went sprawling onto the pavement (ouch), but the person she had run into managed to spin them both in a move that made her think *Crouching Tiger, Hidden Dragon* and set them both upright.

She looked into Kazuki's eyes, and her heart skipped a beat.

Maybe she was just a woman who was attracted to a man.

A competent, handsome man whose smile turned a winter wind into a summer breeze.

和希

KAZUKI was still in the habit of following Aurelie's running schedule, but without the binding to direct him, he couldn't coordinate where they ran.

So he was fairly shocked when she barreled into his arms the day after his Medieval Europe final, wearing a Yale sweatshirt that rivalled her flannel pajamas in size.

Usually her expressions were restrained and nuanced, but she gaped at him. Her cheeks were already pink from the wind, but they deepened to red.

He couldn't help it; he laughed. A deep belly laugh, that spread from his gut out to his shoulders, lifting worries he had only half-acknowledged.

Aurelie laughed too, in a higher counterpoint but just as wholeheartedly. They weren't quite hugging, but his hands held her shoulders—he had twirled her to avoid falling, a use of momentum that he'd learned in *karate*—and her hands rested at his waist.

It was delightfully intimate and closer to the line than anything he'd done since her birthday.

Though crying on him had made Aurelie more receptive to his company, he'd been careful to keep things platonic. He showed her the trails behind Kasuga-Taisha, the ones he had abandoned when the binding had led him to Aurelie instead. He introduced her to various culinary specialties and comfort foods that he thought she'd enjoy.

And Aurelie was starting to reciprocate. She had cooked him dinner, she texted him a several times a day, and now she stood inches from him in a not-quite hug.

"Maybe we should run side by side," she suggested, her head cocking like a bird as she smiled up at him. "To avoid running into each other."

"That implies mutual responsibility," he argued. "I think you ran into me, and I saved us." He winked, and she laughed again.

"Then you don't want to run with me...?" she started to pull away.

"I'd be happy to," and he fell into step beside her.

And when they parted ways, they agreed to meet again tomorrow.

At lunch Kazuki related all this to Emiko, who propped her chin on her fist and nodded slowly to herself.

"Sounds like dating to me," said Emiko. She rubbed her chin with the knuckle of her forefinger. "I think it's time to push it. Ask her out."

"You're the one who said I need to be sneaky," said Kazuki. He was scared, but he didn't want to admit it. Then he realized he had crossed his arms defensively over his chest. He forced himself to relax them and sit back.

Emiko smiled sympathetically. "Yes, but after sneaking, eventually you have to pounce, don't you? Clear the air, make a confession..." She waved both hands vaguely.

Kazuki ran his hand through his hair. "I don't want to push her. I think I should let her ask for more."

Emiko rolled her eyes. "I think, Kazuki-*san*, that if

you are waiting for her to make the first move, you are going to wait a long time. She's very, very careful."

オーレリー

"IS it weird for a woman to make the first move in Japan?" Aurelie asked as she contemplated her berry-crowned custard.

She and Ōkami sat on either side of a small wood table in the cutest pastry shop that Aurelie had ever seen. It was all cream and pink with heart labels and *anime* style artwork telling a simple love story on the walls. (Maybe the mural was to blame for her preoccupation with her own unsatisfactory romance).

Ōkami had a beautiful confection of a cake in front of her—Aurelie would have loved to try it, if it weren't for its obvious use of flour.

Ōkami seemed less tempted, for the cake sat untouched. (Again Aurelie thought of eating disorders and wondered if she should lead an intervention. Were they close enough? How did one even bring it up? She'd Google it later).

"Of course!" laughed Ōkami. "This is 2022!"

Aurelie took a scoop of her dessert. The tangy berries melded perfectly with the silky custard. The bite was finished too soon—and not just because it was delicious. Nervously, she said to Ōkami, "But— sometimes Japan feels very socially conservative."

Ōkami shrugged. "Would you want a man who thought less of you for asking him out?"

I would if it were Kazuki, thought Aurelie. She couldn't help it. She may have avoided drugs her entire life, but Kazuki was more addictive than any stimulant.

However, Ōkami had a good point. If Kazuki was interested in her (if, if, if), then he wouldn't be put off by her confessing first. He wasn't that type of person.

"Are you going to make a move?" purred Ōkami.

"Maybe," said Aurelie. Ōkami smiled at her, and if it was a slightly predatory grin—well, Ōkami always looked hungry, and it made all of her expressions a little predatory.

22. SEDUCED

恵美子

EMIKO found the delicate ombre of the pink and white blossoms on her long *kimono* sleeves more interesting than President Matsumo's graduation speech, but her good mood was in no way impaired by his long-windedness.

After four years, she was about to receive her diploma. She was sitting with the rest of the English majors in the gymnasium. Actually, if it weren't for the ubiquitous white medical masks, Emiko could have forgotten the pandemic. Last year, the ceremony had been cancelled. Emiko had worried that theirs would be as well, but it had proceeded almost as it would have two years ago. Sure, there was a large plexiglass sheet on the podium (the diplomas were to be passed through the narrow slot at the bottom), and families had been asked to watch the ceremony online rather than attend in person, but...

She was grateful.

Most of her cousins collected their diplomas first, and then it was Emiko's turn.

As she bowed and collected the green leather folder containing her diploma, Emiko cried. It was both an end and a beginning.

和希

SOME of Kazuki's cousins had headed straight home after graduation, but most, including Emiko, had agreed on a celebratory *karaoke*.

So he was both pleased and conflicted when Aurelie sent him a text in the early afternoon asking to see him that night.

He typed and deleted a reply three times before settling on,

> I'm free from now until 18:00. Then I'm going out with cousins. Can you meet early? Or do you want to join?

The reply seemed to take forever to come. Kazuki almost messaged her that he could cancel.

> I can meet you at 16:00. OK?

OK.

Kazuki cast a quick glance over his apartment and moments later, he was cleaning. Not that it was a disaster—living by himself, he didn't make much of a mess. But he opened the windows to freshen the air, and he ran the microfiber mop over the floor. And he changed his sheets.

Not that he expected her to touch them, but they might smell? It had been over a week...

He closed the windows again twenty minutes before she was due to arrive to eliminate the draft.

And then, because he was getting nervous for no clear reason, he stretched out on his bed and streamed one of his favorite slapstick scenes, where a tiny woman accidentally beats up a group of thugs. He was cracking up over the male lead's disbelief when his doorbell rang.

Kazuki closed the app and opened the door.

Aurelie stood on the stoop, her eyes on the ground and fingers playing Flight of the Bumblebee on her white palazzo pants.

"Come in," he said.

She did so without meeting his eyes. She fumbled with her oxfords—at least it gave her restless fingers a task—and Kazuki tried to figure out what was different about her. Besides her agitation, which wasn't that uncommon really.

Her hair, he realized abruptly. *It's wet. It wasn't raining though.*

Had she hurried home from work, showered, and then come here? But why?

Maybe she spilled something on herself.

She settled her shoes, aligned and pointed toward the door, and stepped into his apartment.

"I wanted to talk to you," she announced.

"Sure," Kazuki said, keeping his voice casual. "What's on your mind?"

"I've decided not to have an *omiai* with Aoki Kento-san."

"Oh. Why's that?"

"We won't bind anyway."

Kazuki had to resist the urge to tap his own thigh—it seemed he was picking up her nervous tic.

"I see," he hedged. "You don't want a binding anyway."

She whirled on him, at last meeting his eyes. Her dark eyes, so opaque now that their binding was broken, seemed to be lit from within. "Yes, I do! But—but—with you!"

Kazuki heard and understood and yet he didn't believe. "You do? That's not what you thought a month ago."

Her face fell, and she took a step back. "I'm sorry to impose on you. It's already settled between us, I shouldn't have..."

She was going to leave.

Kazuki caught her hand, anchoring her to him.

"It isn't settled between us," he said. "Not at all."

And he kissed her.

It wasn't like in Nara Park, when their desire was all consuming and harmonious.

It was awkward, fumbling, and oh-so-sincere.

He was so aware of everything—the way her lips quivered and then pressed more insistently against his. Her fingers bunching the front of his shirt. Her legs shaking as if they couldn't support her weight—well, he could. He pulled her body tight and realized that she was still wearing her coat. He slipped a hand between them to remedy that but found he couldn't manage the oversized buttons singlehandedly.

He started chuckling and pulled back to use both hands. She helped, starting at the bottom while he started at the top.

He almost said something, almost clarified what it was they were doing, but—*kuso!*—it was too fragile.

Instead, as soon as her coat hit the floor, he grabbed her hips and pulled them into his and kissed her. Her hands tangled in his hair—too tangled, and he winced when they jerked.

But he didn't stop kissing, and her lips parted. He tasted oden, and he smiled.

She ended up pressing her lips into his teeth because of that, and they both started laughing again.

"God, is this what it's always like for humans?" she asked. "How do they bear it?"

Kazuki shook his head. And yet he knew, he understood. Even though it wasn't perfect, it was burning. Real.

He swung her into his arms, and she yelped in surprise.

He dropped her on his bed—a little harder than he meant to, and he started to apologize.

She hooked his belt loops with her fingers and pulled him down to her, wrapping her legs around his waist.

He wasn't sure how long they kissed, his body rocking ever so slightly into hers, his hands pinning her wrists to the bed as their lips, teeth, and tongues became acquainted.

He knew there was no rush, and he intended to savor every moment.

オ ー レ リ ー

AURELIE'S head was spinning, and a great tension was filling her. She felt like every inch of her skin was taut and full of nerve endings—even the slight abrasion of her lace bra against her nipples as Kazuki moved made her want to scream. She was at the edge of a precipice, and she wanted to jump.

Feeling wild, she pushed Kazuki onto his back and straddled his hips. She tried to undo the pretty pearl buttons of her blouse but her fingers were too eager. Kazuki lifted his hands to help, and someone hissed (her, she hissed), "Rip it!"

He obliged, sending buttons flying. They both froze for a moment, stunned by the violence, and then Kazuki pulled off his shirt.

Aurelie's hands found the muscles of his chest, caressing the valleys and ridges that had haunted her dreams.

His hands went to her back and after two fumbles, he managed to unhook her bra. He slipped the straps off her shoulder, and the cups caught on her peaked nipples, hanging there in an oddly sensual moment before she lifted her hands from his body to rip the bra away.

He sat up as she did so, rocking his pelvis into hers and making her gasp—but not as much as she did a moment later, when he bent her backward and pulled one nipple into his lips.

She was supine and spineless, but one of his arms supported her back and his hand cradled her neck. His other hand found her other nipple, gently pinching and rolling it, and she couldn't help but quiver and make all sorts of vulnerable noises.

With great effort, she lifted her own hands to his hair, caressing his head gently before sliding them to his shoulder and down his back.

But he suckled harder, and her efforts to be tender were foiled—her hands became claws, her nails pressing into his back. (How trite!)

And then he groaned and flipped her onto the bed beneath him.

He robbed her of his warmth immediately though, and she cried in protest.

He grinned at her, a slightly shaky expression as he removed first her pants and then his own. She ripped off their underwear since he had missed them.

His penis popped free, standing at attention, and a tiny bead appeared at its tip, crying for her.

She opened her mouth and pulled it in.

He cried out, panicked.

"No, no, you mustn't!" he admonished.

和希

WHEN Aurelie took him into her mouth, Kazuki nearly climaxed.

Afraid of coming without her, he pressed her back into the bed and used his knee to part her legs. She spread her thighs wide and lifted her pelvis, inviting him in.

Having at last found their rhythm, Kazuki slid inside her with one fierce stroke, earning a cry of approval from his beloved's throat.

He took a deep breath, feeling the unbelievably perfect pressure and heat, and making sure he could hold on a little longer.

Withdrawing slightly, he thrust again; she whimpered and clenched around him, but he knew she wasn't quite there.

His mouth found hers, and one of his hands returned to tease her nipple.

Her fingers dug into his butt cheeks, urging him to thrust faster and harder.

He obliged, and she screamed into his mouth.

Her convulsions were more than he could resist, and he joined her.

HUNTED

YES!
HA!
Now?
NOW!
Now!
NOT QUITE.
But we're hungry!
SO HUNGRY.
How much longer?
NOT UNTIL HE LEAVES.
THAT HALF-GROWN PUP?
He's chew toy!
YOU'VE FORGOTTEN. HE'S A PROTECTOR.
How do you know?
THINK OF WHAT HE DID TO GOPI.

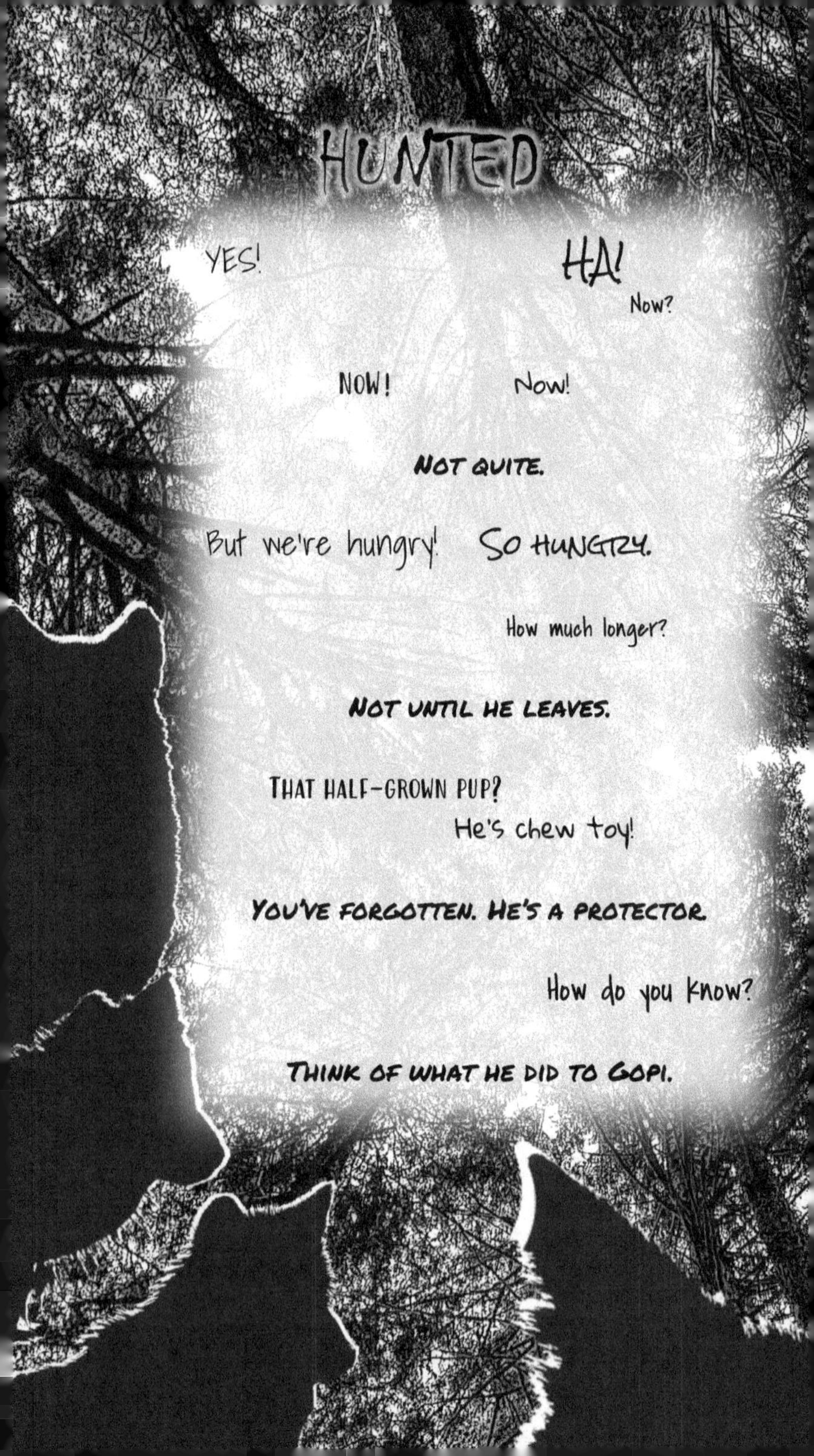

You killed Gopi.
Because he almost exposed us.
But the boy beat him.
Hmm.
So we wait.
How long?
Grrrr.
Don't growl at me.
As soon as they separate.
A few hours, maybe.
But...
We've already waited this long.
A few more hours are nothing.
That's right.
Fine!
Fine!
Fine.
Just a little longer...

23. UNBOUND

オーレリー

AURELIE'S head was pillowed on Kazuki's chest, and she could hear his heartbeat. Every part of her was hypersensitive—his ridiculously smooth sheets pressed a thousand kisses on her skin and his warmth eased through her like a hot bath.

One of his hands started rubbing lazy circles on her back.

Aurelie flinched and ruined an almost perfect moment.

His hand froze. "I'm sorry—"

"No," she said, "It's—" He had caught her by surprise. And that was wrong.

The binding hadn't been restored.

Aurelie blinked rapidly, denying the tears that

suddenly pricked her eyes.

"The binding," Kazuki said, his arms wrapping around her.

Aurelie nodded. Past the lump in her throat, she asked, "How did you know?"

和希

HOW did Kazuki know she was upset about the binding?

Because *he* was upset. Awareness that the binding hadn't been restored was nearly a physical pain, even though his elders had warned him that it wouldn't be easy. (And yes, the sex had been easy, albeit a little awkward). He had wrapped Aurelie in a tight hug, willing the distance between them to be completely eliminated, so that their hearts would connect once again.

He was disappointed when that didn't happen.

"I was thinking about it, too," he told her. He pressed his lips against her hair—still damp—and added, "I'm sorry."

"*You're* sorry?" She raised her head, her dark eyes wide. "If either of us needs to apologize, it's me. *I'm* sorry."

"I snapped the binding," Kazuki reminded her.

She flinched. "You could only do so because I had kept it so weak in the first place." Contrary to her words, her fingers convulsed punitively on his shoulders. He winced, though it didn't hurt much.

Her fingers relaxed and rubbed his shoulders soothingly. "I'm sorry," she apologized again.

But there was something else she wasn't saying. Something that needed to be brought out and analyzed if they wanted to move forward.

He lifted his hand to brush back her hair and found it trembling ever so slightly—he hoped so slightly that she didn't notice.

"Were you upset that I snapped the binding?" Kazuki asked.

Aurelie's face blazed, and Kazuki knew she had been.

"You must have been shocked at—at what you saw," Aurelie stammered. The first time he had heard her stammer, come to think of it. "In my head, I mean."

It hadn't occurred to Kazuki that she might think he had broken the binding because he scorned her. He wanted to reassure her, to make sure she understood him—how he wished she could feel what he felt!

Choosing his words carefully, Kazuki said, "I was pretty shocked. But—I was trying to protect you."

"Protect me?" Her brow furrowed.

"*Obā-chama* was using our binding to dig through your past. She was coercing you."

"Oh. Oh. No—yes, but no. She did force me to reveal memories that I had kept suppressed for a long time. But—it was like vomiting when you have food poisoning. It feels horrible in the moment, but so much better after. If you never get it out, it stays inside, making you sicker and sicker..."

She abruptly changed the subject—except Kazuki realized that it wasn't abrupt for her.

"Is this wrong? You were my student. I just

intended to talk, but we…"

"I already finished my work for your class," he reminded her, "and the prohibition of sexual relationships between professors and undergrads is to prevent someone abusing their authority to coerce someone. I do not feel coerced—and you no longer have authority over me. I graduated." Belatedly, he wondered if that was rude. "I mean, I respect you—"

She laughed—giggled, really—and pressed her face into his neck. A moment later, she pulled back again, her face once again tight with worries. How quickly she must process for her emotions to shift so rapidly!

"That's true," Aurelie acknowledged, "but you are still fourteen years younger than I am."

Kazuki wanted to interrupt, but he forced himself to wait for Aurelie.

Her eyes darted to his and away as she said, "Obā-chama acted like the binding is all that matters but—your mother at least was unhappy with it. My mother—she had me at sixteen." Aurelie shook her head so vigorously that her short blond hair shivered around her face.

Kazuki didn't understand what she was trying to say. To him, it was as if she had listed many unrelated facts.

Trying to shuffle out the sense, he said, "Sixteen is too young. I know that occasionally bindings occur then, but then the couple waits to have children." And then, with sudden insight, he said, "I'm not sixteen. I'm also a willing—eager partner. And we have time. We don't have to have children right away."

She plucked at the sheet. "How can you be so, so

calm?" She swallowed. "At first I feared the binding because I didn't want to end up like my aunt, but now—aren't you afraid that I'm like...my father?"

Never had that occurred to Kazuki. But he forced himself to think about it rather than dismiss it out of hand. "Didn't Shigeru suggest having sex to you?"

Aurelie flinched. "How did you know?"

"Wouldn't your father have accepted such a proposal? Why didn't you?"

Aurelie looked blank. "I couldn't. I wasn't attracted to him."

"That's how it is for most of us, isn't it? Physical intimacy is only appealing with one partner? We are attracted only to our fated mates."

She started to object to his word choice, so Kazuki amended, "Only to particular beings whose pheromones are irresistible, if you prefer."

She grinned. "I do."

"Your father was an exception in the species."

Her mouth snapped back into a line. "Yes. I guess so." She thought for a moment. "You're right that Unseen in general don't seem to be allosexual, but he must have been."

"Allosexual?"

"Feeling sexual attraction more or less all the time. Most humans are that way, or so it seems. But we are mostly asexual until a switch flips."

Kazuki had never given the matter a great deal of thought, but he appreciated the way that sorting through theories and phenomena calmed Aurelie. When she started geeking out, she stopped worrying.

"I wonder—is no one in your clan that way?"

Kazuki shrugged. "I don't know. I certainly have never heard of any infidelity." He wracked his brain for gossip, and the only relationship outside of a binding he could think of was Haruko's infamous affair. But he didn't want to expose her to Aurelie, not when the family never talked about it. "I think your father must have been an anomaly."

Aurelie nodded, slowly, her gaze drifting around the room. It settled on Kazuki's bedside table, and her brow knitted briefly. Then she leapt up, pulling the comforter with her. "It's six o'clock!"

Kazuki didn't know why that was important.

"You said you were going to *karaoke*!"

Ah, yes, so he had. But he wasn't letting Aurelie out of his sight.

He snagged her close and rolled her under him. "That was before I had something better to do." He waggled his brows to make her laugh.

Which she did, but she immediately objected. "If we're going to do this—I don't want to isolate you from your family. That's a sign of a toxic relationship." Her fingers fluttered.

Kazuki didn't think there was any chance of her fear coming true, but he suggested, "Then come to *karaoke* with me. Integrate with my family."

There was such a deep yearning in her eyes that Kazuki held his breath.

"I'd like that...but won't I be a damper on your party?"

"Damper?"

"Like—won't your cousins feel unable to relax with a professor there?"

He smirked. "Yes, tonight you have to be my girlfriend, not a professor."

He pulled her from the bed.

オーレリー

AURELIE stared at her own reflection in Kazuki's bathroom dumbfounded. A ripped sweatshirt and some coke bottle glasses without lenses (Kazuki said they were stylish) had indeed turned her into Kazuki's girlfriend rather than a professor. She supposed it helped that she was quite young for an Unseen (no crow's feet or upper lip hair, like humans in their thirties had to deal with).

"I still look foreign though," she pointed out. "If one of my students saw me like this, they might still recognize me."

Kazuki took the thick-rims off her face and stroked one of her pale brows with his thumb.

"A little mascara," he suggested.

"I don't have any," she said. (Darkening her lashes looked somewhat ridiculous).

He winked. "I do."

"Why?" she asked in surprise.

"The usual reason," he said, "for thickening my lashes."

Aurelie was quite shocked and looked closely at Kazuki's face.

He laughed. "I'm not wearing it right now. But I do sometimes."

He produced the wand, and Aurelie let him apply it, since he obviously knew what he was doing and she didn't. (She vaguely remembered reading an article that said you should never share mascara because of eye infections or something, but she decided not to worry about it).

After a few minutes, he replaced the glasses and directed her to the mirror.

Were her lashes really that long? It did look a bit weird with her super pale skin but with the hood pulled up and the glasses on...

She felt strangely like the years had fallen away. For her, college had been a tense time. God, her life had been a tense time. How different would it have been, surrounded by a large Unseen family? Instead of feeling paranoid anytime someone started to get too close, she would have a dozen confidants.

She turned suddenly and grabbed Kazuki by the front of his shirt and pulled him close for a kiss.

He looked dazed when she released him, and she slipped her arms around his waist. "Thank you," she said, "for—for everything. I don't—I don't deserve— but I'm so grateful."

He pulled her close and kissed her again. He probably had intended it to be light, but it changed quickly, so desperate were they for each other.

Kazuki whispered at her ear, "I think we could be a little late—"

Aurelie pushed him back (she couldn't step away, as he had been pressing her into the door frame) and declared, "We have to leave." She grinned to soften her words. "That can wait for later."

Kazuki covered her mouth, his eyes wide with alarm. "Haven't you ever seen a movie? Saying that will make something terrible happen."

Aurelie snorted—was she really dating a film studies major? "Kazuki," she said, "there's no script here. Just you and me."

Then she blushed again.

24. TROUBLED

惠美子

EMIKO knew things were going well between Aurelie and Kazuki, but when they walked into the *karaoke* parlor holding hands, she couldn't believe it. Aurelie looked like a different person; it was like translating a familiar word only to learn it had a secondary definition.

In an oversized sweatshirt and some ridiculous glasses that Kazuki thought were cool, Aurelie was a far cry from the polished professor of class. Emiko didn't think their binding was restored, but it looked like Kazuki's sneaking was working.

Her stomach flipflopped with an anxiety that she didn't have time to examine, and Emiko stretched her lips so much that her cheeks ached as she surged forward to greet the couple.

Aurelie's face brightened when she saw Emiko, and they clasped hands. The nervous energy in Aurelie's grip softened Emiko's forced grin into a genuine welcoming smile. Emiko remembered that she liked Aurelie, and she was happy for her and Kazuki. Her nerves were because she felt self-conscious in front of the cousins. She didn't want people gossiping about her, maybe pitying her.

Emiko tugged Aurelie away from Kazuki and performed introductions as if she were the one who had invited Aurelie.

Kano asked Aurelie, "So you haven't been bound? Are there many unbound in your clan?"

Aurelie released Emiko's hand to focus on Kano. Even with the disguise, her professorial demeanor seeped through—there was something very elegant, very controlled about Aurelie, and Emiko thought, *I want to be her when I grow up.* Then she blushed because maybe she was already grown up? She was an adult, anyway.

"The only Unseen I know well are my mother and sister, both of whom are unbound."

"That doesn't make sense," objected Kano. "If your mother is unbound, how could she have children?"

Kazuki stepped forward then, clearly ready to defend Aurelie, but she didn't need it.

"Sex is possible without a binding," she remarked, "if distasteful. My mother's generation was afraid the family would die out and there were far more women than men. Some decided that it was worth the distaste to try to keep the species alive." Her eyes swept the group. "They would cry from joy if they knew how many of us there are."

Emiko could see horror and embarrassment on Kano's face. Hoping Aurelie didn't see it too, Emiko asked brightly, "So, have you ever been to *karaoke* before?"

和希

KAZUKI didn't love Emiko taking Aurelie from his side—she felt so right there—but he didn't mind too much either. Emiko's active solicitation of Aurelie's company won over Kano and by extension Ryōta, and soon the rest of their cousins were cheerfully greeting her as well.

Pulling Kazuki aside, Ryōta asked, "So you did bind?"

Kazuki hesitated, not wanting to share the details, yet unwilling to lie. But Aurelie heard the question and answered for him.

"We were called at the beginning of the term. However, our relationship violated the professor-student fraternization rules so we kept things between us."

Ryōta snorted. "Those rules are for humans!"

"And they run the world," Kazuki reminded him. "We are all supposed to follow human mores as much as possible."

Ryōta flushed and snorted; Kazuki met Aurelie's eyes and found her smiling.

Kazuki pulled her back to him, one arm over her

shoulder. That was better.

Food started arriving, a big assortment of fresh fruit and processed snacks, as well as adult beverages and tea.

Kazuki stayed clear of the alcohol and knew that Aurelie noticed. He had never been a big drinker, and though he hadn't considered giving it up entirely before, prioritizing her comfort over social expectations seemed utterly natural.

Although there was no binding between them, none of the cousins seemed to notice. They danced, they sang, they held hands. Kazuki felt light and free—and Aurelie looked nothing like his professor. She kept laughing and flushing. Her cheeks were so pink that he would have thought she was wearing blush if he hadn't applied her only makeup himself.

She was awkward, but at ease with it, if that made any sense. Kazuki barely stopped himself from laughing when Kano offered Aurelie a Calpis Soda.

"Cow piss?" Aurelie echoed in confusion.

"Yes, Calpis," agreed Kano, oblivious to how it sounded in English.

Kazuki took the bottle and a swig with a wink to reassure Aurelie. She accepted it, but still looked nervous as she took her first sip.

"So when will you get married?" asked Emiko.

Aurelie's sip went down wrong; maybe she'd been right to be nervous. As Kazuki patted her on the back, he hedged, "We have to talk to my parents and *Obā-chama* first."

"And *my* mother," added Aurelie, once she was

breathing normally. "I think I need to visit the US before we make any plans."

"The US?" Emiko looked at Kazuki, as if to see what he thought.

Kazuki smiled and nodded. "I need to meet Au-*chan*'s family, too. We'll go together."

Aurelie's eyes widened, and he worried she might contradict him. But she leaned into him, and Kazuki pressed a kiss to her temple.

"The US..." Emiko said once again. Kazuki wanted to ask her what she was thinking about, but he was distracted by Ryōta belting a rock song.

茂

"GO to the US?" Shigeru wasn't sure if Kento was mocking him or not. Kind of a weird guy, Kento. Shigeru had once caught him doing a *kanji* crossword during a family picnic. For, like, two hours, and he finished the whole thing.

"But the clan prohibits international travel," Shigeru reminded him. "*Kuso*, I even had trouble getting my business trip to Okinawa approved!"

Kento nodded. "But Dubois-*sensei* has family in the US, family she hasn't seen in years. Someone needs to go find them."

Shigeru rubbed his chin. "But you and I are both busy with work. Doesn't it make more sense for someone unemployed to go? Kazuki-*kun* or Emiko-*san*."

Kento smiled faintly, a superior sort of smile, but Shigeru didn't mind. Kento was insanely smart; Shigeru wasn't surprised that he saw something that

Shigeru didn't.

"Haruko-*san* told me that the reason Dubois-*sensei's* clan was in trouble is a lack of male Unseen. She only has female cousins."

Shigeru nodded, and then it clicked. He said, too slowly, "She has only female cousins—there's no men? So—they are all unbound."

Kento nodded again.

Shigeru started to laugh.

Time to get a passport.

オ ー レ リ ー

"I COULD have gone home alone," Aurelie told Kazuki, her fingers intertwined with his. She loved his fingers, long and slim. (She never had asked if he played piano—but he was so good at music, she should).

"You could have, but I couldn't," Kazuki winked above his mask.

Aurelie giggled, like a schoolgirl. She *felt* like a schoolgirl. Not that she would ever admit that aloud, but... She felt so light. The world was softer and cuter than she'd ever realized. *Kawaii*, like all the mascots that Japanese adored.

"Do you really want to go to the US with me?" she asked.

Kazuki nodded. "I already have a passport."

"Oh?" That didn't seem significant to Aurelie, but he squared his shoulders as he said it. Then she remembered, "The family doesn't support travel abroad, do they? So why..."

"I applied for one in November," he told her, his

thumb stroking her knuckles.

"You're a confident one, aren't you?"

"Favored son," he whispered in her ear.

Aurelie giggled again.

She told him about the former farm where she had grown up. "Dan—my stepfather—was a farm vet. Lisette took over his practice."

"Did you like Vermont?" he asked her.

"Vermont means 'green mountain.' I liked that—there are so many beautiful places there. And it was a good place to live if you needed to keep to yourself."

"But you didn't want to?" he pursued.

"I guess not. Even though I kept to myself everywhere else I went, too. But it was not a choice. Until..." She met his eyes.

His eyes were so dark, yet they were soft and warm. He nodded, like he could hear her thoughts.

She wished he could. The binding was all that was needed to make this perfect.

Kazuki helped Aurelie pack—well, really he invaded her privacy while she packed, but that was okay. Almost... nice. Because it meant he cared.

There was so much to be said between the two of them—Aurelie laughed at the time Yuriko took him around town dressed in her old skirt because she wanted a baby sister, and everyone had called him pretty.

"You *are* pretty," Aurelie told him. Feeling incredibly daring, she reached out a hand and stroked his cheek. "Gorgeous, like a model," she said.

"Gorgeous?" he repeated, then laughed. "That's

what I thought about you."

By the time they reached Kazuki's place though, neither of them wanted to talk anymore. There was something much more urgent to occupy their mouths.

A short time later (perhaps embarrassingly so, though Aurelie knew nothing about how long it usually took Unseen to climax), they lay panting in Kazuki's bed, a fine sheen of sweat coating both of them.

She felt so vulnerable, yet so safe. With Kazuki, she could give him everything, show all of herself. He knew exactly how neurotic she was, how obsessive and overly analytical, but he thought she was smart, and strong, and *gorgeous.*

And she suddenly thought she knew what she had to do for the binding to come back. She had to trust Kazuki—and she did. So she said three words that she couldn't remember ever saying out loud.

"I love you."

25. SEPARATED

NOTHING happened.

The binding didn't return, up didn't become down, and... Kazuki didn't speak.

Maybe the first two were too much to ask for, but shouldn't Kazuki say something?

Aurelie almost said it again—*I love you*—but she knew he had heard her the first time. It was pathetic to say it again.

He dropped a kiss on her forehead. "Good night."

And that's when Aurelie understood.

She wasn't the reason that the binding hadn't been restored.

She had been sure it was her fault because she was the broken one, the one with generational trauma and skeletons in the closet, the one who was afraid of her own nature, but it was Kazuki who no longer trusted.

She had pushed the golden boy away too many times, and he was afraid to open up to her again.

Maybe that was it; maybe she'd ruined the gift that life had brought her, and it never could be restored.

"Good night," she mumbled, though it no longer felt quite so good as before.

和希

KAZUKI knew that the expected reply to *I love you* was *I love you, too*, but the words got lost on the way to his mouth.

Or maybe it would be more accurate to say they hit a roadblock—Aurelie's words from December.

It's not love. It's biology.

Had she truly changed her mind? Or was she just saying it?

If she was just saying it, did it cheapen the words to say it back? Was this the moment of mutual understanding, the happily-ever-after that *I love you* was supposed to signal?

Kazuki knew how to say "love" in five languages, from watching famous films and popular shows.

And yet, he had never said it to a person. He loved directors, he loved actors, he loved music, food, and the outdoors. Maybe he loved his family? He didn't think of it that way. Their connection was so much more; it didn't need to be articulated. In fact, was Aurelie's profession evidence that they were broken? Their binding had failed, and so they were reduced to verbal expressions rather than the true emotional connection that Unseen were supposed to have.

The binding, *Obā-chama* had once explained, superseded the emotion of love. It was greater than the passion humans felt for each other, and that was important. "Love" had been how *Obā-chama* referred to Haruko's fleeting affair.

His parents' care for each other was evident without them ever saying the word love. They'd do anything to protect each other, they were affectionate, and they clearly enjoyed each other's company. Kazuki felt that way about Aurelie—oh, and he desired her too. He wanted to build a life with her, to have children.

Part of him *knew* that was what she was trying to convey. In dramas, if a lead faltered like Kazuki was doing, he would asked his secretary or higher-EQ friend what love felt like so that the audience could groan at his naivety, and his best friend would flick Kazuki in the head and say this *was* love.

But hadn't everyone been telling him that dramas were about humans? That Unseen were different? Unseen were called and bound; they didn't fall in love. It could be the same thing—a script writer would say that not caring that someone was fourteen years older or that they were a foreigner showed love. But the words felt strange to Kazuki.

He suddenly realized that he had been silent too long. In fact, had Aurelie already fallen asleep? Maybe the words hadn't meant much to her, and he had been overthinking it.

"Good night," he murmured and kissed her temple.

オーレリー

AURELIE woke to an empty bed in the morning. She was upset and yet also relieved. She had had strange dreams, where one of the deer from the park explained to her that she was unlovable. And then it turned into a wolf and chased her. She was wearing a red cloak (she had vaguely known she was Little Red Riding Hood, and that she needed to bring some cookies to *Obāchama*), but the cloak caught on something, and the threads tangled her legs so she fell.

She woke before the wolf could bite her. If Kazuki had been in bed with her, she probably would have yelled at him.

She didn't know why she cared so much that he hadn't said he loved her, but she did. She started to get up when she realized she could hear Kazuki's voice. He was on the tiny balcony. Aurelie turned on stealth mode.

She slipped from the bed and snagged her running clothes. Then, on the balls of her feet, she crept to the bathroom.

When she re-emerged, Kazuki was still on the balcony; Aurelie realized he was on the phone. With Emiko maybe, or another family member.

"Well, you don't say it, do you?" His voice was a little too loud, his words a challenge.

He listened for a moment, and Aurelie cursed the fact she couldn't hear the person on the other end.

"No, of course I like her, but... I mean, we're mated. The binding—well, isn't saying it insulting?"

Aurelie's profession of love had *insulted* him?

"Well, I think it's important to be honest. Trust is the foundation of a happy relationship."

Trust—he wants me to trust him when he doesn't love me?

"How would I know? Well, I've watched—"

Aurelie had heard enough.

She crept to the door, tied her sneakers, and let herself out.

She wasn't familiar with the area around Kazuki's apartment though, and today concrete and car exhaust weren't going to cut it. The bus to Nara Park was pulling up, and Aurelie jogged to catch it.

She'd go where the trees were tall, the air was fresh, and she could pretend that the rest of the world didn't exist.

Unfortunately, the rest of the world didn't cooperate.

No sooner did she get off at the park's stop than Ōkami hailed her.

"Dubois-*sensei*! Where are you headed? Oh, this is my husband."

Ōkami was beaming as she walked up, a man in a tacky brown fleece right beside her.

和希

IT was unpleasant, but Kazuki was doing his best to listen to Yuriko's lecture without defending himself.

"Kazuki-*kun!* Life is not a drama. Seriously. Understanding mechanics of a relationship trope doesn't translate to understanding a relationship."

"So you would have me lie to her?"

"I still don't get why you think it's a lie," Yuriko said. "You've been obsessed with her for months. You've told me how wonderful she is in at least twenty ways. What do you feel toward her if not love?"

"I'm scared! Okay? I'm scared. I don't—this doesn't feel real. And if I say I love her—if I love her—aren't I a fool?"

There was silence. After a moment, Kazuki repeated her name, not sure if she had bumped the mute button or something.

"I'm still here," Yuriko snapped. Then, "The binding didn't return, huh?"

Kazuki froze. He'd been so careful to omit that. "How did you know?"

"If it had, it wouldn't be so scary."

He considered that. "Yeah." And then he blinked. "If the binding doesn't return, I can't take over the clan. I'll have to do something outside the home."

"Sorry," said Yuriko.

"I don't care about that, really, as long as we can be together. But—I don't even know if she meant it," Kazuki added bitterly.

"And she doesn't know how you feel, but she said it anyway. You really think she's a liar? That doesn't match what you've told me before. She's always been straightforward with you, hasn't she?"

Kazuki flushed—because Yuriko was right. Aurelie was straightforward, so she probably *had* meant it. And he had left her hanging.

He was a coward—and it was even worse because

Aurelie was so scared to commit. She had been hurt so badly, and yet she had still taken a risk for him.

"I'm an idiot," Kazuki announced.

"Acceptance is the first step," said Yuriko. Then she suddenly shouted, "*Che!* Those dang strays got into the garbage again! I've got to go."

"Oh, okay," Kazuki said, and she hung up before he could say good-bye.

He slipped inside and looked at Aurelie. Or rather his empty bed because she wasn't there.

In fact, she wasn't in the apartment at all.

And then a red string appeared in front of Kazuki.

オーレリー

"HELLO, Ōkami-*sensei*, and Ōkami-*san*, too," Aurelie said, doing her best to sound friendly and cheerful. She cast another glance at the husband. Why did he look so familiar? Had they met before? Was his picture on Ōkami's desk? "Are you taking a walk together?"

It wasn't a particularly nice day—cloudy if not quite overcast, and it was only in the mid-fifties. But Ōkami and her husband were beaming enough to make up for the missing sun.

"Indeed! Won't you join us?"

Aurelie wanted to say no, but she didn't want to be rude... and... maybe the distraction would be good for her. And if it weren't sufficient, well, she knew that Ōkami loved giving relationship advice. Maybe her husband could offer a male perspective. Of course they couldn't understand the binding, but maybe talking it through might be helpful anyway.

As they walked, Ōkami's husband smacked his lips. *Damn, but he gives me sociopath vibes*, she thought.

And suddenly she knew, knew where she had seen him. Even though that didn't make sense—he was obviously Japanese. Wasn't he?

"Have you ever been to France?" she asked her father's old neighbor.

The one who had told her that her pregnant aunt had committed suicide from shame.

26. TREED

和希

IT was hard to see, for black smoke obscured Kazuki's vision, but the red string glowed brightly, the only clear path forward in a haze of danger.

Kazuki wanted to run; he forced himself to grab sneakers, as well as his wallet and cell. He saw the bus pulling away as he exited his apartment, so he gave into his impulse and ran. When he passed a rack of green rental bikes though, he swiped for one. And then he was off again.

The string guided him. He veered to the right, cutting between two cars. It was a narrow gap and both were moving, but he made it effortlessly. As for the drivers—they didn't even seem to see him. Then he took the sidewalk to avoid a red light. It was crowded, but the string showed Kazuki the path.

His thighs were burning—he should add some biking to his running workouts—but he didn't consider stopping.

He knew time was short.

At last he turned down a narrow, tree-lined road that climbed steadily toward the primeval forest. At its terminus, he dropped the rental bike in the dirt and took off on foot.

Low-hanging branch—duck. Fallen log—leap. There were cobwebs—he swept them aside with one smooth motion of his arm.

And then he froze.

His breath was harsh pants; he needed to recover before—before what?

What was waiting for him?

And then the string pulsed, and Aurelie screamed ahead of him.

He charged forward.

オーレリー

"NO, never been to France," said Ōkami, answering for her husband.

"I meant—of course," Aurelie shook her head. What had she been thinking—of course Ōkami's husband wasn't—who she had thought he was.

"Tell me about Kazuki," said Ōkami.

"Kazuki-*san*," said Aurelie.

"What's that?" asked Ōkami.

"You should call him Kazuki-*san*. Or Hayashi-*san*.

How could you forget the *san*?" Shaking hands wasn't Japanese either. Why was she shaking Ōkami's husband's hand?

And Ōkami's hand too?

Were they shaking hands, or were they pulling her somewhere?

Why was she so dizzy?

Why was she following them?

She tried to pull her hands away, but she couldn't. They were all tied together with horrid black strands that looked so charred that they should have crumbled away.

But they were strong; they held Aurelie tightly.

"Who are you?" she asked.

"I'm your friend, dear. Ōkami, remember?'

"Is Akido-*sensei* okay?" she asked, though she didn't even know why.

"Of course. It was just a car accident."

There was a low growl to her left.

Aurelie turned and looked, and past Ōkami was the massive dog that had attacked her by the garbage cage.

No, there were two of them—or if not the one that had attacked her, ones that looked similar enough to be mistaken for it.

Were they really dogs? Or bears?

Or—or—wolves?

"Let me go," cried Aurelie, and this time she ripped her hands free from theirs, and the black threads did crumble to a fine soot.

She whirled to run back the way she had come, but her path was blocked by more wolves. (Not really wolves; not the endangered animals in zoos; but the wolves of which *Obā-chama* had spoken).

Ōkami and her husband were gone—or they were the wolves.

Holy fuck, were they werewolves?

"Werewolves aren't real," Aurelie said.

The answering growl demanded to differ.

Aurelie sprinted away from them, toward the closest tree, her mind suddenly terrifyingly clear.

The trees will hide you.

She leapt for the lowest branch.

She caught it—and teeth caught her leg.

Aurelie screamed and kicked her other foot. Her sneaker smashed its nose.

The moment her leg was free, she hauled herself up onto the branch. Her leg hurt like the devil—a quick glance showed a whole lot more crimson than the sweatpants were supposed to have.

Aurelie forced herself to breathe deep and she stretched out on the branch, her fingers clinging to the deep groves and her feet braced against the trunk. She looked down.

There were seven oversized monsters circling below her. One of them had blood on its muzzle.

I'm going to be eaten, she thought and started giggling. Or crying. She couldn't tell which.

And you thought that French bastard was dangerous! Japan was supposed to be safe!

It didn't make sense though. If these monsters lived in Japan, the Hayashis would have encountered them before. If they had come from abroad—well, it wasn't like a pack of overgrown canines could board a plane.

Except Ōkami could have—and her husband who Aurelie had met in France. Maybe.

This isn't happening, Aurelie thought, suddenly confident she was still dreaming. Little Red Riding Hood, wasn't it?

And then one of the beasts managed to slam into the branch that she was clinging to. Aurelie couldn't help but shriek.

This was happening, even if it made no sense. Aurelie reached for the branch above her and hissed in pain when she tried to put weight on her leg.

The branch beneath her quivered again as another oversized wolf hit it.

She moved up a branch.

What's the plan, Aurelie? How long are you going to sit in a tree?

Forever, if need be.

"Look," she called, "can't we talk about this?"

She didn't expect an answer, but she didn't have any weapon but her mouth and mind.

One of the wolves went to the base of the tree.

Don't tell me it can climb!

It stretched bizarrely, like a mirage in a desert.

Ōkami then stood there, though her short hair was wild and spiky, and she was wearing a full body fleece.

Aurelie wanted to reject what she had seen, but she couldn't. Magic was real—or at least something so inexplicable, so contrary to the world she knew, that it might as well be called magic.

和希

KAZUKI stumbled to a stop, confused by what he saw. A pack of massive canines had treed Aurelie. Kazuki was vaguely reminded of *Twilight*, but these things were a whole lot scarier than those CGI wolves.

And they reeked of smoke and carrion. That was what convinced him they were real. He wasted a moment wishing, for the first time in his life, that he had a gun. Of course, it wouldn't be very helpful since he had never used one before.

Kazuki grabbed a stick as thick as his wrist, only for it to fall into a dozen mushy chunks when he brought it down on the first wolf's back.

The creature whirled on him, showing a terrifying number of teeth in a dark brown face.

Kazuki's hands were empty, and he reached for the only thing he could—the red string, also as thick as his wrist now.

He wrapped it around the wolf's neck and began to choke it, but that wasn't enough.

He could kill it this way, he was sure, but he couldn't choke the whole pack at once.

As if they had the same realization, two other wolves lunged at him and a third howled its fury.

Kazuki couldn't handle this alone.

But he wasn't alone. He had Aurelie, and together they had the whole world, dozens of web-like strings connecting them to everything. He pulled on the cobwebs, and power poured into him. He felt so hot, like he might spontaneously combust. A growl ripped from his throat, and he faced his enemy.

オーレリー

LIKE a maiden in a tower awaiting her knight, Aurelie clung to the tree branch. And Kazuki came, swinging a branch like a sword. Aurelie was horrified—she knew that Ōkami and the pack offered her death, but dying alone was preferable to dying with Kazuki.

She truly did love him—his thoughtfulness, his singing, his confidence, his sentimentality. She was happier knowing he was in the world.

"Get out of here!" she screamed, but Kazuki didn't even seem to hear her. In fact, there seemed to be something wrong with him—for a moment, she didn't see a knight but a monster.

And then something grabbed Aurelie's foot. She recalled Ōkami, too late. Aurelie tried to kick the other woman—or whatever she was—to knock her off the branch, but Ōkami's long claws dug into the bark and Aurelie's sneaker.

She reached for something that Aurelie couldn't see—until she could. Like walking into a dark house on sunny day, wobbly patches of light seemed to dance in front of her. Dark red, they resolved themselves into threads.

The red strings of fate.

Aurelie remembered that terrible story and suddenly feared that she and Kazuki might leave nothing but ash behind. Her mother and sister would never know what happened—just that she went to Japan and never returned. The Hayashi clan would hate foreigners forever, for robbing them of Kazuki.

For bringing the wolves.

A howl rent the air. Both she and Ōkami paused to look.

Aurelie wished she hadn't. All the other wolves had turned on Kazuki, who was...

What was he doing? His expression was odd, faraway, like he couldn't even see the wolves. Aurelie screamed as one leapt straight for his throat.

But instead of biting Kazuki, its teeth sunk into a deer instead. One of the sacred deer of Nara.

It wasn't alone—there were suddenly ten or twenty deer, mostly young bucks, among the wolves. They slashed with their antlers and kicked with their legs. Aurelie had never seen anything like it.

It was unnatural.

It was supernatural.

Somehow, Kazuki was driving the deer with the red threads. Ōkami leapt down from the tree into the fray. Aurelie pressed her face against the bark, letting the ridges dig into her cheek, the scent of moss filling her nostrils. She felt a little more grounded, more real.

She lifted her face, still hoping against hope that the world would be normal again.

But nothing had changed.

和希

THERE was power all around him, in the plants and trees, in the birds and the deer, and in Aurelie and himself.

Kazuki didn't fight the pack with his hands, he

fought them with magic. With the bindings that connected the world.

He needed more; he needed enough power to smother the wolves into oblivion.

And he saw it—pure and pulsing, in Aurelie's womb.

He reached for that power, ready to use it to save their lives. But when he touched it, he realized that power was his son. Just a tiny cell, not even a fetus yet, but full of potential. His and Aurelie's child, the babe of the morrow.

Kazuki struggled for a moment. He knew that the raw potential contained in the child, the not-quite baby, was enough to save them. If he didn't claim that power, he'd have to rip it from the forest. To sacrifice the animals and plants around them.

He started reaching for the cell, only to realize he wasn't the only one. The half-woman, half-wolf holding Aurelie's foot was also reaching for it.

In that moment, Kazuki saw that he and Ōkami were the same. Wielders of the red thread, slaves to their appetites, creatures that consumed the connections around them.

Monsters.

Kazuki saw that and chose to be better. Instead of seizing the pulsing power of the fetus, he shielded it by wrapping his and Aurelie's red string around it.

And he grabbed the forest around him.

The tree Aurelie was in creaked in protest, but one branch snapped, falling directly into Ōkami. She bent backward and fell to the ground.

Two songbirds trilled their terror before diving at

the eyes of the wolves biting Kazuki's arms.

Then the deer arrived, and Kazuki was with each of them, his consciousness split two dozen ways. His hands flexed and his muscles knit; the bucks kicked their hooves into the wolves' sides and gouged with their antlers.

The wolves tore their throats and bit their bellies; Kazuki yelled, tasting blood in his own mouth.

The seedlings around them shot up, twining around the wolves' paws, tangling them so the deer could attack again.

The world was blood, dirt, and death cries.

Kazuki stood amidst it, almost drunk, until all fell silent.

Black smoke drifted slowly up, the wolves' bodies wholly gone.

The only proof that they'd even been here was the broken and bloody corpses of the deer.

27. CHOSEN

和希

KAZUKI felt nauseous, but he didn't vomit. Instead, he walked over to Aurelie and stretched his arms up to her.

She stared at him, her mouth gaping, tears trickling down her cheeks.

Kazuki wondered what she saw. He kept his arms extended.

Aurelie slowly lowered herself from one branch to another, then dropped the last few feet into Kazuki's arms. He caught her weight against his chest and slowly lowered her until her feet rested on the ground and her head on his neck.

They stood there, silent, feeling the weight of what had happened, doubting their own impressions, smelling the rotten-ocean odor of blood.

"What were they?" asked Aurelie. "Have you ever...?"

"No," said Kazuki, "I don't know." He stroked her head. "We had better go to the Forest-Heart Home. Can you walk?"

Kazuki's own leg was throbbing in phantom pain. He could feel everything Aurelie felt now, her thoughts mingling with his own. The binding was restored, at least as strong as that first morning after they had made love the whole night.

"I can," Aurelie started to step. She didn't stumble, but Kazuki felt her pain. He swung her up in his arms, ignoring his own bites.

Aurelie gasped. "Your arms! And there's no way you can carry me all the way out of the woods," she protested.

"True," said Kazuki, more of a grunt than a word. He would have explained more, but it wasn't worth the breath. He carried her a short distance, to a large rock, and set her on it as gently as he could manage. Kneeling, he lifted her leg into his lap.

Kazuki had never seen a bite wound before; in fact, he was not great with blood. There was a lot of blood soaking Aurelie's pant leg.

Aurelie pulled off her sweatshirt and then her t-shirt, leaving only her sports bra behind. She started binding her leg with the t-shirt. Belatedly, Kazuki tried to take over, but she shook her head.

Her lips quirked, and she said, "You vomiting on my leg or fainting isn't going to help anything."

That's right, the binding went both ways. She could

feel everything he felt and thought now.

"How are we going to get to the Forest-Heart Home?" Aurelie asked. "Won't people ask questions if they see my leg—or your shirt for that matter?"

Kazuki looked down at himself. There were several blood sprays across his torso—not to mention his bloodied forearms. They had nothing on Aurelie's leg though. He peeled off his long-sleeved shirt—his undershirt looked fine. Even if going around sleeveless before the spring equinox would catch some eyes. Aurelie took his outer shirt and ripped strips that she wrapped around his forearms. It looked odd, but *maybe* like a fashion statement?

"That'll do," Kazuki declared. "Public transit is out, and it would take a while for anyone to get us—I know, there's a car rental nearby."

"You have a license?" Aurelie asked.

"Yeah. I'll get the car and pick you up. You just need to wait a little closer to the road."

He glanced back at the dead deer.

Aurelie caught his chin and turned his face to hers. "Don't look at that."

He nodded once.

And then, almost contradicting herself, she asked, "Should we call the authorities?"

He laughed, not that it was funny, he was just so keyed up.

"I don't think so. What would we say—some massive wolf-beasts attacked us and the deer killed them and they turned to smoke?"

"They looked the same as that 'dog' outside my

apartment, didn't they?"

Kazuki nodded.

"And—did you see Ōkami-*sensei*, too?"

"I—yes, I guess so. But she was…"

Aurelie nodded. "I ran into her and her husband—a guy in a terrible fleece—I think I met him in France…"

Kazuki abruptly remembered the weird guy who he had seen outside both Aurelie and his own apartments.

"I'm not sure exactly what happened. I don't remember walking into the woods. Everything is foggy. But suddenly I realized they were going to attack me, and there was a whole pack, so I climbed the tree and one of the wolves half-shifted into Ōkami-*sensei*, to follow me." She shuddered, and Kazuki put a hand on her shoulder. He didn't know what to say. The red string was one thing, but this was something else.

Aurelie put her hand on his and asked, "Why did the deer kill them?"

Kazuki didn't want to answer, except he knew that she already knew. "I made them. I made them fight for us." He closed his eyes briefly. "Was that wrong? I put our lives over theirs…"

"I consider you more important than a hundred deer, sacred or not," Aurelie said. Kazuki wrapped his arms around her and escaped the reek of blood by inhaling the rose scent of her hair.

オ ー レ リ ー

AURELIE waited for Kazuki on the edge of the primeval forest, just in sight of the road. She was freaking out, of course.

What if someone saw her? What if a *police officer* saw her? Her position and leg wound weren't illegal, but they were definitely sketchy. Would she be connected with all the dead deer? How long would it take to find the deer anyway? Would they look for whoever killed them? Or would the bite wounds lead them to believe it was an animal attack?

A creepy, unnatural animal attack.

Aurelie pressed her back against the tree and willed herself to blend into it, like a chameleon. At one point, she could have sworn a biker on the road looked directly at her, but he didn't stop, thank goodness. Probably he preferred to mind his own business, like Aurelie herself.

Or maybe she blended better into the woods than she realized, for when Kazuki came, he swept his eyes right over where she sat.

"Au-*chan*?" he called, uncertainly.

"I'm here," she said, half-rising. His eyes latched onto her, and he hurried to help.

He opened the passenger side door and buckled her into the seat himself. Unnecessary, but sweet.

Aurelie felt so exhausted that though there was much to say, she sat without speaking. She knew Kazuki sensed her desire for quiet, but once they were on the highway, he spoke anyway.

"We should discuss a few things before we arrive," he told her. He cleared his throat, and Aurelie tried to stay relaxed. "You said you wanted to go home before we get married, but under the circumstances, I think we had better wed, at least legally, as soon as possible."

Aurelie processed that. There was one more thing she had felt, with the... the magic.

"I'm pregnant," she said baldly. It didn't make it feel more real though.

"Yes—it's early, but I—I felt it. You--?"

"Yes," she agreed. "So you're worried—you want to make sure I and the child can return to Japan. That legally, it's considered yours."

Kazuki nodded. "There's a lot of regulations because of the pandemic right now. I'm afraid if you leave the country..."

"Yeah," said Aurelie. "I understand." She'd feel the same way.

She didn't like getting married in a rush though, not so soon after he graduated, not before everything was settled with her family. And—hadn't they more or less agreed they'd wait before having children? (Was there Unseen birth control? Condoms would have worked...)

But she should have thought of those things before sleeping with him yesterday. (Had it only been yesterday?) Had she known they would sleep together when she had gone to his house?

She had known. Of course she had—why else would she have showered?

She started crying, again, or maybe she had never fully stopped.

Kazuki took the first exit they came to and pulled over at Lawson convenience store.

"Aurelie," he said, "I love you."

Her eyes fell shut. Damn this binding, which let him feel her worries. "You don't need to say that," she told him. "I agree with you, not with... whoever you were talking to. I'd rather you be honest with me than say what I want to hear."

"I'm being honest," he told her. "It just took me a little while to process it—I'm not as clever as you are."

She shook her head, her eyes still pressed shut.

Something soft and warm encircled her—not literally, though it felt so palpable as to be physical.

The binding. He was doing something with the binding. And then Aurelie was in his mind, his memories, walking those paths as he had in her own.

和希

Forest-Heart Home, Kyoto Prefecture, Japan - May 2008

KAZUKI curled into a ball in the recess under the dining table. He'd been playing there, pretending it was his cave, when *Ōba-chama* had entered with someone. A woman, probably his cousin, though Kazuki didn't remember her name.

"Sit down, Haruko-*chan*," said *Ōba-chama*.

Kazuki wondered if he should declare his presence. It wasn't against the rules to play in the dining room; it was generally considered a common space.

Why had *Ōba-chama* brought "Haruko-*chan*" in here at all? Why not to *Ōba-chama*'s room?

"Explain yourself," said *Ōba-chama*, "why did you have an affair with a human?"

Kazuki went rigid with shock. Even close friendships with humans were viewed with skepticism. An affair—a lover? Who would do such a thing?

Kazuki was now unwilling to reveal himself. He wanted to hear more, and he was afraid of admitting what he had already heard.

"I loved her," said Haruko.

"Love! What is love?" scoffed *Ōba-chama*. "It is the binding that guides our lives, which shows us who we are to be with, and how to care for each other. Love is a human emotion."

"But she saw me," said Haruko. "And she loved me. I needed her, I needed to be seen. I chose her over the clan."

"That's not a choice you are allowed," said *Ōba-chama*, and for the first time in his life, Kazuki feared her. "You owe your life to the clan; you cannot choose to give it elsewhere.

"And now you will stay here, at the clan home, until you remember that. You are dismissed."

Kazuki was shaking, scared.

He was waiting for *Ōba-chama* to follow Haruko out, but she didn't. After a few minutes, she said, "Kazuki-*kun*, come out."

Kazuki didn't want to. Slowly, he uncurled his body, and stuck his head out between the floor and the table.

Ōba-chama patted the seat on the couch beside her.

Reluctantly, Kazuki took it.

"I'm sorry, I was here—"

"I know," *Ōba-chama* cut him off. "I brought Haruko-*san* here because I wanted you to hear what I said to her."

"Why?" asked Kazuki.

"Because your life belongs to the clan even more

than Haruko-*san*'s does. Someday you will take over my role, leading the family and making sure we aren't discovered."

Kazuki nodded, even though he didn't ever want to tell someone they couldn't love.

オ ー レ リ ー

Off Highway 163, Kyoto Prefecture, Japan - March 2022

"AU-*CHAN*," Kazuki said, "I couldn't say I loved you because I thought love was wild and irresponsible. While the binding was about logic and protecting the clan. But I'm no longer sure what the difference is because, like Haruko-*san*, I would choose you. I would choose you over the clan, over my pride, over any position. I will give you my everything. I love you."

Aurelie swallowed. She opened her eyes and turned to Kazuki. He was, of course, already looking at her. With those big emoji heart-eyes that had so unsettled her in October.

"Attraction happens," Aurelie said, "but love is a choice." She had already made the choice, and surely Kazuki could feel that, but she needed to say more. To acknowledge how much it meant to Kazuki. "Thank you for choosing me. I choose you, too. I will face whatever comes with you, and I will give you my everything, too. I love you, too, Kazuki-*san*."

He leaned forward, his eyes locked on hers until the last possible moment, and then they fell shut.

His lips, soft as flower petals, covered hers.

Aurelie closed her own eyes and kissed him back.

It was terrifying and wonderful all at once. Wonderful because it was a milestone, the moment they knew they were a team.

Terrifying because their partnership was new and untested. Unlike the dramas that Kazuki liked, which ended with the couple's confession, their story was just beginning.

GORGED

Appalachia, West Virginia, US

AAIIIEEE!

Gone, gone, gone!   FREE!

Free to eat, free to rend.

Eat!   EAT!

Starving.   Go, go, go, goooo!

Let's go!

Let's bite, let's rend, let's tear, let's gnaw, let's eat!

...

So full.   So tasty.   Ahhhhhh.

What about tomorrow? Next year?

What will we eat then?

ACKNOWLEDGMENTS

Before we get to the writing, I want to thank my wonderful sister-in-law, Wanxi Yang, and my dear friend, Joseph Griggs, who have talked to me about the thrills and challenges of marrying and living in a foreign country. Those conversations drove my decision to write a cross-cultural romance.

Next, my beloved husband and de facto editor, Joshua Pawlicki for brainstorming, reading partial drafts, and telling me that yes, he wants to read more.

Then, thanks to the "cheerleaders" - my amazingly patient and supportive sister, Helen Luk, who read the first few chapters in fall 2021 to help me decide whether or not to continue, and then waited almost a year to get the rest of the story; Normand Manning, who read my first draft the day I finished it and said it was my "best yet"; and Gail Hanson, who lets me call all hours of the day and always says I'm right!

Thanks to Genevieve and James Zola, who both seem to know what it is I am trying to say and tell me to say it! I might write books without you, but it has been the feedback from the two of you that has allowed me to break through my mental blocks. If you love Kazuki, thank James because I was preparing to eliminate his romantic streak until James convinced me otherwise. If you appreciated the Unseen lore, thank Genevieve who told me she wanted MORE!

Nicole Wells - whose novel UpSpark touched my heart - humbled me with her detailed and thoughtful feedback.

Ciara Hartford – who writes absolutely stunning epics about elves that I can't wait to buy – gave me some much-needed reassurance when I was doubting my vision, which is often the most precious gift an alpha-reader can provide.

I had six beta readers for this book: James Hanson, Matilda Williamson, Margaret Ball, Faith Enoul, Cheryl Chudyk, and Edith Hanson. Thank all of you for catching errors and your boundless support! I truly appreciate it.

Because I knew I would be self-publishing this book from its conception, I spent a lot of time reflecting on its aesthetic while writing. I am very grateful to those who helped me achieve the right feeling: Tricia Siudut Allen, who advised me on the frame and interludes; Faith Enuol, Helen Luk, Howard Burr, Joshua Pawlicki, and Ellora Sen-Gupta for sharing photographs; and of course, Darin Nagamootoo, who made a cover even better than my vision.

Last but far from least, thank you to one of my favorite people ever: Henmi Megumi! She answered so many questions about address, names, pandemic protocol in Japan, et cetera, and always did so with enthusiasm and patience! The student has become the teacher. Remaining mistakes are my own!

BOOK DESIGN

I dithered for a long time over this book's cover, but when I saw a beautiful and haunting silhouette by my friend Darin Nagamootoo, I suddenly had a clear vision. So in the midst of final edits, I messaged him about creating cover art, and he agreed! You can find more of Darin's magical art on Instagram @wellnessartist.

Following my three-year-old niece's advice, I decided to include photographs for each chapter. Most of them are from my times in Japan, and were taken by both me and my travel companions. Additionally, wolf photographs (including chapter 26 and the interlude silhouettes), were all kindly shared with me by the amazing Ellora Sen-Gupta. The wolves are from Wolf Hollow, a sanctuary in Massachusetts. Find Ellora and Wolf Hollow on Instagram @hellorainyday and @wolfhollowma.

The text is Spectral designed by Production Type and the chapter titles are Candara by Gary Munch for Microsoft. The interludes feature a variety of fonts, all from Google Fonts or Microsoft: Chiller, Shadows into Light, Covered By Your Grace, Modern Love Caps, Rock Salt, Permanent Marker, and Gloria Hallelujah, Julee, Cavolini, Solitreo, and Nanum Pen.

ABOUT THE AUTHOR

Edith Pawlicki lives in Connecticut with her husband, twin sons, dog, and two rabbits. She fell in love with words in fourth grade and finds writing necessary to free the worlds and characters in her head. When she isn't busy being a mom and author, she enjoys cooking and learning new things. Like Aurelie, Edith taught in Japan; like Kazuki, she's obsessed with dramas and tropes. In addition to *The Unseen*, she has written an epic fantasy series called *The Immortal Beings*, a YA science fiction novel, *Minerva*, and a regency romance which is free to newsletter subscribers. Find her and her books at edithpawlicki.com or on Instagram @edithpawlicki.

www.ingramcontent.com/pod-product-compliance
Lightning Source LLC
Chambersburg PA
CBHW060851210726
48293CB00006B/1754